DEADLY GAME

D S BUTLER

Deadly Obsession
Deadly Motive
Deadly Revenge
Deadly Justice
Deadly Ritual
Deadly Payback
Deadly Game
Lost Child
Her Missing Daughter
Bring Them Home
Where Secrets Lie

❀ Created with Vellum

For Chris

CHAPTER ONE

BENNY MORRIS STOOD in front of the Rose Hill Community Centre, shuffling from foot to foot impatiently.

They were late.

"Late, late, late," Benny muttered, slapping his hands together and stamping his feet.

A man walking past gave him a startled look and then hunched his shoulders, fixing his eyes on the ground and giving Benny a wide berth.

Benny was used to people keeping their distance. His size made people go out of their way to avoid him. At six foot five and eighteen stone, Benny Morris was a big man. His brother, Rob, told him his size was something to be proud of because it made people respect him and think twice before taking liberties.

An elderly woman walking towards him with a shopping trolley took one look at him and crossed to the other side of the road.

Benny waved and grinned at her, a nice big smile, showing all his teeth, but that just made her scurry away faster.

Rob, said he shouldn't worry about people like that, but he couldn't help it. He wanted people to like him.

He looked down at his freshly polished shoes. Shiny shoes were important to Benny. His trousers swung around his ankles because he kept pulling his trousers up too far. Rob told him off for doing it and said he looked like a simpleton, but Benny wanted to have his trousers high up on his waist, just like he wanted to have shiny shoes.

He looked at the Star Wars watch strapped to his wrist and muttered to himself again, "Late, late, late."

He looked in the direction the girls normally came from, past the Fried Chicken Palace and the bus stop. He saw the girls every morning, and they were normally here by now.

Rob wasn't going to be happy. Benny bit his lip as he imagined his brother's reaction.

He wasn't usually allowed to work with his brother.

"Don't blow this Benny," Rob had said that morning. "There'll be big trouble if you do."

He knew exactly what would happen if he did mess up. They wouldn't go to McDonald's for tea, and Benny wouldn't get his present.

He'd had his heart set on getting a new Xbox for ages, and Rob had promised to get it for him just as long as he brought the girls to the alleyway behind Celandine Gardens.

Benny bounced on the balls of his feet. "Come on, come on," he muttered.

He wished they would hurry up. The sooner they got here, the sooner he could have his Xbox. He grinned. If he was really lucky, his brother might even have time to get the Xbox today. He could spend the whole afternoon playing online.

He smiled and waved to a little boy who walked past with his mother.

The little boy waved back, but his mother yanked on the boy's hand before quickly crossing to the other side of the road.

Benny sighed.

His brother didn't like to be kept waiting. He'd probably get told off now.

The excitement of having a new Xbox faded. If his brother were really angry, he'd forget about Benny's present, and there would be no trip to McDonald's, either. It would be beans on toast for dinner. That's what happened last week when he'd done something wrong, and Benny hated beans. They were too little to stay on his fork.

He broke out into a broad grin when he saw the two girls walking towards him.

"Hello," he shouted out, unable to wait until they reached him.

He bounded over to them, and they both grinned at him.

He liked the girls. They'd been working in the centre for a few weeks. The staff changed a lot at the centre, and he'd never liked anyone as much as the two girls. They weren't scared of him. They taught him how to use computers, showed him funny YouTube videos on the Internet and told him how good the new Xbox was.

"Hi, Benny," they said in unison.

"What are you doing out here?" Ruby asked. "The centre should be open already. You can go in if you like."

Benny nodded. He knew that. He'd been coming to the centre for years before the girls had arrived. This morning was different. He had something to do.

He licked his lips and closed his eyes, trying to remember

what he was supposed to say. He needed to get the words exactly right. Otherwise, he wouldn't get the Xbox.

"I need you to help me," he said. "I found a bag of puppies in Celandine Gardens. I didn't know what to do, so I left them there. Can you come and help me?"

"Oh, how horrible. How could somebody do something like that?" Lila said. She patted Benny's arm. "Let's go and get them."

"We can call the RSPCA," Ruby said.

Benny nodded and smiled even wider.

His brother would be proud of him. Things were going exactly to plan.

He hummed to himself as the girls chatted about a program that had been on telly last night.

"This way," he said confidently as he led them across the cobbled courtyard.

He stepped into the alleyway and turned back to smile at them again. "It's just down here."

He was so excited he wanted to run to the end of the alley, but he knew his brother wouldn't be happy if he did that. That wasn't part of the plan.

So he walked slowly, and the girls followed him.

After they'd been walking for a couple of minutes, Ruby said, "Hang on, Benny." She wasn't smiling anymore. "How much further is it? We're going to be late for work. Perhaps you should get the puppies and bring them back to the centre."

He shook his head. No. He couldn't do that. That wasn't the plan.

"Are you pulling my leg, Benny? Are you sure you found some puppies?" Lila asked, grinning at him.

Lila was his favourite. She was always telling jokes and

making Benny laugh, and she even laughed at *his* jokes, which Rob said weren't funny and didn't make sense.

He turned back and gave the girls a sly smile. He hoped they wouldn't be angry when they found out he'd tricked them. He thought they would understand if he told them about the Xbox. He didn't mind sharing. They were welcome to use it any time they wanted.

He opened his mouth to tell them the truth when his brother's voice sounded at the end of the alleyway.

"Good job, Benny. You'd better get yourself off home now."

He smiled, but when he turned back to the girls the smile slid from his face. They looked scared.

"It's all right," Benny said and started to explain about the Xbox, but his brother cut him off, and Benny saw another man step out of the shadows.

The man had a big nose and wore a baseball cap. He lunged forward, shouting and swearing, and Benny took a step back, not sure what to do.

He looked to his brother for help as he always did. Rob was clever and would know what to do, but his brother didn't say anything. He didn't even tell the man off for shouting at Benny.

One of the girls screamed, and the nasty man grabbed her by the throat.

Benny looked at them in horror. "No, don't hurt her. Let her go."

"Stay out of it," his brother ordered.

Benny's hands were shaking as he lifted them and pressed them hard against his ears to block out the sound of the girls' screams.

"No," he sobbed. "This wasn't the plan."

"Go home, Benny," his brother shouted at him.

Benny didn't like shouting. It scared him. He began to moan and shake his head.

The nasty man laughed as he punched Lila on the side of her head, and she fell to the floor in front of Benny.

"No!"

The man in the baseball cap turned to Rob and said, "He'd better come with us. The bloody fool will probably run off and tell somebody."

Benny watched in horror as the man put a hood over Ruby's head. She was wriggling, trying to escape when the man in the baseball cap punched her in the stomach.

Benny's lip wobbled. "Stop hurting her."

"Shut your gob and make yourself useful. Carry the other one," the man in the baseball cap snapped.

Benny looked down at the floor. Lila, the girl who'd laughed at all of his jokes, was laying motionless in front of him. There was blood on her lip.

Benny's eyes stung with tears as he looked at his brother for help.

"Come on, Benny," Rob said. "Pick her up."

Benny's hands were shaking as he leant down and scooped the poor girl up. He lifted her as gently as he could, and her head lolled back against his arm.

With tears streaming down his face, he followed his brother and the man in the baseball cap.

CHAPTER TWO

JACK MACKINNON MUTTERED a curse under his breath as the lawnmower came to a dead stop. He'd thought a cordless, battery-operated mower was a good idea, and it was fine, apart from the fact it ran out of juice after twenty minutes.

He took out the battery pack and headed towards the house to put it on charge.

It was his last day of leave, and he'd been intending to enjoy it. Unfortunately, his idea of enjoyment and Chloe's didn't go quite hand-in-hand. So far he'd had to mow the lawn, fix the shower screen and repair a leaky pipe under the kitchen sink, and he still had to go and buy a replacement light for the main bathroom.

Chloe had gone out with her daughter, Katy. They were having a girls' day, a treat for Katy because she'd done so well in her end of year exams.

When he entered the house and put the battery on charge, he heard a noise in the sitting room and realised he wasn't alone. There was someone else in the house.

Chloe and Katy weren't due back for another couple of hours. He noticed a bag of laundry dumped on the kitchen floor by the washing machine and realised Chloe's eldest daughter, Sarah, had come home.

She'd been at university in Kingston and had told Chloe that she wouldn't be returning for the summer because she got herself a job as a club promoter. That hadn't gone down very well with Chloe, who thought her eldest daughter should have more ambition and should be planning a long-term career.

"Sarah?" Mackinnon called out as he walked through the kitchen and into the hallway.

Sarah wandered out of the sitting room. She had dyed her hair dark auburn, almost purple, and wore a pair of jeans and a loose top that slipped down off her shoulders.

"Oh, Jack. I didn't realise anyone else was home."

He looked over her shoulder into the sitting room and noticed that one of the cabinet drawers was open. For a long time, he and Chloe had kept cash there. Not much, but enough for things like paying the window cleaner or the pizza delivery driver, but they'd stopped doing that after the money had started disappearing. They both knew it was Sarah, but she'd denied it.

He knew she was lying now, too. The lawnmower may have been battery-operated, but it was still bloody noisy, and she would have heard it as soon as she entered the house as all the downstairs windows were open.

"Is Mum not here?" Sarah asked, sounding bored as she walked back into the sitting room and plopped herself down on the sofa.

Mackinnon shook his head. "She's gone out for the day with Katy."

She saw him looking at the open drawer and smirked, almost daring him to mention it.

He took a deep breath instead and said, "Do you want a cup of tea. I was just about to have one."

She nodded. "Yes, okay. Do you know when Mum and Katy are due back?"

"Probably not for a couple of hours," Mackinnon called over his shoulder as he walked towards the kitchen.

He was surprised to see Sarah follow him in. She leant against the kitchen counter, watching him as he filled the kettle.

He switched it on to boil and then turned to face her. "Is there something wrong?"

Sarah bit down on her lower lip as though debating whether or not to trust him. Then she took a deep breath and let it out in a sigh. "I suppose you could say that."

Mackinnon put the two cups he'd just taken out of the cupboard down on the kitchen counter.

There was something about Sarah that put him on edge. He was always expecting her to get into trouble. He supposed it was the job that made him expect the worst of most situations. He sensed something was wrong.

He knew Sarah had got herself into trouble. He just didn't know how bad it was yet.

"Do you want to talk about it?"

Sarah twisted her hands, staring down at her fingers.

He thought she was going to say it was none of his business, and he wouldn't have been surprised, but she didn't.

"I need money," she said. "Can you help me?"

"What do you need the money for?" Mackinnon asked.

He thought it was a reasonable question, but obviously, Sarah didn't. She scowled at him.

"I know what you're thinking."

"Really?"

"Yes, you're so easy to read. It's pathetic. You're thinking, Sarah's messed up again. Sarah, the black sheep of the family. Nothing like Katy, who doesn't do anything wrong, ever."

"So let me get this straight. You're asking me for money in the same breath as calling me pathetic?" Mackinnon asked dryly.

Sarah's cheeks flushed, and Mackinnon immediately felt guilty. If Sarah was in trouble, she should be able to confide in him.

"Sorry, let's start over. If I can help, I will. What do you need the money for?"

Sarah pursed her lips and shook her head. "It doesn't matter. I'll ask Mum."

The kettle came to a boil, and Mackinnon poured hot water into the mugs. He couldn't be bothered to faff about with the teapot.

He was about to press Sarah again when the phone rang.

It was his work mobile. It looked like his leave was going to be cut short.

"Can you finish making the tea?" Mackinnon asked Sarah as he reached for his mobile, even though he was pretty sure he wasn't going to get a chance to drink it.

He answered the phone. "Mackinnon."

The voice of Detective Chief Inspector Brookbank said, "Mackinnon, you're needed at Wood Street. ASAP. How soon can you get here?"

Mackinnon's attention switched from Sarah's problems to work mode. The DCI wouldn't be calling him unless there was something big on the horizon.

"I'm in Oxford," he said. "I can be there in an hour and a half."

"Just get here as soon as you can," Brookbank said. "We've got a case that could escalate quickly."

Brookbank wasn't usually so cryptic. If he wasn't giving details over the phone, it either meant he didn't have the details or he was with someone, preventing him from talking freely.

"I'll head in straightaway," Mackinnon said.

He scribbled down a quick note to Chloe as he told Sarah he needed to go to work.

"Unless you wanted to talk about this problem and why you need money." Mackinnon felt duty bound to offer.

Sarah shook her head and walked out of the kitchen, leaving the tea unmade on the counter. "Whatever," she said.

CHAPTER THREE

IT TOOK Mackinnon an hour and a half to get to Wood Street Station. A quick check on the traffic app on his phone told him it was quicker to get the train than drive, and so he had come to London via Paddington.

He nodded hello to the sergeant on the desk and swiped his ID card to get into the secure area of the police station. He was intrigued by the lack of details Brookbank had provided. He'd checked the news, but came up blank. These days, it seemed the press often got wind of a crime before the police did. But the DCI's voice had a steely edge to it on the phone, which made Mackinnon think this new case was a big one.

He reached the open plan office area and dumped his gear on the desk. DCI Brookbank had a glass-fronted office with a window, looking down onto the courtyard. There were renovations going on in the station, but they were taking a long time, and everyone had been moved around. DCI Brookbank's temporary office wasn't much bigger than a rabbit hutch.

The DCI looked up, caught Mackinnon's eye and then waved him over.

As he walked over to the office, Mackinnon saw the familiar grey-haired head of DI Tyler.

He opened the glass door, and Brookbank nodded at him.

"Shut the door behind you, Jack."

Mackinnon did as he asked and then sat down in a chair beside Tyler.

"There was an incident this morning. We believe a seventeen-year-old girl has been abducted. Her name is Ruby Watson. She didn't arrive for work, although her parents told us she set off to go to work at seven forty-five this morning. Two hours ago, her mother received a text message."

Brookbank's eyes drifted down to the paperwork in front of him, and he lifted up a piece of paper scrawled with his distinctive handwriting.

"We have your daughter. Await further instructions."

"Is that all?"

A seventeen-year-old going missing for a couple of hours wasn't usually cause for alarm, but this text message certainly added a sinister aspect.

"Yes, that was all," Brookbank said. "We have already looked into the text message, and it originated from a pay-as-you-go mobile. Trying to ring that mobile number has not been successful. The phone is obviously switched off, but we're trying to pinpoint where the text message was sent from."

"There was a case not long ago," DI Tyler said. "A similar situation. A teenage girl didn't show up for work, and her parents received a text message. It turned out the girl and her boyfriend were behind it. They were trying to extort money from the parents."

Brookbank nodded. "We don't think that is the case here, though. Right now, we are treating this as a genuine abduction. Her father, Peter Watson, is an investment banker. He is worth a lot of money, and his daughter would be a valuable target."

"Have the parents heard anything more from the kidnappers?" Mackinnon asked.

Brookbank shook his head. "No. There's a police officer with them now, and I am assigning a trained family liaison officer. DI Tyler will be heading up the enquiry," Brookbank paused to nod at DI Tyler and then looked back at Mackinnon. "He requested I bring you in, and I agreed. The team is assembling in incident room one. I'm sure I don't need to remind you time is paramount in cases like this."

Mackinnon nodded.

"Right, you'd better get started," Brookbank said.

DI Tyler and Mackinnon got to their feet, left Brookbank's office and headed for incident room one.

Mackinnon had been right; this case was a big one and time sensitive. Recovering the abduction victim within hours was the best case scenario. The longer the person was held, the less chance there was of a successful outcome.

"We are going to get set up in incident room one," Tyler said, "but we'll spend a lot of time working closely with the Watson family. They are very wealthy and live in a penthouse just within the city limits. Their apartment even has its own rooftop garden, and they also own a number of other apartments in the building, and as one of them is currently empty, they've offered us the use of that if we need to set up a temporary base there. I think it's a good idea to have officers there in case the abductors get in touch."

Mackinnon nodded. "Who is working the case?"

"At the moment it's just the City of London Police. The girl went missing in the city, and she lives about a quarter of a mile away. It's our jurisdiction."

"Press?"

Tyler frowned. "No press yet. We want to control the information that gets released to the media. We don't want to spook the abductors, and we don't want any have-a-go heroes."

As they reached incident room one, Mackinnon stood to one side to let Tyler enter the room first.

Most of the team were already gathered inside.

DC Webb was perched on the edge of a table near the front of the room, fiddling with his laptop. He'd overdone the hair gel as usual, and Mackinnon could smell his aftershave as soon as he stepped in the room.

DC Charlotte Brown was already there, too. She looked pensive but offered Mackinnon a smile as he walked in. Her hair was tied back neatly, and she wore black trousers, black boots and a grey blouse.

DC Collins was there, too, looking neat and tidy as usual. He was sticking a photograph to the whiteboard and was the only one who actually called out a greeting to Mackinnon and Tyler.

Tyler walked to the front of the room and put the folders he'd been carrying on the table in front of him.

"Right, let's get down to business. We'll have support staff joining us shortly. This morning, seventeen-year-old Ruby Watson didn't arrive for work at Rose Hill Community Centre." Tyler paused to nod at the photograph of Ruby Watson on the whiteboard. She was a fresh-faced girl, smiling happily in the photograph. "She has been working there on a voluntary basis for the past three weeks. It's a summer placement. She is an A-level student at City College.

"We are considering this an abduction because her mother, Claire Watson, received a text message from an unknown individual claiming they had her daughter and to await further instructions.

"The text message hasn't given us much to go on at the moment. Other than we know it was sent from a pay-as-you-go sim card. The tech team is working on that.

"Ruby's parents are extremely well off. Her father, Peter Watson, is an investment banker. He also owns properties within the square mile, residential and commercial. The family's money could be the motive behind the abduction, but we can't rule out other possibilities at this stage. It's possible that this could be a revenge attack, perhaps the abductor is someone the parents or Ruby herself has upset."

He turned to Charlotte. "DC Brown I'd like you to start looking into Ruby's background. Boyfriends, friends, Social media. Did she have any enemies?"

"How many enemies could a seventeen-year-old girl have?" DC Webb piped up.

"You'd be surprised," Charlotte said dryly as she sat down at a desk and opened her laptop.

DI Tyler turned to Collins next. "I want you to trace her last known movements. She was last seen by her parents leaving their apartment this morning. We need to get hold of all CCTV that could show us where she went next. We know her usual route to work, according to her mother. She left home at seven forty-five this morning."

Collins nodded. "I'll get on it straightaway."

Finally, Tyler turned to Mackinnon. "You're with me, Jack.

We're going to go and meet the parents and ask them some very difficult questions."

Mackinnon nodded and picked up his jacket. It was warm and muggy today and he'd prefer to be without it. He'd like to ditch his tie, too, but appearances were important in their line of work. If you dressed well, people had more confidence in your abilities. DI Tyler always wore a suit and tie but looked a little crumpled and worn around the edges.

So despite the heat, Mackinnon shrugged on his jacket and straightened his tie.

Mr and Mrs Watson were living through every parent's worst nightmare, and Mackinnon knew things were going to get worse.

Their daughter was missing, and they'd want to be out there scouring the streets. Instead, they'd have to sit in their apartment and be grilled by two policemen, prying into their personal lives. It wasn't a part of the job Mackinnon enjoyed, but he knew questioning the Watsons would give them the best chance of getting Ruby back unharmed.

And at the end of the day, that was the most important thing.

CHAPTER FOUR

TYLER DROVE TO MOOR LANE, which was on the very edge of the square mile. It was within walking distance from Wood Street Station, but with a case like this when every moment counted even a few minutes saved by taking the car made a difference.

He parked the Mondeo in the underground car park. Parking in the City was scarce, but the basement car-park was vast and full of Range Rovers and Porsches. Like most things in life, if you had enough money, you didn't have to worry about trivial things like finding a parking space.

They got out of the car, and Tyler pointed to the right. "The entrance is over there. There is a private lift to the penthouse. How the other half live, eh?"

Mackinnon didn't answer. He was too distracted by the Audi R8 they were walking past.

A short man, wearing a navy blue uniform, with *security* printed above his breast pocket, stood beside a set of glass doors. He looked at them warily as they approached until they held up their warrant cards.

"DI Tyler and DS Mackinnon. We're here to see the Watsons," Tyler said.

The short man moved to open the door for them as he said, "What's happening then? You're the second lot of police to turn up today."

"It's a private matter," Mackinnon said. They would have to question him at some point, but right now they wanted to keep things as quiet as possible until they had more details.

The man looked offended. "Well, if it involves the security of this building, I really should be in the loop."

Mackinnon smiled. "Of course. When we have some information to share, you'll be the first to know."

The man frowned as though he didn't know whether to be mollified or annoyed. "This way." He led them around the corner to a mirrored hallway and the lift. "Just press P for the penthouse."

"Thanks," Mackinnon said.

Tyler didn't bother to respond. He was too busy scrolling through messages on his phone.

"Collins has managed to find Ruby Watson on a CCTV camera outside the building at seven fifty this morning. He's tracing her route now," Tyler said after the security guard was out of earshot.

They stepped inside the lift and pressed the button. The walls were mirrored, and the floor had a lush carpet.

Stepping out into a luxurious lobby covered with marble, Mackinnon found it hard to believe this sumptuous apartment block was less than a quarter of a mile away from the notorious Towers Estate.

There was only one door on this level. Tyler knocked, and

the door was opened by a uniformed officer. They held up their warrant cards, and the officer took a step back.

"The family liaison officer has just arrived, sir. She is talking to the family now."

As the officer spoke, a young woman appeared behind him. "I'm Kelly Johnson, family liaison officer. I've been speaking to Ruby's parents. If you want to follow me, I'll introduce you to them."

They followed Kelly along a wide corridor and into a room with huge, floor-to-ceiling windows that gave a panoramic view of London, with St Paul's taking centre stage.

Sitting on a cream sofa, with at least a foot separating them were Ruby Watson's parents. Claire Watson had recently been crying. Her eyes were red, and she clutched a tissue in her left hand. She looked up at Mackinnon and Tyler hopefully as they entered the room.

"Have you found her," she asked, her eyes darting from Mackinnon to Tyler.

"Not yet," Tyler said. "But we are doing everything we can. We are currently tracing Ruby's movements."

Her face fell, and her dismay twisted Mackinnon's gut.

Peter Watson's face was unreadable. He sat stiffly on the sofa as though he would rather be anywhere but sitting beside his wife.

"Surely there is something we could be doing. It's ridiculous to be stuck here, while Ruby is out there somewhere..." The rest of his sentence faded away as he stared miserably at the ground.

"It's best if you stay here. Because the people who have taken your daughter will probably try to contact you again," Tyler said. "Now, we're going to ask you both some questions. They may seem intrusive, and I apologise in advance, but the more information we have, the better chance we have of getting Ruby back home safely."

Claire Watson nodded. "Of course, we'll tell you anything."

Peter Watson nodded. He wasn't as openly emotional as his wife, but it was clear he was struggling to hold it together.

Tyler nodded at Mackinnon, indicating he should begin questioning the couple. He started with a couple of easy ones.

"You've checked with all of Ruby's friends?"

Claire Watson nodded. "Yes, that was the first thing we did. We've already told the other police officer this."

"It might seem like our questions are rehashing old ground, but it's important we confirm the facts as quickly as possible. Our colleagues are already tracing Ruby's movements, and this won't take long."

"To be honest, the friends we called were Ruby's classmates from school, but she is seventeen years old, Detective," Peter Watson said. "We don't know every single one of Ruby's friends."

His wife bristled as though her husband's words were an affront to her mothering skills.

"I know all of her friends, at least, everyone who is important in Ruby's life. Her best friend, Kirsty, is in Capri for the summer. In fact, most of Ruby's friends are abroad." Claire Watson began to pull apart the tissue she'd been clutching.

"She could have a few casual acquaintances we don't know," she added grudgingly.

"And has she been going to work regularly before today?"

Both Peter and Claire nodded.

"Yes, when I got the text message, I didn't phone the police straightaway," Claire said. "I thought it was some sort of horrible hoax, and I phoned the community centre. I spoke to

Diane, the woman in charge, and she told me Ruby wasn't there."

Claire Watson's voice quavered, and her husband took over.

"She told us she hadn't arrived for work this morning, but Ruby has never missed a shift before. She's never even been late. Diane said she was one of her most reliable volunteers."

"Why is Ruby working at the centre?" Tyler asked.

It was a good question. The Rose Hill Community Centre catered for adults with learning disabilities and adults who struggled to find steady employment due to a lack of education. A skeleton staff ran the programs and were assisted by unpaid volunteers like Ruby.

It was a commendable job, but as a well-connected seventeen-year-old girl with rich parents, a holiday in Capri with her best friend would have been tempting. With her friends holidaying in Europe for the summer, why had Ruby chosen to remain and volunteer for a program in London?

Claire Watson let out an impatient little huff. "It's voluntary work. Ruby thought it would be helpful on her university application. Just because we have money, it doesn't mean our children don't know it's their duty to contribute to the community."

Tyler nodded but didn't make any further comment.

"Is Ruby's passport still here?" Mackinnon asked.

Peter Watson nodded. "Yes, and she wouldn't have left the country to join her friends on holiday without telling us if that's what you're implying."

Mackinnon sensed Peter Watson was close to losing his temper. As far as he knew, they were wasting time with pointless questions while his daughter was missing. He couldn't know the extent of the investigation and how many

22

police officers were working to bring his daughter home. He saw the family liaison officer and Tyler and Mackinnon, but there was a whole team of support staff working behind the scenes.

Mackinnon took a breath and prepared to ask the next question. He had a feeling Peter Watson wasn't going to like it.

"Is there anyone you can think of who would do this?" Mackinnon asked.

"No! We've already been through all of this," Claire Watson said as she shredded her tissue into small squares. "Why would anyone want to take our daughter?"

Mackinnon didn't answer her question, but he looked at Peter Watson. The lines around the man's mouth became more pronounced as he clenched his teeth. Mackinnon suspected he was holding something back.

"Any problems at work? Disgruntled employees?" Mackinnon prompted.

Peter Watson hesitated for a moment and then shook his head. "No. Nothing like that. I can't imagine who would want to do this. To be honest, I assumed it was down to money, but we haven't had a ransom demand yet. What do you think that means?"

Peter Watson was obviously used to taking charge. In his profession, he was the one who asked questions and directed the meetings.

"I'm not sure we can read anything into that just yet," Tyler said. "It's quite possible we will have a ransom demand in the next twenty-four hours."

Mackinnon asked, "Does Ruby have a boyfriend?"

Claire Watson shook her head. "No. She was seeing someone last year, but it fizzled out. It wasn't anything serious. She's still young. She has plenty of friends but not a boyfriend."

"Not that we know of," Peter Watson added.

His wife turned to look at him. "What do you mean by that?"

"Just that she could have a boyfriend we are unaware of."

Claire Watson looked away and shook her head again. "No, she doesn't. I would know if she did."

Mackinnon pressed on. "Any problems with friends recently? Had she fallen out with anyone?"

Peter Watson's hands tightened into fists at his sides, showing his frustration. "No. This isn't some kind of silly teenage tiff. Someone has taken our daughter."

In the awkward silence that followed, Mackinnon was aware of the steady, thumping beat of music. It had to be coming from somewhere in the apartment. The sound-proofing in this place had to be very good because if you'd paid a few million for a three-bed apartment, you'd be pretty miffed if you could hear your neighbour's music.

"That music, is it coming from your son's room?" Mackinnon asked.

"Yes," Peter Watson said, his eyes narrowing slightly in disapproval.

"Do you think we could have a quick chat with him?"

"Why?" Claire Watson asked. The question came out quick and sharp.

"He's only a year younger than Ruby; perhaps he knows something that could help."

Claire Watson shook her head. "I don't think so. They're not very close."

"Still, we'd like a word with him," DI Tyler cut in.

He spoke politely but in a tone that indicated he wasn't going to accept a refusal.

It was such a delicate balance. Mackinnon felt for Ruby's parents. Their family had been pulled apart and their world tilted on its axis, but as investigators, they weren't here to make friends. They were here with one objective: to find out what had happened to Ruby.

With a sigh, Peter Watson got to his feet. "I'll get him."

He walked off to get his son.

"Have there been any disagreements in the family recently?" Tyler asked when Peter Watson had left the room.

Claire Watson's eyes flashed angrily as she glared at DI Tyler. For a moment, Mackinnon thought she might take out her frustration on him, but she didn't.

"I know what you're thinking, detective. But she wasn't unhappy at home. Ruby hasn't run off on her own accord. It's not in her nature, and it doesn't explain the text message, does it?"

Before either Tyler or Mackinnon could answer, Peter Watson entered the room with his son.

"This is Curtis," he said and then sat back down on the sofa next to his wife.

Mackinnon turned to look at the surly youth who had just walked in behind his father.

He had a long thin face and didn't look like either of his parents.

The first thing Mackinnon noticed was that he didn't seem particularly distressed over his sister's disappearance.

He wandered over to an armchair and slumped down into it. His arms dangled over the sides.

"Curtis," Mackinnon said. "Thank you for agreeing to speak to us. You must be very worried about your sister."

Curtis nodded, but he still didn't look upset. In fact, Mackinnon was positive he could see a smirk on the teenage boy's face.

"Yeah," he said. "I reckon she'll probably turn up."

"Turn up?" Tyler prompted. "What do you mean?"

"Well, it was only one text message. It's probably a prank."

Mackinnon's gaze drifted from Curtis to his parents. Curtis looked relaxed and confident as he sprawled in the chair while his parents looked uptight and scared. They didn't contradict their son, though, which Mackinnon found very odd.

"Do you think this could be a prank, Mrs Watson?" Tyler asked.

"No, of course not. Ruby would never do such a thing. Curtis is just… Curtis," she said, exasperated.

Curtis leant forward in his chair. "Well, I suppose we'll see, won't we?"

Those words wounded Claire Watson, and she flinched. She didn't reprimand or argue with her son. Instead, she started to cry.

"That's enough Curtis," Peter Watson said and nodded, excusing his son. "You can go back to your room."

But in Mackinnon's opinion, it hadn't been nearly enough. Curtis was definitely someone they would need to question further.

But Tyler was in charge of this one, and he wasn't going to push it. "We'll set up a small base on the seventh floor of the building as long as you have no objections."

"That's fine," Peter Watson said, looking distracted as he gazed over Tyler's shoulder, his eyes fixed on Curtis as he walked back to his bedroom.

"Is there anything else you think we should know,

anything that could be helpful?" Mackinnon asked, sensing the interview was coming to a close.

Claire and Peter Watson exchanged a nervous glance. There was definitely something.

There was a long pause before Peter Watson finally sighed and said. "I don't see how it can possibly be relevant, but Ruby and Curtis are adopted. We adopted Ruby when she was five years old and Curtis when he was seven."

Mackinnon nodded. "Were there any problems with the adoption?"

"Not at all. Why would there be? Everything was perfectly aboveboard," Claire Watson snapped.

"I meant were there any issues with Ruby's biological family? Perhaps a relative who wasn't happy with the adoption?"

Peter Watson shook his head. "No, Ruby's biological mother was a heroin addict, estranged from her family, and nobody knew who her real father was. We haven't heard a peep out of them since Ruby was five."

As Tyler wrapped things up and thanked the Watsons for their time, Mackinnon noticed Claire Watson's behaviour had changed. When they'd arrived, she had looked heartbroken and distraught. Now, as she glanced at her husband and then looked furtively down at the floor, the change in her demeanour was dramatic. She looked like a woman who had something to hide.

CHAPTER FIVE

JANICE GEORGE ROLLED over in bed and groaned. She'd had a skinful at the pub last night, and her head was killing her.

She would have slept for longer, but the baby was in the next room, screaming her head off.

"Where the hell is Lila?" Janice moaned as she curled up and put the pillow over her head.

When she didn't get a response, she felt the bed next to her and realised it was empty.

She sat up in bed quickly, and her head spun. She put a hand on her forehead and looked bleary-eyed at the empty space in the bed next to her.

Where the hell was her good-for-nothing husband? She'd had so much to drink last night she couldn't even remember if he'd come home with her. She frowned, trying to piece together the events of the previous evening.

They'd left Lila, their eldest daughter, looking after the baby, she remembered that much. Janice thought the least Lila could have done was stick around to look after the baby this morning as well. She must have known her mother would have one hell of a hangover.

Janice yawned and rubbed her eyes, smearing last night's mascara all over her hands.

One look at the clock on the nightstand told her that Lila had probably already gone to work.

Janice grunted. That was a waste of time. It wasn't *real* work. It was voluntary. Janice told Lila they were taking advantage of her, but her daughter was too headstrong to listen.

She had no idea what Lila was playing at. She walked around with her head in the clouds most days.

Lately, she'd been talking about applying for a course at college next year. Ridiculous. The girl needed to get out into the real world and start earning some money.

Janice flung back the duvet and climbed out of bed, scratching her head.

She'd put her hair up last night and hadn't bothered to take out the little hair grips before she went to bed. Now, they were digging into her scalp painfully.

She stumbled towards the baby's room pulling out the hair grips as she went.

"All right, all right, I'm coming," she said as she walked along the hallway.

God, she felt like death warmed up this morning. She needed to get some strong coffee into her, pronto.

Before she got to the baby's room, she pushed open the door of Lila's bedroom and stuck her head in just to check she wasn't home. She wouldn't put it past the cheeky cow to pretend she was out.

But her bedroom was neat and tidy, and her bed was made.

It didn't look like Janice had any alternative. She would have to deal with the baby herself. She walked into the baby's room and winced at the screams.

"Oi, keep it down. Your mother's got a headache."

Baby Ella had no intention of quieting down. Her little cheeks turned bright pink as she screamed even louder.

Janice leant down and scooped the baby up, and tried to shush her as she walked to the kitchen. The baby's nappy was dry, so at least Lila had changed her before she left. She jiggled her up and down with one arm as she tried to prepare a bottle.

She should have made the bottle before picking the baby up, but her head wasn't with it this morning.

It seemed to take forever. There was no way she could make a cup of coffee with a baby in one arm, so she decided to feed Ella first. Her caffeine fix would have to wait.

She carried the baby into the front room, and that was when she saw her husband sprawled out on the sofa.

How on earth did he do it? He hadn't even stirred. He'd slept through all of Ella's screams. Lucky sod.

Janice collapsed back onto the sofa and held up the bottle so Ella could feed.

When she'd finally got the baby to take the bottle, she saw her mobile phone on the little coffee table. She reached for it.

Then she saw the text.

"We have your daughter. Await further instructions."

BACK AT WOOD STREET STATION, Mackinnon caught up with Collins and Charlotte. He'd left DI Tyler back at the Watsons'

building. He knew Tyler wanted to be on the scene in case the Watsons received a second text message.

They were still setting up the communication equipment needed for the apartment on the seventh floor. Usually, the equipment would be used for a mobile incident room, but in this case, the closer they were to the parents during the investigation, the easier things would be.

Charlotte had been hard at work investigating the background of Ruby's biological parents.

They couldn't ignore the real parent angle or the possibility that another relative had tried to get at Ruby. Sometimes resentment and family rifts lingered for a long time. The Watsons might consider Ruby's adoption done and dusted and her real parents forgotten about, but that didn't mean her biological family felt the same.

"Jack, how did you get on?" Charlotte asked as Mackinnon walked up to her desk.

"Okay. Her parents are very upset, which you'd expect, but the brother is a little strange. His reactions aren't quite...normal."

Charlotte frowned. "What do you mean?"

"He's a little odd. He told us he expected Ruby would turn up, and he doesn't seem worried in the slightest."

"Do you think he knows something we don't? He could know who abducted Ruby, or maybe he thinks it was a staged abduction?"

Mackinnon shook his head. "I really don't know. Curtis is only sixteen, so we have to tread carefully. We were only able to question him briefly before his parents sent him away again. They said he and Ruby aren't close, but he's definitely someone we need to look at. The family liaison officer, Kelly

Johnson, is great. She's experienced, and I hope she's going to be able to talk to Curtis and get him to open up."

Charlotte leant back in her chair and tapped her pen on the desk. "Let's hope so. Collins has tracked Ruby from the Watsons' apartment building to Rose Hill Lane. She was picked up on a CCTV camera very close to the community centre around the time she was expected to turn up for work. He is contacting the community centre, and as they've got their own CCTV, hopefully, we can get a better angle and see Ruby more clearly. She was literally yards away from the building, but for some reason, she didn't turn up for work."

Mackinnon frowned and before he could reply one of the phones rang. It was on an empty desk behind them.

"I'll get it," Mackinnon said and left Charlotte scrolling through a list of names on the computer.

Right now, they hadn't heard anything more from the abductors, so they needed to use this downtime to collect as much information as possible. No matter how small or insignificant a piece of information might seem, it could be a clue that led them to Ruby.

He picked up the phone and thanked a member of the support team, who told him the communications team were heading out to take the equipment they'd requested to the make-shift incident room at the Watsons' building.

As he hung up the phone, Mackinnon saw DCI Brookbank striding through the doorway. Everyone looked up.

Brookbank didn't bother with any preamble. He took a quick look around the room and then announced, "We've got another one."

CHAPTER SIX

MACKINNON AND CHARLOTTE arrived outside Buddleia Court on the Towers Estate less than ten minutes after hearing the news another girl had been abducted. They stepped inside the dark entrance hall and paused by the lifts.

"It looks as though it is working. Do you want to chance it?" Charlotte said, looking at the dented metal door of the lift, which was still marked with traces of old graffiti.

The family they were visiting lived on the fifth floor. On most occasions when he had visited the Towers Estate, Mackinnon had avoided the lift. Today, thankfully, the only smell coming from the lift was bleach. Even so, he nodded towards the stairwell and they walked briskly up to the fifth floor.

As soon as they reached the landing, they saw a woman clutching a baby. She had panic written all over her face. It had to be Janice George.

"Are you the police?"

Mackinnon nodded and showed her his warrant card. "I'm Detective Sergeant Jack Mackinnon, and this is my colleague,

Detective Constable Charlotte Brown. We've come to talk about Lila. Is it all right if we come in?"

"Yes, of course. Is there any news?" She asked and then shouted out to her husband, "Toby! The police are here."

From the other end of the passage, Toby George appeared. He was a small, thin man with wispy, brown hair that was greying at the temples and standing on end. He looked as though he'd only just woken up.

"We have a team looking for Lila now. We'd like to ask you some questions so we can find her as soon as possible."

"Questions?" Toby George looked at them blankly.

Janice shifted the baby to her hip and waved her hand, gesturing for everyone to move into the sitting room. "Of course they need to ask us questions. They need to know about Lila."

The small sitting room smelled stale, and Mackinnon noticed a couple of empty beer cans sitting on the floor beside the sofa.

Janice George sat down in an armchair, balancing the baby on her knee. Her husband remained standing.

"Can we see the text message you received?" Charlotte asked.

"Yes, go right ahead. My mobile is on the coffee table." Janice jerked her head in the direction of the phone but then looked away quickly as though she couldn't stand to look at it.

"It's just someone having a laugh, isn't it? There are some sick people about."

She put all her hope into that question, but the frantic look in her eyes told Mackinnon she knew how serious this was.

"We have to treat this text message as genuine at the

moment," Mackinnon said. "Have you called any of Lila's friends?"

Janice looked as though she might be sick. She closed her eyes and leant forward, resting her chin on the baby's head.

"I've called a couple of them," Toby said. "But none of them have seen her. She's not hanging around with the same group of friends at the moment, so it's hard to know who to call. To be honest, my head is all over the place."

Charlotte nodded and smiled reassuringly at Toby. "That's all right. I'm sure we can help you contact Lila's friends. Now, can you tell me when you last saw Lila?"

Toby ran a hand over his unshaven chin. "Well, we saw her last night before we went out. She was looking after the baby for us so we could have a night out. I didn't see her this morning. I slept in."

"Mrs George?" Mackinnon prompted. "Was that the last time you saw Lila, too?"

Janice's eyes were shining with unshed tears. Her body was trembling as reality started to set in. "Yes, I saw her last night before we went out. She's a good kid. She loves her baby sister and doesn't mind babysitting. When I saw her room was empty this morning, I just assumed she'd already left for work. It's not a proper job. She volunteers at the community centre on Rose Hill Lane. It's a travesty really. They don't pay her a penny." Janice turned her head to look at her husband. "If one of those weirdos she helps... If one of those bastards has done something to my Lila, I swear to God..."

Toby took a step forward and put a hand on his wife's shoulder. "We don't know that yet. It might have nothing to do with them."

"How long has your daughter been volunteering at the Rose Hill community centre?" Charlotte asked.

"She's been working there most of the summer. I told her she was wasting her time and would be better off getting a proper job, but she is mixing with a different type of person now. She's got herself some new friends, and they've put ideas into her head."

"What sort of ideas?" Mackinnon asked.

Toby shook his head. "It's nothing really. She's just made friends with a girl who is going to university next year. Lila's decided she might like to go to college."

Charlotte shot a glance at Mackinnon, and he nodded. He knew what question she wanted to ask next.

"Does your daughter know Ruby Watson?"

Janice blinked and looked up to her husband. "No, I don't think so. I don't recognise the name."

Toby frowned. "Who is she?"

"We believe she was abducted, too, possibly by the same person who has taken Lila," Mackinnon said.

Janice's face paled. She muttered a curse, stood up, thrust the baby at her husband and rushed out of the room. Five seconds later, they could hear the sounds of vomiting.

Toby George sank into the seat his wife had vacated and hugged the baby to his chest. She began to squirm and grizzle, sensing his distress.

"What do we do now?" Toby asked. He looked lost.

"We're tracing your daughter's movements so we can find out where she was taken and when. If you have any ideas about why Lila would be targeted, you should tell us now."

Toby shook his head. "I have no idea. We haven't got any money so they can't have targeted her for that. What about the other girl you mentioned? Ruby, wasn't it?"

Mackinnon nodded. "Yes, Ruby Watson. We are not sure why she was targeted yet. We have been keeping the abduction quiet and out of the press. If things are made public, it could hinder the investigation. Although members of the public will want to help and phone in information, we will get inundated with calls and we won't know which ones are genuine. Right now, we think it's sensible to keep the press out of it, and that means keeping people who know about Lila's disappearance to a minimum."

Janice appeared in the doorway. She was trembling and crossed her arms over her chest, hugging herself tightly as though she were worried she might fall apart.

"Do you know if Lila was caught up in anything? An estate feud? Or drugs?"

Janice let out a bitter laugh. "She doesn't get involved in stuff like that. Just because we are not hoity-toity snobs doesn't mean our Lila is involved with drugs. She might do a little bit of pot here and there, but doesn't everyone?"

Mackinnon guessed that was a rhetorical question.

"Ruby Watson's parents are very wealthy. So far, they have only had one text message the same as you. It's possible we may get a ransom demand in the next few hours."

Janice put a hand to her forehead. "Oh, God. What has Lila got herself involved in? I knew she had been hanging around with someone who was filling her head with daft ideas for the future. I told Lila she should just settle for what she had and make the most of it. But Lila's always been a dreamer. She just wanted to better herself. Our daughter is a hard-working, sweet girl. Please find her for us."

Charlotte reached out and squeezed Janice's hand. "We will do our very best."

CHAPTER SEVEN

WHEN MACKINNON and Charlotte left the Towers Estate, they went their separate ways. Charlotte returned to Wood Street Station to report back to DI Tyler, and Mackinnon headed to the Rose Hill community centre.

He knew DC Collins would already be there, accessing the centre's CCTV, but as both girls were last seen just outside the community centre, Mackinnon wanted to talk to the staff himself. People attending the centre may have witnessed something important without realising it at the time. Things that may have seemed innocent to a casual observer could now take on a new meaning.

The Rose Hill community centre was set at one end of a pleasant square. Numerous young trees had been planted to try and improve the landscaping in the area and bring some greenery and interest to the concrete blocks surrounding the square.

There were a couple of new, glass-fronted buildings scattered around the square, but the majority of the buildings had been built in the late sixties and looked like ugly, grey concrete slabs.

The community centre itself was a single-storey, red-brick building, partially covered by a facade decorated with primary colours.

The community centre had been funded by one of the big banks in the city. They described it as their contribution to supporting the local community. The difference in wealth was huge in this area of the city. On the one hand, wealthy traders and bankers were conducting multi-million-pound deals, and on the other, some residents were struggling day-to-day to make ends meet.

The glass front doors were open, and Mackinnon walked straight in.

The entranceway was a large room in itself. The long windows let in plenty of daylight, and the walls were painted a brilliant white, making everything seem bright and cheerful. There were a couple of bookshelves lining either side of the room, and there were bright yellow tables and chairs set out along the edges of the room.

The room was empty apart from a young woman with pink hair, who had her head bent over a book, muttering to herself.

To his right, there was another door, and through the small glass panel, Mackinnon could see there were many more people in that room.

He opened the door and went inside. The murmur of voices trailed away, and a number of heads turned his way, looking at him curiously. Most people at the centre were dressed casually, and Mackinnon stood out in his suit and tie.

They probably had pegged him immediately as a police officer, but he didn't mind that.

A woman, who Mackinnon guessed to be in her mid-fifties, made her way towards him.

"Can I help you?"

Mackinnon nodded and pulled his ID out of the internal pocket of his jacket. "Yes, I'm Detective Sergeant Jack Mackinnon. I believe my colleague is already here?"

The woman smiled. "He is. We've set him up in a room where he can look through the CCTV footage. My name is Diane Swanson," she said and held out her hand for Mackinnon to shake.

"He's actually working in my office at the moment as we've got a course on today. The centre isn't usually so full."

Mackinnon nodded. "I can see you're busy. But if you could spare the time, I would really like to ask you some questions about the centre and Lila George and Ruby Watson."

Diane frowned and tucked her grey curls behind her ear. "Has something happened to the girls?"

Although nobody wanted a tidal wave of press complicating matters right now, there was no point in a complete information blackout. The police needed to ask questions and they needed answers urgently. People were much more likely to try to help if they knew the police were trying to help two girls in danger.

"They haven't done anything wrong have they?" Diane asked.

Mackinnon shook his head. "No, they haven't done anything wrong."

Diane Swanson seemed to appreciate the fact Mackinnon didn't want to talk about the situation in front of a room full of people. She nodded to the door behind him. "Let's go through there, into the kitchen. We can talk privately."

Mackinnon followed her into the kitchen area which was very small, but functional. There was a toaster, microwave and a kettle all lined up next to a tiny sink.

Diane picked up a mug from the draining board and asked Mackinnon, "Would you like a coffee?"

Mackinnon shook his head. "No, thank you. I'm fine."

"You won't mind if I make one while we are in here?" Diane asked. "I don't usually get time to make myself a coffee when I'm working, so I'm going to take advantage of this."

Mackinnon leant back against the kitchen counter. "We've been looking at other CCTV in the area and we found that both Lila and Ruby were just outside the building this morning, but it doesn't look like they entered."

Diane nodded as she spooned some instant coffee into a mug. "That's right. Your colleague said they'd been seen outside, but neither of them turned up for work this morning. It was most unusual. This is the first time they've missed a shift."

"How long have they been working here?"

"Just for the summer. So about three weeks now. Ruby is in the middle of her A-level course, and I think Lila is hoping to go to college next year so they'll both be leaving us in September. They're working here as volunteers so it's not paid employment, but it is the kind of thing that looks good on a CV, and in Ruby's case, I'm guessing she's going to use it for her university application."

She switched the kettle on and then opened the fridge, taking out a pint of milk and then looked up at Mackinnon. "You think something bad has happened to them, don't you?"

"Both girls are missing. Their parents are understandably

very concerned. I need to know anything you can tell me that might help us find them."

Diane put a shaking hand to her mouth. "God, how awful. Their poor parents."

She closed her eyes and ignored the kettle as it came to the boil. "I can't understand why anyone would want to hurt them. They work hard, they're cheerful, and they're great with the regulars who visit the centre."

Diane shook her head as though she was lost for words.

"Were you aware of any arguments between the girls themselves or anyone in the centre?"

Diane shook her head. "No, I'd never heard a cross word between them. They got on very well with everyone here."

There was an abrupt knock and the door was flung open. A young woman with dark, spiky hair and a diamond stud in her nose pushed past Mackinnon to get to Diane.

"You said that CV would work. You said if I put down everything you told me, they'd give me a job. Well, they didn't." The young woman almost spat the words at Diane.

Mackinnon had to fight the urge to order the young woman out of the kitchen.

There wasn't much room in the kitchen area as it was, and although the young woman was only petite, her anger seemed to fill the room. She folded her arms over her chest as she stared accusingly at Diane.

"I don't have time for this now, Charlie," Diane said. "I'm sorry you didn't get the job. If you can just wait five minutes, we'll talk things through."

The girl narrowed her eyes and turned to look at Mackinnon, no doubt blaming him for the fact Diane didn't have time for her.

"Oh, I see. I guess I'm not your favourite pet project anymore."

The girl turned and whirled out of the room.

Diane smiled apologetically. "I'm sorry about that. Most of the people we help here are grateful, but sometimes their frustrations can get the better of them. Sorry, I've lost my thread. Did you ask me a question?"

"Have you ever seen anyone waiting for one of the girls outside? Or did either of the girls mention a boyfriend?"

Diane put a hand to her forehead and was quiet for a moment, trying to think. Then she shook her head. "I'm sorry, I wish I could be more help, but they didn't really confide in me about things like that, and I don't think I ever saw anyone waiting for them outside. Even if there had been someone waiting for them, I'm not sure I'd notice."

Mackinnon opened his mouth to answer another question but before he could there was another knock on the door.

He turned angrily, expecting it to be the young woman again, but instead he saw Collins standing in the doorway.

"Sorry to interrupt, Jack, but I've got something you should see."

Mackinnon turned back to Diane and apologised before following Collins through the centre and into a small office area at the back of the building.

Inside the office, there was a desk piled high with papers and a garish abstract print in fluorescent pink and green hung on the wall behind the computer.

Collins sat down at the chair in front of the computer station and pointed at the screen.

Sometimes it was easier to use CCTV in situ because there were multiple playback systems and not all of them were compatible. It would cost the police a fortune if they had to acquire playback software and machines for every single system.

"Have you found them?" Mackinnon asked as he leant down to take a closer look at the screen.

Collins nodded. "Yes, and they are not alone."

CHAPTER EIGHT

MACKINNON AND COLLINS didn't talk as they watched the video playback on the computer screen. They watched as a large man approached Ruby Watson and Lila George. The man didn't attempt to hide his face or shy away from the cameras. Either he didn't know they were there, or he didn't care.

"He's a big lad," muttered Collins.

Mackinnon tensed as he waited for the inevitable confrontation between the girls and the man approaching them. He immediately had a very uneasy feeling about this. They were watching something that had already happened, something that couldn't be changed.

Mackinnon frowned as the video playback continued. There was no altercation, no fear shown by either of the girls.

"They know him, Mackinnon said. "Look how she touches his shoulder, and they're both smiling."

Collins nodded in agreement. "Do you think he is someone from the centre?"

Mackinnon straightened. "Let's ask Diane if she can identify him."

He walked around the desk and then stuck his head out of the office door and caught Diane's gaze. She was standing a few feet away, cradling her mug of coffee.

"Could you spare us a minute?" Mackinnon asked. "We'd like you to identify someone if you can."

Diane nodded and put her coffee mug on the table beside her before walking towards him. "Absolutely."

She shuffled behind the desk and joined Collins in front of the computer screen.

She didn't need to look at the screen long before she said, "Oh, yes, I know who that is. It's Benny Morris. He's a nice lad and…." Her voice trailed off, and her face paled as Collins continued the playback, which showed Benny Morris leading the girls away.

Diane looked up at Mackinnon, blinked a couple of times and then swallowed hard. "Benny didn't show up for his IT class this morning," she whispered.

"What can you tell us about him?" Mackinnon asked.

Diane shook her head as though she were overwhelmed. "I think it's better if you ask Eddie, Eddie Longbridge. He spent a lot more time with Benny than I did. He takes the IT classes, you see."

Mackinnon nodded, and Diane scurried off to go and find Eddie.

After she left the office, Collins turned to Mackinnon and said, "He's got to be involved, hasn't he?"

"He's a person of interest, for sure," Mackinnon said. "Even if he had nothing to do with the girl's disappearance, he's the last person we know who saw the girls before their mothers got the text messages. So we need to talk to him as soon as possible."

The door open behind Mackinnon, and he stood to one side as Diane walked into the office followed by a short man with large muscular arms. Eddie Longbridge had a crewcut and carried himself with an angry air. From his build, Mackinnon guessed Eddie worked out many of his frustrations at the gym.

"What's all this about then?" Eddie asked brusquely.

There was a section of society who didn't particularly like helping the police. People who had had a brush with the law in the past and felt hard done by, or people who felt let down or victimised by the police. From the way Eddie was glaring at them, Mackinnon sensed that Eddie was one of those people.

They were going to have to tread carefully to get the information they needed from Eddie Longbridge.

"They want to know about Benny," Diane said, looking at Eddie.

The frown didn't leave Eddie's face as he spoke. "Benny's a nice lad. He's got learning difficulties, but he's a gentle giant. He's been coming to the centre for years and he loves doing the IT classes. I don't imagine he'll ever get a full-time job, but it does him good to get out and about."

"Lila George and Ruby Watson have gone missing. When was the last time you saw them?" Mackinnon asked.

Eddie visibly tensed and paused before answering. "Yesterday. When they came to the centre."

"Have you ever seen anyone hanging around waiting for them, or did they ever mention any problems?"

"Problems? Like what?"

"Problems with ex-boyfriends or anyone at the centre?

Would they have told you if they were worried about someone here? We think someone has taken the girls and we're trying to discover who that may have been."

Eddie shook his head.

"Do you think Benny would have taken the girls against their will?" Collins asked.

Eddie scowled. "No! Benny knows right from wrong. He would never hurt those girls. About a year ago, he found a bird outside with a broken wing. Benny was in tears over it. He couldn't hurt a fly."

"Do you have his address? We'd like to have a word with him?" Mackinnon addressed the question to Diane, but it was Eddie who answered.

He drew himself up to his full height, which compared to Mackinnon wasn't very tall. He folded his arms and said, "I don't think I like the way this is heading."

"We need to speak to him because—" Collins started to say.

But Eddie interrupted, "Oh, yes, I'm sure you do. So you can railroad the poor sod into confessing to something he didn't do."

"No," Mackinnon said coldly. "We want to speak to him because he was the last person to see Lila and Ruby before they went missing."

That shut Eddie up, but he still didn't look happy.

Mackinnon turned to Diane. "We can get a warrant so we can access your records, or we can find out his address by other means, but all that's going to waste time. And as we think Ruby and Lila could be in danger, time is a luxury we don't have."

Diane shook her head. "A warrant won't be necessary. You can have his address."

Diane moved back towards the computer, and Collins vacated the chair so she could sit down.

With a couple of taps on the keyboard, she accessed the information from the computer.

"Benny used to live in sheltered housing, but he moved in with his brother last year after their mother died."

She hit print, and the small printer beside the potted plant on the desk hummed to life.

She handed Mackinnon the printout. "My gut feeling is that Benny is not involved. He's never been violent... He's never shown any anger towards women at all. Please, treat him gently. He's a sensitive soul."

Mackinnon took the address printout, but he didn't reply. He wasn't going to make any promises he couldn't keep.

CHAPTER NINE

WHEN MACKINNON and Collins left the community centre, Collins went directly to meet Charlotte at Wood Street. Tyler was organising the visit to Benny Morris' property. They needed to speak to him as soon as possible as he was their first major lead.

Mackinnon would have liked to go himself, but he had been given another job to do. He had a printout of Benny Morris and the girls from the CCTV to show Ruby Watsons' parents.

He entered Drake House, walking into the cool marble lobby from the street level entrance this time. The luxurious apartment block was less than a five-minute walk from the community centre. The contrast struck Mackinnon again. There was a stark difference in wealth between different sections of society in this area. In this building, each apartment cost millions of pounds. The community centre, less than a quarter of a mile away, helped the most deprived population.

Mackinnon was glad he didn't live in the Towers Estate, but there was something about Drake House he didn't much like either. The million pound apartments were incredibly well-designed and fitted with all the latest, luxurious fittings and furnishings, but Mackinnon found them soulless.

The last time he'd visited the Watsons' apartment it had struck him as odd that they had so few personal items on display. It was more like a show apartment than a real home.

He told the doorman he was there to see the Watsons. The doorman had been questioned by Tyler earlier and was eager to know if there was any news. Mackinnon simply shook his head. If there had been any news, he wouldn't have shared it with the doorman before speaking to Ruby's parents.

The doorman called the apartment and announced Mackinnon's arrival, and then watched Mackinnon as he headed for the lift. As the lift ascended, Mackinnon took a quick look at the image he'd printed out of Benny and the girls. This wasn't going to be easy. He was going to have to show this picture to Mr and Mrs Watson and they would immediately assume the worst, but that couldn't be helped. If they knew Lila George or Benny Morris that could help the police unravel the motive behind this kidnapping and could be crucial in solving the case.

He folded the printout in half and put it back into his pocket as he reached the front door to the apartment.

He lifted his hand to ring the doorbell, but the door opened before he could do so.

"Is there any news?" Claire Watson demanded.

Mackinnon shook his head. He didn't want to give her any false hope. "I'm here to ask a few more questions, and I have a photograph I'd like you to have a look at."

Claire Watson seemed to deflate before his eyes.

"I see," she mumbled.

She turned away and walked back into the living area of the apartment, leaving the front door wide open.

Mackinnon closed it behind him and then followed her.

Peter Watson was pacing in front of the huge floor-to-ceiling windows. He looked furious and Mackinnon sensed he was going to be looking for somebody to take that fury out on. He had a feeling that the next ten minutes were going to be exceedingly difficult.

"Have you managed to track them down yet?" Peter Watson demanded. "I can't understand what's taking so long. How can someone just disappear in this day and age? Why did nobody see anything?"

"Peter, come and sit down. He wants to ask us more questions and show us a photograph," Claire said wearily.

Photograph seemed to be the magic word. Peter Watson rushed over, his eyes searching Mackinnon for the photograph. "Where is it, then?"

Mackinnon fished it out of his pocket and laid it flat down on the coffee table so both Claire and Peter could see it.

"Do you know this girl?" Mackinnon asked, pointing to Lila George.

The Watsons poured over the picture and Claire Watson's breathing grew ragged. Mackinnon knew it was because she'd seen the image of Benny Morris talking to the girls. He wished there was something he could do to make this easier, but there wasn't.

"The girl," Mackinnon repeated. "Do you recognise her?"

Peter shook his head. "I've never seen her before. Is she a friend of Ruby's?"

"Her name is Lila George. We know she was a work colleague of Ruby's." Mackinnon paused for a beat before delivering the worst news. "She has also gone missing, and her parents received the same text message."

Claire Watson gasped, and her hands covered her mouth as she shook her head. She was still looking at the photograph. She couldn't take her eyes off Benny Morris.

"Did... Did he take them?"

"We know that Benny Morris used the community centre and he knew your daughter and Lila. We are currently tracking him down and..."

Mackinnon's phone buzzed in his pocket, and he took it out to silence it, but as he did so, he saw a message from Charlotte.

No answer at Morris' address. Getting a warrant.

Mackinnon shoved his phone back in his pocket.

Claire Watson shook her head. "I don't understand. So Ruby actually went to the community centre but she didn't go to work?"

Mackinnon nodded. "It looks that way. Both girls got as far as the community centre but then they walked away."

Claire Watson looked up at him, her eyes wide with horror. "They walked away... With him?"

Mackinnon nodded.

Peter Watson couldn't sit still any longer. He stood up, curling his hands into fists at his sides. "Have you spoken to him yet?"

"Officers have visited his address, but he wasn't home. We're getting a warrant and..."

"There's no time for that," Peter Watson said, his hands clawing through his hair. "We don't have time to wait for a stupid warrant. Give me the address and I'll go myself."

Mackinnon didn't bother to tell Peter Watson to calm

down. There really wasn't any point and it would only make him angrier.

"I have to stress that Benny Morris was known to be a friend to both of the girls, and there's no indication he would have harmed them. All we know is he was the last person to see them before we lost track of the girls on CCTV. That's why we need to speak to him. We need to find out what happened next. I know it's not easy, but try not to think the worst. This is positive news. We have a fresh lead and somebody we can talk to about what happened to Ruby."

Peter Watson snorted in disgust and turned around, walking away as though he couldn't bear to look at Mackinnon or the photograph any longer.

"Sorry to interrupt, here's the tea." Kelly, the family liaison officer, put the tray down on the coffee table. Her eyes flickered over the photograph and then she looked at Mackinnon and gave him a small smile.

Kelly knew better than anyone how hard it was to deal with victims of crimes when they were angry and the only person they could direct their fury at was the police officers helping them.

The mugs of tea sat on the coffee table but nobody touched them.

Mackinnon had got what he came for. It was his job to find out whether the Watsons had known Benny or Lila George, and it seemed to be quite clear that they didn't.

He felt sorry that he was going to be leaving Kelly to deal with the aftermath his visit had caused by showing the parents the photograph, but it couldn't be helped.

Mackinnon was just about to get to his feet and excuse himself when he heard a noise behind him.

He turned and saw Ruby's brother, Curtis, in the open

plan kitchen. Curtis opened the cupboard and shut it again noisily, pulling out a bowl and setting it on the kitchen counter.

He pulled out a box of cereal from another cupboard and began to whistle as Mackinnon watched him. He took a carton of milk from the fridge and poured it all over the cereal and then began to eat.

There was something very odd about that boy, Mackinnon thought.

While he was here, he decided it might be a good idea to talk to Curtis again. "Curtis, I'd like to have another quick chat with you, if that's okay?"

Curtis smiled. "Sure," he said, waving his spoon around. "But I'd better eat this first. I hate it when my cornflakes go soggy."

CHAPTER TEN

RUBY WATSON'S mind was going around in circles. How could this have happened? She kept thinking of things she should have done differently. There must have been something she could have done to escape.

They'd snatched her at eight a.m. in central London.

She'd felt *safe*. Safe enough to follow Benny without any alarm bells ringing.

She had been completely oblivious to any danger until she and Lila had followed Benny across the cobbled square and into the quiet alleyway. That was when the first alarm bells had started to jingle.

But it was some stupid sense of politeness that stopped her refusing to go with him. She didn't want to hurt his feelings, and she'd been with Lila. She hadn't considered anything truly bad could happen to them in broad daylight a few metres away from the community centre.

But as they'd walked further down the alley, the brick

walls seemed to close in around her, and alarm bells rang louder with every step she took.

Her palms had grown sweaty, and she'd glanced over her shoulder, looking back longingly at the safety of the children's play area.

"Maybe we should do this later," she had said, trying to smile and act like she wasn't afraid. "I don't want to be late for work."

Then she saw the other two men in front of them, and Ruby knew she was in serious trouble.

One wore a baseball cap pulled low, shading his eyes, but she could see his smile, a cruel, twisted smile.

There was something evil about the man who loomed in front of them. Something inherently bad.

She'd tried to step back but crashed into her friend. Trying to get away, she'd reached out, grazing her arm on the rough brick wall. The path was too narrow, and Lila wouldn't move. She hadn't sensed the danger yet.

She'd seen the bemused expression on her friend's face turn to panic as realisation dawned on her. She opened her mouth to scream, but the man in the baseball cap was too quick. His fist collided with the side of her face, and Lila crumpled to the floor.

Ruby had pushed off the wall, preparing to run. All her senses were on high alert as adrenaline flooded her system.

Her scalp burned as he yanked on her hair, pulling her head back. He slapped her with the back of his hand, not as hard as he'd hit Lila, but hard enough to leave her dazed for a moment. She hadn't seen it coming.

She turned and staggered, still stunned from the blow.

She heard the man in the baseball cap laughing behind her, and Benny telling him to stop.

Yes, she thought. Yes, that's right, stop. Let me go. Listen to Benny.

But he didn't. She felt his sour breath against her ear as he reached up and pulled her hair again, yanking it down and making her cry out in pain.

"You're not going anywhere," he said.

She wanted to turn away. She wanted to see her friend get to her feet and run. At least one of them had to escape and get help.

But she couldn't see anything apart from the evil eyes of her captor, staring down into hers.

She bucked against him, kicking out hard, and she knew that her blows were hitting home because he huffed and grunted as her heel connected with his shins.

His grip loosened a little, and she managed to jerk herself free, but he grabbed onto her arm, his fingers digging painfully into her flesh.

She kicked out again and hit him back with her free hand.

"Feisty one, isn't she?" he asked, chuckling. "I thought you said she'd go quietly."

Not a chance, Ruby thought. She knew if she didn't escape now, there was a chance she never would. She clawed at his face, but his hand tightened around her neck, forcing her back against the wall. Her head hit the brickwork with a sickening thud. He stuffed a rag in her mouth.

At first, she thought she'd been knocked out because everything went black and then she realised he'd pulled something over her head, something that smelled bad... stale and musty... a hood.

He'd lifted her upper body and ordered his partner to grab her legs. She felt his arms encircling her torso and somebody else reaching for her ankles. She'd kicked out and felt her foot connect with something soft. That earned her a fist in her stomach.

She'd gagged and gasped for air, winded by the blow. She still struggled as hard as she could, but it was no good, they held her tight and carried her away.

It had seemed to take forever until all of a sudden they'd let her go, and she'd hit the floor with a metal clang.

She'd tried to calm herself down and work out what had happened. The rag they'd put in her mouth made her want to gag.

Suddenly the hood was ripped off, and as she looked around, she realised she was in the back of a van.

She stared up at her tormentor; all her fight had ebbed away. All Ruby could think was, *why us?* Her friend, Lila, lay unconscious on the floor of the van, beside her. The man in the baseball cap had hit her too hard. She had a trickle of blood running from the side of her mouth.

Oh, God. Don't let her be dead. Please don't let her be dead.

"Sit back and get comfortable, girls," he'd said as he secured her wrists behind her back and checked the rag was firmly stuffed in her mouth. "I've got plenty of fun planned for you."

CHAPTER ELEVEN

At that moment, Benny Morris was sitting on a hard-backed chair outside the room he knew Ruby and Lila were being held in.

He wanted to go into the room and talk to them, but the nasty man wearing the cap had locked it.

Rob had told him the nasty man's name was Marlo. He had introduced them, and Marlo had smiled at Benny in a way he didn't like. It wasn't a nice smile.

Marlo was a bad man.

Benny was confused. He had once heard somebody say he wasn't the sharpest knife in the drawer. But he didn't usually worry about that. Not every knife needed to be razor sharp. As his mother used to say, everyone had their place in this world.

After their mother died, Rob had taken care of him and Benny trusted him absolutely, which was why he couldn't understand why Rob liked a man like Marlo.

Benny knew that Marlo was a bad man no matter what Rob said.

Rob was in the kitchen with Marlo now. The door was shut, and they were talking in whispers. His brother had given him a packet of cheese puffs and a can of Coke. He loved cheese puffs, but today they tasted slimy, and he couldn't finish the packet.

Benny didn't understand what was going on. Rob had told him he needed to bring Ruby to Celandine Gardens. He said he was doing a bit of business to get some money together so he could buy Benny an Xbox, but everything had gone wrong.

There was no sign of Benny's Xbox here and he knew that they'd hurt Ruby and Lila.

Rob told him to be quiet and sit still and stop asking questions. He told him the girls were fine, but Benny couldn't believe it. He'd seen Lila had been bleeding.

Benny sniffed and wiped his nose on his sleeve. It was horrible in the flat. There was no proper daylight because they were down in the basement.

Benny hated the dark and still slept with a nightlight. Rob had tried to get him to sleep without it, but it didn't work. Danger lurked in the darkness. Ever since he was a little boy, his mother had forever been telling him off for leaving all the lights on in the flat, but Benny knew things could hide in the shadows and it scared him.

A few months ago, Rob had threatened to take his nightlight away. He said Benny needed to grow out of it, but if Rob took his nightlight away, Benny had a plan to buy another one. He'd seen one in a shop.

He thought he heard a noise coming from the room where the girls were being kept and tried to listen, but he couldn't hear anything other than the hushed whispers coming from the kitchen.

Benny got up and pressed his ear to the door. He really wanted to talk to the girls and tell them everything would be okay, but Rob would be furious if he did that.

Benny sat down again and put his hands against his ears. He hated the whispering.

As he rocked back and forwards in his chair, his foot caught the half-full can of Coke, and it spilt all over the carpet.

"Oh, no," Benny said as he leant his huge frame down to pick up the Coke can with a shaking hand.

He walked to the kitchen and opened the door to tell his brother about spilling the Coke. It was an accident so he couldn't be angry with Benny. People weren't allowed to be angry over accidents.

But when he saw his brother's face, Benny froze. Rob looked very angry.

"I thought you said you could control him." Marlo's voice came from the other side of the kitchen.

Benny's head whipped around, and his lower lip wobbled as he held out the empty can of Coke. "I had an accident," he said.

Surely even nasty Marlo couldn't be angry if it was only an accident.

Rob moved closer to him and put a hand on Benny's shoulder. "It's all right, Benny. Don't you worry. I'll clear it up in a minute."

But Benny couldn't take his eyes off Marlo.

Rob glared at Marlo over a shoulder. "Don't worry, Benny. Marlo is just a bit on edge. I tell you what, why don't we put the telly on?"

Benny nodded. "Okay then."

Rob took the empty can of Coke and threw it in the bin. Then he led Benny along the hallway, past Benny's empty chair and into the front room.

When they were alone, Benny turned to his brother. "I don't like Marlo. He's a bad man."

Rob sighed and nodded. "We've got to put up with him for a little bit longer, Benny."

"Why can't we go home?"

"We can, soon, but first, we've got to do a little bit of business and get some money together. I've got to get you that Xbox, don't you remember?"

Benny rubbed his eyes. He didn't care about the Xbox anymore. He just wanted to leave and go home.

"Are Ruby and Lila okay?"

Rob nodded as he switched on the TV for Benny. "Oh, sure. They're fine. I tell you what, I was thinking I'd get them some lunch. What do you think they'd like?"

"McDonald's," Benny said immediately.

CHAPTER TWELVE

Rob left Benny in the front room watching the TV and went back to the kitchen where Marlo was hiding out.

They were holding the girls in a two-bedroom basement flat, which had been empty for a few months before Marlo had claimed it. He didn't have much furniture. There was one single bed pushed against the wall in the main bedroom, and the bedroom the girls were being kept in didn't have any furniture at all.

There was a huge TV in the front room, though, and a leather settee, which Rob hoped would keep Benny happy for a little while longer.

Benny didn't like to be out of his comfort zone, and truth be told, Rob was worried. He'd had no intention of getting Benny involved in any of this. But Marlo had insisted it was the easiest way to get Ruby Watson where they wanted her without being watched by any prying eyes.

When Rob walked into the kitchen, he saw Marlo crouching over a large white container.

"What's that?" Rob asked as he tried to look over Marlo's shoulder.

Marlo slammed the lid on the white container and lifted it by a small metal handle before shoving it behind the bin.

He grinned at Rob. "Patience is a virtue. All will be revealed in good time."

As Rob watched Marlo stand up and lean over a selection of mobile phones on the window sill, inspecting each one carefully, he felt a wave of dislike.

He should have known better than going into business with Marlo. He had a feeling this whole thing was going to spiral into the most epic failure.

"I hope you'll be able to keep him under control from now on," Marlo said mockingly, not bothering to turn around.

"Don't be too hard on him. Benny will be fine."

"Good. I'm not having a retard messing up my plans."

Rob felt an icy wave of fury flood his body. Through gritted teeth, he said, "That's my brother you're talking about."

The tone of Rob's voice finally got Marlo to turn around.

He smirked. "No offence, mate. I don't know why you bother. It would drive me nuts having him hanging around all the time."

"Yeah, well, I'm not you, am I?" Rob said. He needed to get out of there and away from Marlo before he snapped. "I'm going to get some food for the girls and Benny. McDonald's. Do you want anything?"

Marlo nodded absentmindedly. He either didn't know he'd upset Rob or he just didn't care. Rob suspected it might be the latter.

"Yeah, get me a Big Mac meal," Marlo said. He picked up

one of the phones that were set out in front of him on the windowsill and peered at it closely.

Rob couldn't resist asking, "Have you sent another text message?"

Marlo put the phone back on the windowsill and turned around. He gave Rob a small smile. "I'm going to send one after lunch."

Rob nodded. That was good. The sooner this was over, the better as far as he was concerned.

"How much are you going to ask for?"

Marlo's eyes were hooded, and he looked shifty. "I'm not going to ask for the money just yet."

Rob's forehead prickled with sweat. What the hell was he playing at?

"Why not?" Rob demanded.

Marlo chuckled. "Don't be so impatient. All in good time. I just thought we should have a little fun first."

Why had he trusted Marlo? This had to be the most stupid thing he'd ever done. Of course, he was going back on his word. It was Marlo. That was what he did. He should never have got involved in Marlo's little plan, and now he'd got Benny wrapped up in it, too.

He tried to control his anger and be persuasive. He knew Marlo was stubborn, and if he protested too much then Marlo would make life even more difficult for him and Benny.

"Come on, Marlo. You promised me money. The rent is due, and I need the cash. Besides, we need to return the girls as soon as possible. I don't like them being here. It makes me uncomfortable."

Marlo licked his lips. "You'll get your money, Rob. Don't worry about that. We're just going to play a little game first."

CHAPTER THIRTEEN

THE ATMOSPHERE in Wood Street Station was tense. Tyler had acquired a search warrant for Benny Morris' address, but the search had yielded nothing to go on so far, and there was still no sign of Benny or his brother, Rob.

DI Tyler led the search at the Morris brother's address himself. The block of flats had front facing hallways, which were open to the elements. This created a number of problems. A resident had hung their washing outside, making it difficult for the officers to get past.

They had a multitude of tools at their disposal to get inside the property, such as the Enforcer, a battering ram jokingly referred to as the big red key, and a specialised team, but Tyler was sure he didn't need any of that. For one thing, there was no way to approach the flat without being seen, and a load of officers dressed in black tactical gear would soon attract people's attention. He didn't want to give Benny the fright of his life, causing him to panic and do something he might regret.

Then there was the evidence from the CCTV. Most of the cameras around the Towers Estate were down. As soon as they were repaired, somebody would smash them up again. This was mainly because of the drug dealers operating on the estate. The dealers didn't want to be observed for obvious reasons. This meant security was lax, and in this day and age, modern policing relied heavily on surveillance equipment.

Thankfully one of the cameras opposite the Morris brother's block of flats was working. It showed Benny Morris and his brother leaving at seven a.m. and didn't show them coming back. There was only one entrance to the flat, and since they lived on the third floor, Tyler thought it was very unlikely they would be able to climb high enough to access the balcony at the back of the flats, so he was confident they hadn't returned.

The attitudes of the residents living in the Towers Estate varied quite considerably, but the majority of people were sick and tired of the drugs on the estate. Others were perfectly happy for things to continue the way they were. But all the residents seemed to have one thing in common, Tyler noted, and that was an unwillingness to help the police.

Officers had called at various flats in the immediate vicinity, and nobody admitted to seeing anyone of Ruby Watson's or Lila George's description that morning. In fact, most people wouldn't even admit they knew Benny Morris or his brother Rob.

The sheer size of Benny meant he wasn't an easy guy to miss, so he knew the residents were holding back. But the CCTV evidence didn't lie. Even if Benny Morris had been involved in the girl's disappearance, he hadn't brought them back here.

The first thing he'd noticed when he entered the flat was

that there was no smell other than that of old cooking and a whiff of some spray deodorant. That was one of the things as an experienced officer Tyler dreaded when he entered a property — the smell of decay, the smell of a dead body. And that definitely wasn't the case here.

The girls had only been taken that morning, and a quick look around the flat didn't reveal anything to indicate a crime had taken place there. There was no blood, no obvious weapons, no drug paraphernalia and no stolen goods.

They couldn't rule anything out until they'd conducted a proper search, though. Tyler had taken a deep breath and left the other officers to it as he went outside.

The block of flats wasn't as tall as some of the others at only seven stories high. All around the blocks of flats towered above him, reaching to the sky and making him feel claustrophobic.

He ran a hand through his grey hair and muttered a curse. His home life had been crap just recently and he had thrown himself into the job full force.

He'd never had any desire to be a career copper. He'd fallen into doing the detective exams and progressed from there, being lucky to be in the right place at the right time when promotions rolled around. He'd always been one to take the easy way out, and he'd been pretty lucky through his career. This was his first big case as SIO. He'd been involved in others, of course, even headed up some enquiries, but this was different. The buck stopped with him and that was scary. If he screwed up, the life of two girls could be at stake.

He'd hated watching the video that Collins had brought back from the community centre. To see those girls smiling, looking happy and then disappearing from view, swallowed up by the Towers Estate, made him feel sick.

"Where did you go?" Tyler muttered.

He stood there for a moment considering his next move. He needed to find Benny Morris. His gut told him, even if Benny wasn't involved in the abduction, he would have information. And right now information was exactly what they needed.

His mobile phone rang and he took a quick glance at the screen and saw it was DC Collins. He pressed answer and waited for Collins to speak.

"I've gone through the cameras," Collins said. "There's no trace of them. They disappeared into the Towers Estate after we lost sight of them at Rose Hill Community Centre, but we've got no record of them coming out again. Of course, they could have come out in a vehicle, maybe on a bus?"

Tyler almost smiled. "I hardly think they've gone out for the day on the bus, Collins. But vehicles are a possibility. Make sure you get the number plates of all the vans that left the Towers Estate. In fact, make that cars as well. They could have been put in the boot of a car or even on the back seat, so let's get a copy of the license plates of every vehicle that left the Towers Estate between eight a.m. and—"

"That's a lot of cars," Collins said.

"I'm aware of that, thank you," Tyler said sarcastically, and then wished he hadn't snapped at Collins. He was known among the other officers as being a bit of a curmudgeon, even someone who was willing to cut corners occasionally, but now he was in a position of authority, he should make sure he was worthy. He should be leading by example not making pithy comments.

Still, he wasn't about to apologise. He didn't do apologies.

"Just try your best, Collins. We know they came into the

estate, so we've got two options. Either they went out in a vehicle, or they're still here."

Tyler looked around at the numerous tower blocks and felt his heart sink. It would mean a door-to-door enquiry among residents who really weren't interested in helping, but he couldn't think of a better way to do it.

After he hung up on Collins, he dialled Mackinnon's number.

"Jack, I need you to meet me at Drake House. We need to give the Watsons an update. I'll meet you there. Then after that we'll have to go to the George's. I want to check up on the family liaison officer, Glenn Calvert. I think he is relatively new at this, so I want to make sure he is feeling comfortable with his role."

* * *

HALF AN HOUR LATER, Mackinnon met Tyler in the lobby of Drake House and noticed how much greyer Tyler looked. It wasn't just his hair. He wore a grey suit with a grey tie and he reminded Mackinnon of the old Spitting Image puppet of John Major.

"What's the latest? Mackinnon asked as he approached.

"The team is still searching the flat, but it doesn't look like we're going to find anything. I think we have hit a dead end, but I would feel a lot better if we could speak to Benny."

Mackinnon nodded. "When I showed the Watsons the still from the CCTV to see if they recognised Benny Morris or Lila George, they were incredibly upset and angry, and Peter Watson isn't going to be happy that we haven't managed to speak to Benny yet."

DI Tyler sighed as they headed towards the lift. "Let's hope we find him soon. Even if he is the gentle giant Diane and Eddie wanted you to believe, I still think he's involved somehow."

"Have the team managed to dig up any more information on either family's background?"

Tyler shook his head, and as they stepped out of the lift into the marble lobby of the penthouse floor, he said, "Bits and pieces. We'll have a full update at the briefing."

During an investigation like this, it was important to speak to the parents regularly, and also important not to fob them off with a lower ranked officer. They needed to speak to the person in charge of the team. It was Tyler's job to reassure them the police were doing everything they could, although it seemed as though they were up against an impossible task right now.

Tyler looked tense and on edge as they approached the Watsons' front door.

"It's a difficult case," Mackinnon said. "But the DCI knew you could handle it."

Tyler scoffed and rolled his eyes. He didn't do sentimental, but despite his reaction, Mackinnon knew he appreciated the support.

Mackinnon raised his hand to ring the doorbell when there was an almighty roar from inside the apartment.

Adrenaline flooded his system as the door flew open.

CHAPTER FOURTEEN

ROB WAITED in line at McDonald's, jangling the change in his pocket. The place was packed as was usual for lunchtime. He bit down on the inside of his mouth. How could they call this fast food when they were taking forever to serve each customer?

He was eager to get back to the basement flat. He didn't trust Marlo for one second. The sly bugger would probably take advantage of Rob's absence. He wouldn't put it past him to send the text message on his own before Rob got back. Marlo liked to be in control and prove to others he was the one in charge.

The past few hours had revealed a lot about Marlo's character. He probably didn't even care about the money. The whole thing was like some kind of crazy power trip for him.

He'd been unnecessarily violent with the girls when they confronted them in Celandine Gardens. Rob had been worried he was really going to hurt them, but since they'd got them back to the flat Marlo had left them alone.

He had noticed Marlo staring down at Lila when she lay on the floor of the van. Her top had been pushed up, and Marlo's gaze focused on her exposed skin. The look on Marlo's face had made Rob feel sick. Now, he tried to push that image away.

He had enough problems, and he had to put Benny first.

Benny was his responsibility. Rob should never have got him involved because now everything was screwed up.

Rob glared angrily at the people in the queue in front of him. They were all so concerned about getting their burgers and fries and had no idea what was going on just under their noses.

If he hadn't needed cash so badly, he would never have done a deal with Marlo. Instinctively, he had known Marlo was a man to be avoided. He'd met him a few months ago, through a mate at a pub. He'd known Marlo had a reputation for being a complete psycho, but Rob had assumed people had exaggerated. It wasn't unheard of for people to create rumours to add weight to their reputation. But now it seemed as though Rob should have listened to those rumours when he had a chance. Marlo was a devious bastard.

He hoped Benny was doing all right. If he had any sense, he would be doing exactly as Rob told him — staying in the front room, watching the TV and staying out of Marlo's way. He thought he could trust Benny to do as he was told, especially as he had promised him McDonald's.

Rob smiled. It wasn't easy supporting Benny. He was a big lad and it cost a huge amount to keep him in food, but in many ways, Benny was still like a little boy.

Rob had promised their mother just before she died that he would take good care of Benny. He had taken that promise very seriously. He'd even moved Benny out of his sheltered accommodation and into his own flat. That probably hadn't been the wisest choice because now he was responsible for Benny's every move. He felt guilty if he went out without him, and he had cut Benny off from the limited number of friends he'd had in the sheltered accommodation. He couldn't send him back now, though. It would look like a rejection.

As the queue shuffled forward, Rob glanced to his right and saw two PCSOs standing in the line next to his. He sucked in a breath and froze. Were they here looking for him?

Rob didn't know what to do for the best. They weren't looking at him. Maybe they were just here for lunch like everybody else. It had to be just a coincidence.

He took his hands out of the pockets of his jeans and looked around to see if the exit was clear. He decided to wait it out. If he turned around and rushed out, they might notice something was up.

"Oi," a voice said behind him. "If you're not ready to order, you'd better get out of my way."

Rob turned and saw a skinny bird behind him, carrying a snotty nosed toddler on one hip and pushing a baby in a pram in front of her.

"Go right ahead, love. I wouldn't want to get in the way of you and your Big Mac."

The woman looked startled. "You cheeky sod!"

But Rob wasn't paying her any attention. He was watching the PCSOs, who were moving forward in the queue just like everybody else.

It's fine, he reassured himself. Everything was going to be fine. Then he stepped up to the counter and placed his order.

CHAPTER FIFTEEN

KELLY JOHNSON OPENED the door for Tyler and Mackinnon. Her face was pale, and her eyes were wide as she looked up at Tyler and said, "I'm so sorry, sir."

Before Tyler could answer her, there was another roar of outrage from inside the apartment.

Peter Watson was standing in the centre of the living area. The sun streamed through the huge floor-to-ceiling windows behind him. He turned as he saw Tyler and Mackinnon walking towards him. His hair was standing on end as though he had been clutching at it with his hands.

When they reached him, he looked up at them. His face was red, and the corner of his mouth was splattered with spittle.

"She's gone," he said.

He was clutching a piece of paper in his hand.

"Ruby?" Tyler asked.

Peter Watson shook his head. "No, my wife!" He took two

steps towards them and held out the piece of paper. It was a note written by Claire Watson.

"They sent her another message, and she's gone."

Mackinnon read the note over Tyler's shoulder.

I'm sorry. I have to do this alone or they will kill Ruby. I have to do as they ask.

Tyler's head snapped up. "Where's the phone?"

Peter Watson shook his head. He was no longer filled with fury. He looked lost and vulnerable. "She must have taken it with her. I can't find it anywhere."

Tyler didn't take the time to comfort Peter Watson. Right now, that wasn't his priority.

He turned to Mackinnon. "Get Glenn Calvert on the phone, now."

Mackinnon was already dialling. He knew exactly what Tyler was thinking. If the abductors had contacted Ruby's mother, they would probably contact Lila's mother, too.

"Let's look again for the phone just in case," Tyler ordered.

The family liaison officer helped him look behind the sofa cushions as Peter Watson looked on helplessly.

Glenn Calvert answered Mackinnon's call on the second ring. The television was playing in the background.

Mackinnon took a step away from Peter Watson and said, "Glenn, it's DS Mackinnon. Is Janice George there?"

"Yes. She just went to see to the baby."

"Right, listen to me carefully. Claire Watson has received another text message from the abductors and she's left the apartment on her own without telling anyone. We think Janice George could get another message too, so whatever happens, do not let Janice or her phone out of your sight."

Glenn made an audible gulp over the telephone line. "Right. I'll just go and get her."

"I'll stay on the line, Glenn, and I want to speak to Janice, okay?"

* * *

THIS WAS the first major case Glenn Calvert had been assigned as a family liaison officer. He'd done other bits and pieces here and there, but never on the case as huge as this. He thought he had been doing well. Obviously, the family were in bits emotionally, but he was doing his best to set up a rapport between them just like he had been trained.

He had a sneaking suspicion that Janice George looked down on him and thought he was too young for the job, but Glenn wasn't really that young. He was thirty-three, but he had a round, youthful face that made people think he was younger than he was. He tried to keep his voice warm and reassuring and kept calm even when Janice was ranting at him. He hoped that made up for his youthful appearance.

Just before he had received DS Mackinnon's phone call, he had been talking to Toby George. The man was in a state of shock, and Glenn had been trying to put him at his ease by talking about football. Toby had answered his questions about which team he supported and their chances for next year. His replies had been mechanical, but at least he had answered. Glenn felt that was a step in the right direction.

Janice simply ignored him. A little while ago, she informed Glenn and Toby she was going to put baby Ella down for her nap.

As Glenn scrambled to get up from the sofa and rushed into the hallway, he tried to remember how long ago Janice had left to see to the baby. He supposed he should have paid more attention. It was probably about ten minutes ago at least.

Glenn liked his job, and he wanted to keep it. Having DS Mackinnon hanging on the other end of the line made him extremely nervous. DI Tyler was in charge of this investigation and he was well known for his acerbic comments. Glenn hoped he wasn't going to be on the receiving end of a dressing down from DI Tyler.

"I won't keep you a minute, sir," Glenn said as he pushed open the door to baby Ella's bedroom.

"Okay, good. Keep her calm. After I've spoken to her, DI Tyler will be coming straight round."

But Glenn didn't answer. He stared in horror at the room. The baby was asleep in her crib, but there was no sign of her mother.

He stood there for a full ten seconds, willing Janice George to appear before his eyes and then he lifted his phone to his ear again. "Oh, Jesus."

"What?" Mackinnon demanded.

"She's not in the baby's bedroom."

Glenn raced out of the bedroom and along the hallway back to the sitting room. "Toby, where is Janice?"

Toby looked up and blinked a couple of times at Glenn as though he wasn't quite processing words properly.

Eventually, he said, "She is with the baby."

Glenn shook his head. "No, she isn't. The baby is asleep, and I can't find her."

Glenn was aware of the building panic in his voice and he knew it wasn't the correct way to address Toby, but desperation was bubbling inside him, and he knew he had let everybody down. He felt awful. He had been so pleased when they had assigned him the job. He thought people really saw something special in him, but now he was sure he wasn't cut out for this sort of job.

Toby frowned and heaved himself out of the armchair.

"Don't be daft," he said to Glenn. "She hasn't gone out. She would never leave in case Lila came back, or somebody rang with some news. She is probably out on the balcony having a fag."

Glenn could have kissed him. Of course, why hadn't he thought of that? His legs felt weak with relief as he rushed forward to the balcony door.

He pushed back the net curtains and opened the door. The balcony was only four foot by three foot, and other than two flowerpots containing wilting geraniums, it was empty.

Glenn felt his stomach churn.

He raised his phone to his ear. "I'm sorry, sir. She's gone."

CHAPTER SIXTEEN

WHEN ROB ARRIVED BACK at the basement flat, Marlo was waiting for him and tapping his watch. "Do you know how long you have been?"

Rob shrugged. He hadn't been that long. "There was a queue at McDonald's," he said and fished in the paper bag to pull out Marlo's lunch.

Marlo waved his food away.

"We don't have time for that now," he said impatiently. "Give it to your big lump of a brother and make sure he feeds the girls, too. You and I have got work to do."

Rob tried to hide his annoyance. He was sure Marlo got off on pissing people off. If he just went along with his stupid plan for now, hopefully, Marlo would send a text message demanding the money and then they could give back the girls and get on with their lives.

He carried the McDonald's bag into the front room and saw that Benny was still sitting on the sofa in front of the television. He was watching the news, which was very unlike him. Benny liked children's programmes or quiz shows, so Rob knew he was feeling out of sorts, which really wasn't surprising.

Benny was staring straight ahead, his eyes fixed glassily on the television screen. He didn't turn around until Rob spoke his name.

"All right, Benny? I've got your McDonald's. I need to do something with Marlo, so you'll have to stay here for a bit. We are going to lock the door behind us and you mustn't let the girls out of that room. Do you understand?"

Benny fixed his eyes on his brother, and Rob could see he was close to tears. He didn't care what Marlo wanted. Benny wouldn't be able to give the girls the food. He may have been nearly twice Rob's size, but the girls would run rings around him.

Marlo had put up sound proofing in the bedroom, but the rest of the basement flat wasn't soundproofed. If they got out of the bedroom and screamed out loudly enough, the girls would definitely draw some unwanted attention.

"I'm going to give the girls their lunch and then lock their door. I'll put the keys in the kitchen, but you're not allowed to use them unless there is an emergency. Just stay in here, watch the TV and eat your McDonald's. I'll be back before you know it, okay?"

Benny nodded slowly and took the burger and fries Rob handed to him.

"There are more cans of Coke in the fridge if you're thirsty."

Benny nodded as he unwrapped his burger, and Rob headed back out into the hallway. He took a deep breath before unlocking the bedroom door.

It was pitch black in the room. Although the flat was in the basement, most of the rooms had a long, narrow window where the wall met the ceiling, which allowed a small amount of daylight. In here, the window had been covered by the soundproofing material Marlo had used. For some reason, he'd also removed the light bulb.

He heard the girls scurry away from him, like frightened mice. He swallowed back his feelings of guilt and threw the bag of McDonald's food in their general direction. Marlo had left them two large bottles of water earlier.

He quickly stepped out of the room and shut the door behind him. He put the key back in the keyhole when he sensed he was being watched. He turned and saw Benny watching him from the doorway of the front room.

Rob turned the key, locking the girls in. "Benny, I told you to stay in there and watch the telly. Promise me you'll be good while I'm gone."

Benny nodded solemnly. "I promise."

"Aren't you ready yet?" Marlo demanded stalking out of the kitchen towards the front door.

"Almost," Rob said.

He jogged along the hallway to the kitchen and put the key down on the counter. Then he joined Marlo at the front door, pausing briefly to pat Benny on the shoulder as he walked past.

Marlo opened the front door and both men climbed the steps to the pavement. Marlo turned to Rob with a smile on his face.

"Have you got your phone? I hope you've got plenty of battery left."

Rob frowned in confusion and nodded. "Yes, why?"

"Because you're going to be recording the game. Now,

listen carefully because if you mess this up, you're going to land both you and your brother in the shit."

Rob's body tensed and his fists clenched. He longed to ram his fist into Marlo's face, but he didn't. Instead, he said, "I don't respond well to threats, Marlo."

Marlo looked at him for a moment through narrowed eyes and then said, "No one is threatening anyone. This game is important to me. If you do everything right, the next message I send will be for the money, okay?"

Rob nodded. "Fine. I'll do it. Let's just get on with it."

Marlo smiled. "I've already sent text messages to both the girls' mothers. I've instructed them to come alone, but you should keep your distance in case they've told the pigs. The first part of the game will take place at Monument Underground Station. There is a little present waiting for Ruby Watson's mother, the container you saw earlier. She has to throw the contents over someone in the station, and you have to record it, okay?"

Rob stared at Marlo in disbelief. What the hell was he talking about? They didn't have time for this crap.

"You want me to record her throwing the contents of the container over somebody?"

"That's right."

"And what exactly is in this container?"

"Oh, you'll find out soon enough," Marlo said, chuckling to himself. "Just be at Monument Underground Station, the subway entrance outside House of Fraser, to video Claire Watson."

"I can't even remember what she looks like," Rob said.

The smile fell from Marlo's face. "I showed you a picture."

Rob shrugged. "I can't remember."

Marlo let out a huff of annoyance and pulled his mobile

phone from his pocket. He tapped on the screen a couple of times and then held it out for Rob to look at a photograph of Claire Watson. "Take a good look."

Claire Watson looked just like Rob had remembered. He hadn't really forgotten what she looked like. He was just stalling for time. He didn't want to be part of this stupid game.

"When you've finished videoing Claire Watson, you need to get to the bus stop on Bryant Lane. That's where Janice George will be. I suggest you wait opposite the bus stop. You should have a good view from there. And no distractions. The time between both events is tight."

Rob stared at Marlo. He'd gone to so much effort over a poxy game. It was as though he didn't understand how serious the situation was. They had kidnapped two girls and were holding them hostage. If they got caught, they were going away for a very long time. They should be treating this like a business transaction, moving as quickly and swiftly as possible, getting the matter sorted and covering their tracks, but instead, Marlo wanted to play a game.

Rob wanted to tell him where to go. He wished he had the backbone to refuse, go back down into the basement flat to get Benny and get the hell out of there.

But he wouldn't. If he didn't pay the rent next week, they would be out. He was on his final warning. All he needed to do now was play Marlo's stupid game for a little while longer, and he would get his hands on enough cash to pay his rent for years.

He took a deep breath and nodded. "Fine."

The smile froze on Marlo's face. "You don't sound very enthusiastic, Rob."

Rob sighed and ran a hand through his hair. "To tell you the truth, Marlo. I just want all of this to be over."

"Well, you had better get on with it then. Chop chop."

CHAPTER SEVENTEEN

CLAIRE WATSON WAS SHAKING. She couldn't believe this was happening to her family. They were successful and very careful about security. She'd never made an enemy in her life, well, not a real one anyway, not someone who would want to hurt her this badly.

She was only wearing thin cotton trousers and a lightweight blouse because she had rushed out of the apartment without bothering to grab a cardigan or jacket. The afternoon had turned cool, and she wondered if Ruby, wherever they were holding her, was warm enough.

Peter would be absolutely furious she had snuck out of the apartment to do this alone. In his mind, he was the man, so he should be the protector, but the message specifically said Claire must come alone otherwise her daughter would die.

Claire Watson had been almost paralysed by fear when she'd received the message, but if there was one thing that could motivate her to move through that terror, it was her daughter.

She had to be there by two p.m. and she'd forgotten she wasn't wearing her Rolex. She dug around in her pocket for her mobile phone and checked the time. She still had ten minutes and didn't have too far to go now.

She didn't know what this game was all about, or what part she was expected to play. She only knew she would do anything to get her daughter back safely.

Claire couldn't help hoping that it was all a hoax. An elaborate, nasty hoax, and Ruby would be there waiting for her. She could almost picture it even though deep down she knew the abduction was real. Ruby would never have made them worry like this.

Her stomach churned, and she clasped a hand to her belly, fearing she might vomit in the middle of the street. She was entering a busy part of the city now and passed a group of bankers on the way back to their office after a boozy lunch. She didn't understand how everybody could be going about their business as though nothing had happened. She wanted to scream at them. Didn't they realise her daughter was missing? Her world had been turned upside down, and they were merrily carrying out their everyday lives as though nothing had changed.

She was nearly there now, but as she approached the entrance to the alleyway, she gasped in horror.

It had been blocked off. That wasn't right. Where was the entrance? She was sure there had been an entrance here to Merryweather Alley. They'd added a bloody new tower block exactly where she had expected the old entrance to be.

She felt the tears burning in the corners of her eyes. What would they do if she wasn't there on time? Would she forfeit the game? Would they kill Ruby straightaway? She looked around frantically, trying to find another entrance to the alley.

She tried to make herself calm down and think logically. If they'd closed this entrance then there had to be another one further down the street.

It had been a long time since she'd walked around the city. She usually used taxis and hadn't used public transport in years. She had a brand new Mercedes parked in the basement but she never used that either. Parking was ridiculous in central London.

She forced herself to keep moving, her eyes scanning for the entrance, and when she finally saw it, she could have sobbed with relief. She broke out into a run, bumping into a woman crossing the road. The woman stumbled and shouted something after her, but Claire wasn't listening. The woman was not important.

She held her breath as she raced into the alley, but there was nobody there.

What had she expected? Did she think the abductors would be there waiting for her?

She didn't know. But there was nobody here...What was she supposed to do next? She walked down to the end of the alley and looked around, but it was empty. She was alone.

She pulled out her mobile phone again and read through the text message, thinking perhaps she'd got the location wrong.

But she hadn't.

She shivered as she read the message again.

If you want to save your daughter, you must play the game. One girl will live, the other will die. Be at the corner of Merryweather Alley in one hour. Tell no one or your daughter dies.

She put a hand to her head and clutched at her hair. Was this some kind of cruel trick?

She turned in a circle, unable to believe that anyone could be so cruel, and that was when she saw it.

A piece of paper, taped to the street sign, fluttered in the breeze and caught her eye. Below the street sign was a white tub.

Could that be it? Was this some sort of follow the clue game? She reached up, grabbed the note and tried to blink away the tears blurring her vision.

The note was handwritten in block capitals and said,

You have completed the first level. To complete the second level, you must take the white container to Monument Underground Station. Use the subway entrance outside House of Fraser. Choose a platform and throw the contents over a person of your choice.

No peeking before you throw. We will be watching.

Claire turned around, expecting someone to be watching her right then and there, but she couldn't see anyone.

She gazed up at the buildings looming above her. She supposed they could be in there, looking down at her.

Did they have Ruby up there?

She couldn't think like that now. She had to do what they asked. If she did, there was a chance they would free Ruby unharmed.

And she knew that the other mother would do it. Claire's only chance of success was to do it first.

She saw the white container nestled underneath the street sign. It was a five-litre tub and had no labels, just a small metal handle.

There was nothing to indicate what was inside the tub.

But she supposed it didn't really matter. Whatever was in

there, she would throw it over anyone to get her daughter back.

With a shaking hand, she reached down and picked up the container and began to walk briskly towards Monument Underground Station.

CHAPTER EIGHTEEN

ROB WAS WAITING by the entrance of Monument Underground Station. Claire Watson should arrive at any moment,
but would she really participate? Surely she would have told
the police about Marlo's sick game, and they would have
advised her not to take any part in it. That was the sensible
course of action. Even Rob knew that. The more he thought
about it, the more he was convinced that Claire Watson
wouldn't turn up.

The underground station was busy and with so many
people going in and out, Rob had to keep a close eye on the
commuters, so he didn't miss Claire slipping in.

Rob stuffed his hands in his pockets and exhaled a long,
slow breath. If only he could turn back time. He should never
have got involved with Marlo.

When he'd first talked things over with Marlo at the White
Hart pub in Ealing, they'd laughed over the pictures of Claire
Watson and her husband. The couple were quite the
socialites. There were pictures of them in *Hello* magazine and

articles in various social columns about their charity work. He and Marlo had had a good laugh at that. Marlo had said that charity started at home and raised his eyebrows meaningfully.

Rob agreed. He had grown up on the Towers Estate, and all his life he'd seen bankers growing fat and rich while his family and friends grew poorer. Perhaps the Watsons did give some money to charity, but compared to what they kept for themselves it was only a drop in the ocean.

He did feel a little bad about Ruby, though. She'd been doing voluntary work, and Benny really liked her. He said she'd been kind to him. When Rob had mentioned the fact that a girl with mega rich parents worked at Benny's community centre, Marlo had formulated a plan. It had seemed so straightforward at the time. Easy money and nobody was supposed to get hurt.

Lila had been a complete surprise to Rob and Marlo. They hadn't planned on abducting two girls. He had to hand it to Marlo, though. He was a quick thinker. When they'd got the girls in the van, Marlo had copied their contacts to his own phone before they dumped the mobiles.

Rob was convinced now that Claire Watson wasn't coming. He pulled out his mobile phone ready to call Marlo and tell him he was heading back.

But then he saw her.

She looked awful. Her face was pale and pinched, and she had a light sheen of sweat on her forehead. She was carrying the white container and staggering under its weight, bumping into people.

Nobody spared her a second glance, and Rob couldn't understand why. She was clearly a woman in distress, but no one cared. None of the crowds of people rushing past stopped to ask if she was okay or if she needed any help. They were all far too busy with their own lives, most of them looking at their smartphones as they ignored the world around them.

He wished he could reach out to her and tell her that Ruby was okay and wouldn't be hurt so long as she waited until Marlo had finished playing his stupid game. Ruby would soon be back at home with her parents, and everything would be fine. The Watsons would be one hundred grand poorer, which was nothing to rich people like them, and Marlo and Rob would be fifty grand richer.

Claire slipped into the underground station, and Rob followed. He waited for her to purchase a ticket and then pulled out his wallet, tapped his oyster card against the sensor pad and followed Claire down the escalators.

He didn't want to get too close and alert Claire to his presence, so he let three people stand between them on the escalator. But he needn't have worried. Claire was in a world of her own. She was staring blankly ahead, and her whole body was trembling.

A businessman dressed in a navy blue suit, which probably cost a ridiculous amount of money, started to march down the escalator, mindlessly hitting people with his umbrella and laptop bag as he went.

His bag knocked the container, and for one horrible second, Rob thought it was about to tumble down the escalator, but it didn't. Claire guarded it fiercely.

When she reached the bottom of the escalator, Claire only took two steps forward before coming to an abrupt stop. People behind her were trying to get around her quickly, away from the rush of people descending behind them. As the swell of people began to build up behind her, she got a little shove from behind from one of the commuters. That seemed to jolt her into action, and she chose to head towards the platform on her left.

Rob followed her, feeling increasingly nervous. Marlo was a power hungry fool, but Rob wasn't really scared about what might be in the container. He was sure it wouldn't be anything dangerous. Even Marlo wasn't that stupid.

He watched Claire as she approached a couple of people sitting on a bench. Her hands were trembling as she lifted the container and began to peel back the lid slowly.

But an elderly lady hobbled up to the bench, and the young girl who'd been sitting there stood up and let her have her seat. That seemed to throw Claire for a moment, and she hesitated before turning away.

She walked slowly to the next bench, towards Mr Umbrella Man, the idiot in the navy blue suit who had rudely hit everyone with his umbrella and laptop bag on his way to the platform.

He could tell from the way Claire had set her head and swallowed hard that she had chosen her victim.

Rob approved. If anyone deserved to be targeted, it was him.

He fumbled for his mobile phone, tapped on the camera app and began to record. Nobody paid him any attention. It was such a normal sight these days. Rob wasn't doing anything out of the ordinary.

He watched Claire as she ripped off the lid and heaved the container up to chest height. She paused for a fraction of a second before she threw it.

There was an audible gasp from commuters standing nearby. Even though he knew what was coming, a small gasp escaped Rob's lips, too.

The man was covered in bright red paint.

In her eagerness to complete her task, Claire had let go of the container and thrown that along with the contents at Mr Umbrella Man. The paint was dripping from his face and hair. He let out a roar of outrage and shot to his feet.

But Claire was already darting for the exit. Rob knew he should have left too but he was transfixed.

A few seconds passed before he heard an alarm sound, and he knew that staff would be arriving soon, asking questions and looking for witnesses.

It was definitely time for Rob to go.

CHAPTER NINETEEN

JANICE GEORGE ARRIVED at Tanner Street with her heart hammering. She wanted whoever had taken her daughter to be there so she could rip their eyes out with her own hands.

She was scared, absolutely terrified for her Lila, but it was the anger that surprised her. She had a raw, furious need to rip those bastards to pieces.

If they had been standing in front of her now and somebody handed her a knife, she'd be able to stab them in the gut and smile while she did it.

But unfortunately for Janice, there was nobody on Tanner Street, only a paper note taped to the street sign. Janice ripped it in two in her haste to read it.

She swore under her breath as she held the two pieces together. Her grip tightened on the piece of paper as she read.

First level completed. To complete the second level and have a chance to save your daughter's life take the white container to the bus stop on Bryant Lane. You must throw the contents of the container over a person of your choice. No peeking at the contents before you throw. We will be watching.

Janice looked down at the white bucket. She didn't know what was in it but she didn't much care. She reached down to snatch it up and marched around the corner to Bryant Lane.

She wouldn't let herself think about the situation too deeply. If she did, she was scared she would hesitate and maybe even bottle it. She needed to do this for Lila. God knows, she'd let the poor girl down in the past and she wasn't about to do it again. She swore to herself if Lila came home she could go to any bloody college she wanted and she would have Janice's full support.

Janice licked her dry, cracked lips and tried to breathe normally. Her chest felt too tight, as though someone had wrapped a tight band around her ribs.

As the bus stop came into view in front of her, Janice began to shake. She could see there were two people sitting down at the bus stop and another person leaning against the bus stop sign.

She had to pick one of them.

Janice chewed on a fingernail as she slowed down. She needed to be smart about this. If any of them sensed what she was up to and ran away, that would mean she failed.

She didn't understand the purpose behind this game. Was one of the people at the bus stop someone the abductor wanted to punish? But if that was the case, why had they told Janice she could throw it over whoever she liked?

She had a sickening feeling that this was all for the enjoyment of whoever had taken her daughter. They were playing with her life, treating her like a puppet.

But as much as Janice hated the fact they were pulling her strings, she couldn't refuse, not when Lila's life was at stake.

She lifted the container, put one hand beneath it and then began to peel back the lid. She grimaced at the smell and then stepped forward.

A girl sat at the bus stop. She couldn't have been more than eighteen, and she was heavily pregnant, so Janice ruled her out straightaway. Beside her was an elderly gentleman, dressed in a suit and leaning heavily on his walking stick.

How could Janice throw the stuff at an old man like that?

That only left one option. The young man leaning against the bus stop sign. He hadn't even noticed her approach. He wore baggy cargo pants that were splattered with paint and some kind of plaster. She guessed he'd been carrying out building work in the area.

It would have to be him.

She muttered an advance apology and then lifted the container.

* * *

ROB SKIDDED to a halt opposite the bus stop. He'd only just made it in time. Marlo really hadn't timed this very well. Janice George was already there, standing at the bus stop, clutching the container.

Rob could see she had already picked out her victim, a young man dressed in casual working clothes.

He was completely oblivious to Janice's presence. He was preoccupied with his phone, tapping away, unaware that Janice was about to dump a load of paint over his head.

Rob shook his head as he pulled out his phone to start recording. This was such a pathetic waste of time. There was no point behind this silly game, and it had just occurred to

Rob that when the police discovered he had been at both scenes, they would put two and two together.

If they did arrest him, then Rob would spill the beans on Marlo. He owed the man nothing. He was furious with him and determined never to work with him again. As soon as he had recorded Janice throwing the paint, he intended to head back to the basement flat and tell Marlo it finished today. He would force him to send a text message with a demand for money and a drop-off point.

There was no way he was going to waste any more time playing Marlo's stupid game.

"Come on," Rob whispered under his breath.

He just wanted her to get on with it so he could get back to Benny and make sure he was all right. He hated the thought of leaving him alone with Marlo. Anything could happen if he wasn't there to look out for Benny.

He zoomed in using the viewfinder on the phone to get a better view, and he saw Janice's arms tense a fraction of a second before she flung the contents of the container at the man beside the bus stop.

He was tall and that stopped the contents reaching his face. Instead, it splattered over his grey hoodie and cargo pants.

But there was something different this time...

For one thing, the container's contents wasn't red.

Rob had been watching everything through the screen of his phone, but he now looked up so he could get a better view.

The young man wasn't acting outraged or angry like the man at the underground station. Instead, he let out a high-pitched scream, and Rob noticed there was smoke or steam coming off his clothes.

Janice dropped the container by her feet and looked horrified as the young man tried to yank off his hoodie, screaming as he did so.

Whatever liquid Janice had thrown over him was now burning a hole through his T-shirt.

Rob forgot all about the fact he was supposed to be filming the incident. His hands dropped to his sides as he looked on.

He took two steps forward, intending to go over there and help, but then he realised he couldn't. If he did, he would definitely be caught, and if he went to prison, what would happen to Benny? He couldn't leave Benny to face something like this alone. If the police found Benny at the same flat as the girls, they wouldn't listen to Rob if he tried to tell them that Benny wasn't involved.

The young man had flung his hoodie on the floor and ripped his T-shirt over his head. Even from the other side of the road, Rob could see that his chest was red.

Jesus Christ. What had Marlo done?

He'd used acid.

The other two people who'd been waiting at the bus stop had scattered sharpish, but another young man who had been passing had stopped and was now on his mobile phone. Rob guessed he was calling an ambulance and the police.

Janice hadn't run away like Claire. She stood there, horrified, with the empty container by her feet.

Rob knew he had to get out of there and he had to move now. He turned his back on the gruesome scene and charged up the road.

He had been prepared to confront Marlo and force him to demand the money today, but after seeing that sick game unfold before his eyes, he realised all the stories about Marlo were true. He *was* a psychopath.

Right now, the money was unimportant. Rob needed to

get Benny out of there as soon as possible and get him away from Marlo.

CHAPTER TWENTY

MACKINNON DIDN'T NEED to tell DI Tyler what Glenn Calvert had said. The detective inspector had already guessed what had happened from reading Mackinnon's expression.

Tyler shook his head. "Don't tell me. Janice George has disappeared as well."

Mackinnon nodded. "Yes, and she has taken her phone."

Tyler was barely holding his emotions in check. He marched out of the sitting area, through the hallway and straight out of the front door without turning around.

Mackinnon turned to Peter Watson as he began to demand to know where his wife had gone.

"Try not to panic, Mr Watson. We have cameras everywhere, and we will be able to follow your wife's movements. We just need a little time."

"Do you think the abductors have taken Claire now as well as Ruby?"

"There's no reason to think that. We still believe they are

after money, and it's possible they saw Claire and Janice as easier targets."

Peter Watson shook his head. "I can't believe it. Why is this happening to me?"

As Peter Watson spoke, his son, Curtis came out of his bedroom and walked into the open plan kitchen. That boy seemed to get stranger and stranger.

His father had been yelling only a moment ago. Surely there was no way Curtis could have missed that. Even Mackinnon and Tyler had heard him from outside the apartment, and yet Curtis was only now coming out to investigate.

He looked at his father and then turned to Mackinnon. "What's happened?"

When Peter Watson didn't answer his son, Mackinnon said, "Your mother has gone out, and we're not sure where she is. Did she say anything to you before she left?"

He kept his voice calm, not wanting to alarm Claire's son. He needn't have worried. The boy was cool and unruffled by the news that his mother had left the house while kidnappers still had his sister.

Curtis shook his head. "No, but I'm not really surprised. If she told me she planned to go out, I would have tried to talk her out of it."

"You would?"

Curtis nodded. "Of course. It's quite clearly a ridiculous thing to do, especially after what has happened to Ruby. She should have stayed here."

Mackinnon didn't elaborate on the note that his mother had left and didn't tell him they suspected the kidnappers had told his mother she had to go alone in order to save Ruby's life. It was up to Peter Watson to tell the boy the details.

Kelly Johnson stood beside Peter, murmuring reassurances, but Mackinnon wasn't sure Peter Watson was even listening.

"So what happens now?" Curtis asked.

"We are going to track down your mother and keep looking for your sister. I need to head back to the station now, but I'm sure your father would really appreciate your support at the moment."

Mackinnon nodded at Peter Watson, who held his head in his hands as he slumped down into an armchair.

Curtis rolled his eyes. "We're not really that kind of family."

Shocked at the boy's reaction, Mackinnon left the apartment and took the lift down to the lobby. He found DI Tyler outside, pacing in front of the entrance. He was clearly furious.

He looked up as Mackinnon stepped out onto the pavement.

"I should have confiscated their phones," Tyler said. "I should have insisted and said they were part of the investigation."

Mackinnon shook his head. "It's not your fault. We couldn't exactly put them under house arrest. They left of their own free will."

"I wish I bloody had put them under house arrest. If I had, this wouldn't have happened." Tyler shook his head and ran a hand through his hair. "This isn't going to go down well, Jack. It's my first big case, and this is a screwup of epic proportions."

"We'll be able to see where Janice and Claire have gone from the CCTV cameras. They could lead us straight to the abductors. This could be the breakthrough we need."

Tyler took a deep breath and nodded. "Let's hope so. I've

just spoken to Collins and Charlotte, and they're already on the case. They've got footage of Claire Watson leaving this building, and I've just heard by text message from Collins that Claire Watson entered Monument Underground Station. We don't know if she's still there, but there have been reports of an incident. The details are sketchy."

Before Mackinnon could reply, Tyler's phone rang.

He looked at the display with a grim face and then looked up at Mackinnon and said, "It's DCI Brookbank."

He answered the phone, and Mackinnon moved a few steps away, giving him privacy to talk without being overheard.

He thought it would be unfair of the DCI to blame Tyler for this, but in investigations this sensitive, a tiny mistake could have very far-reaching consequences.

When Tyler hung up, he turned to Mackinnon and said, "We need to get back to Wood Street now. There's going to be an emergency briefing, and I expect to get hauled over the coals for this."

CHAPTER TWENTY-ONE

MARLO leant back on the kitchen counter and grinned to himself. Rob wasn't back yet, the girls were quiet, and brain-dead Benny was in the front room listening to some rubbish on the telly.

He couldn't wait till Rob got back so he could see the recordings. He knew he could trust Rob to do a good job. People like him were so easy to manipulate. Sometimes he thought he might like to have more of a challenge, but you couldn't have everything you wanted in life, and at least he had the game. That was very entertaining. It was a stroke of genius on his part really, and it had all come about through luck, not planning. They hadn't expected to get Lila George as well as Ruby Watson, and Marlo could hardly believe his good fortune.

His plan had been to take Ruby and have a little bit of fun with the family before he asked for the money.

He was still planning on asking for money. After all, who didn't like having a bit of extra cash? But at the end of the day, it was the thrill of the game that excited Marlo. He had two sets of parents competing to see their daughters alive again. It was sheer brilliance on his part.

He knew Rob didn't approve. He'd made that obvious, but Marlo simply couldn't care less. Rob was simple-minded, perhaps not quite as simple as his brother, but he would never understand the way Marlo's brain worked. Marlo was intelligent, and he needed more from life than moving from one dodgy job to another.

He opened the fridge and removed two cans of Coke. Carrying them out of the kitchen and along the hallway, he paused beside the bedroom door to check on the girls. He couldn't hear a thing. The soundproofing was doing an excellent job. He could go in there now and terrify the life out of them, but he wasn't interested in that. He knew that a lack of contact was one of the most terrifying things you could do to a person. Their imaginations would be conjuring up all sorts of horrors, far worse than anything Marlo could probably think up.

Terrorising the girls wasn't very appealing anyway. It was the parents Marlo wanted to torture.

They had it coming.

The Watsons, with their obscene level of wealth and their tiny contributions to charity, made him sick. They had their faces plastered all over the society pages when it was people like Peter Watson who had caused the last recession.

Okay, so Marlo had never actually held down a job for more than a week, but that was beside the point. If he *had* wanted a job, he wouldn't be able to get one thanks to bastards like Peter Watson, who had created such a mess of the economy. Plus the fact everyone was prejudiced against Marlo from the start just because he had a criminal record.

He carried the drinks into the sitting room and looked critically at Benny.

He really was a huge bloke. At first glance, he looked like somebody Marlo should avoid, but under more careful scrutiny, it was obvious to see his face was almost childlike.

"Hello, Benny. I've brought you a Coke."

He held it out, and Benny looked at him distrustfully before leaning forward and grabbing the Coke out of Marlo's hand.

"What do you say, Benny?"

"Thank you," Benny muttered, staring down at the can. He seemed unwilling to look at Marlo directly.

Rob had spouted off some rubbish about his brother not liking to be shouted at, but Benny was going to have to get used to it.

"I thought we'd better get to know each other a bit better, Benny. It looks like we're going to be spending a lot of time together over the next couple of days."

Benny looked horrified at that news. "No. I want to go home."

Marlo chuckled and popped the ring pull on his can of Coke before taking a long swallow.

"Well, we don't get everything we want in this life, do we, Benny? You're not going to give me any trouble, are you?"

Benny looked down at the floor and shook his head.

"That's good." Marlo sat down on the sofa and ordered Benny to pass him the remote control.

"Are you going to let Ruby and Lila go home now?" Benny asked.

Marlo narrowed his eyes and turned to face him. "Why? What do you care?"

"They are my friends. I don't want them to get hurt."

Marlo barely resisted rolling his eyes. It was honestly like dealing with a five-year-old. He didn't know how Rob managed to put up with it. "They're not going to get hurt, and they are staying here until we get the money," Marlo said and then smiled maliciously at Benny. "And so are you."

CHAPTER TWENTY-TWO

WHEN THEY RETURNED to Wood Street Station, Tyler went straight to Brookbank's office with a look of grim determination on his face. Mackinnon was quite glad he wasn't the one in charge of the operation. Choices like this were never easy, and mistakes were made as a matter of course. The trouble was, the consequences of mistakes were huge in a case like this.

It wasn't an easy balance. The parents needed to be treated carefully and sensitively, and as he said, Tyler could hardly have put them under house arrest. They had stressed to the parents the importance of staying at home and communicating with the police.

Mackinnon wandered over to Charlotte's desk and noticed her unfinished cup of coffee. When Charlotte was busy tracking down information, she often forgot to drink. He'd lost count of the number of cups of coffee he'd made only for her to let them grow cold.

It made him remember it had been a long time since his last shot of caffeine. His energy levels were flagging.

"It looks like it's going to be a late one," he said, and Charlotte turned around and stretched, rolling her shoulders because she had been sitting in front of the screen for so long.

Charlotte nodded. "Yes. Janice and Claire are both back home now. Claire was lucky to be the one who threw paint over her victim, and due to the circumstances, it doesn't look like the victim will press charges. Unfortunately for Janice, there was acid in her container."

Mackinnon pulled a face. He'd heard the news on the way over. "How bad is he?"

"It could have been a lot worse. He'll recover, but he's going to have some nasty burns and definitely some scarring. Understandably, he is distraught and in a great deal of pain."

Mackinnon nodded. It was almost as if the kidnappers were favouring one mother over the other.

They both looked up as they heard the door to Brookbank's office open, and Tyler came out with a stony-faced expression.

"That didn't take long," Mackinnon muttered to Charlotte.

Tyler headed over in their direction. "Briefing room now," he said gruffly.

The whole team, including the admin and support staff, filed into the briefing room. The lucky ones got a seat around the large table, and the less lucky people leant back against the wall as Tyler brought everyone up to date on the investigation.

"There's a gold meeting tomorrow, which I have the pleasure of attending," Tyler said, running a weary hand over his face. "I'm sure they'll have plenty of ideas regarding strategy, but until then, let's continue the investigation as planned. Charlotte, can you update us on the phone situation?"

Charlotte nodded and said, "They are using a new phone for every text message they've sent so far. After using the phone, they are turning it off and probably removing the batteries as well, which makes life hard for us. We can't trace the phone or its location. We should be able to trace where the text message was sent from eventually, but it's going to take a little while."

Tyler nodded wearily and then moved on, clicking a button on the laptop in front of him, which displayed the second text message sent to Janice George's phone on the white screen behind him.

If you want to save your daughter, you must play the game. One girl will live, the other will die. Be at the corner of Tanner Street in one hour. Tell no one or your daughter dies.

The message sent to Claire Watson was exactly the same except she was told to go to Merryweather Alley half an hour earlier.

"He's making them compete for their daughters' lives," DC Webb said, stating the obvious.

"But why give one woman paint and the other acid?" Collins asked.

"You mean other than the fact he's a sick bastard?" DC Webb said.

Tyler sighed audibly. "I don't know. Is it because he resents Janice George more than Claire Watson?" Tyler let his gaze roam around the room. "How close are we to tracing the whereabouts of Benny or Rob Morris?"

Collins shook his head. "We've spoken to their neighbours and checked out their local haunts. Apparently, Rob often visits the Kings Arms, but no one has seen him today. We do have an officer stationed nearby to see if they come home."

"Inconspicuously I hope?" Tyler's voice was sharp.

Collins nodded. "Of course."

Tyler turned to one of the admin support staff, Evie Charlesworth. "How are we getting along with the mobile technology?"

"It's all set up now," Evie said confidently. "There were a few delays, but now we will get a copy of any text message Claire Watson or Janice George receives."

Tyler nodded "Good. It's a shame it wasn't set up earlier. That could have saved us some headaches.

"When the women followed the instructions in the text message, both found a white container at the scene. From the crime scene photographs, you can see they look like the type of container to hold something like paint. The containers were plastic, not metal, which obviously would be important for transporting acid. They both found a note at the scene, instructing them to throw the contents over a person of their choice. Now, this leads us to believe that he is getting some kind of kick out of controlling the mothers. He's not using them to hurt anyone in particular. He left it up to them to decide who to maim and who to cover with paint."

The anger in Tyler's voice was obvious.

"How many people do we think are involved in the abduction?" Mackinnon asked. "The slight time delay between both events is interesting. I would guess if he is doing this to exert control, he would want to watch, and he couldn't be in two places at one time."

Collins nodded. "They are like his puppets, and he wants to be at the show. He couldn't be in two places at once so he staggered them."

"That's possible. But we can't rule out the fact that there's more than one, and they both wanted to watch. I'm still eager to talk to Benny Morris and his brother Rob. As far as we know, Benny Morris was the last person to see the girls before they were abducted. If he's not involved, he could still hold very important information. Tracking them down and interviewing them is a priority. We also need to shadow the parents all day and make sure they don't leave and try to participate in any more of these games. At considerable cost, DCI Brookbank has agreed to station plain-clothed officers outside the Watsons' apartment building and the Georges' block of flats. If they leave, we will know about it."

"Are they going to be there around the clock?" Mackinnon asked, already feeling sorry for the poor officers who were going to be posted to the Towers Estate all night.

Tyler nodded. "Yes, we've had one screwup. I'm not going to allow another one."

CHAPTER TWENTY-THREE

MARLO DECIDED it was time for a little entertainment. He left Benny in the sitting room and walked towards the bedroom where they were keeping the girls. He put his ear against the door but couldn't hear anything.

The soundproofing worked a treat. It was definitely worth the investment. He had bought it off the Internet and installed it himself. It was a pain in the arse and had taken him ages, but it needed to be done. He couldn't let anyone hear the girls screaming because that would attract unwanted attention.

They had two keys to the bedroom and kept one in the kitchen in case Rob needed to see to the girls, but Marlo kept his own key with him at all times.

He extracted his set of keys from his pocket, selected a long thin key and slid it into the lock. The lock made a quiet clicking sound as the key turned.

As he pushed open the door, light from the hallway flooded the bedroom, and he heard the girls scrambling, trying to get away. He grinned and stepped into the room.

Both girls were huddled in the corner, looking up at him with wild eyes. He could smell the fear in the room.

"Hello, girls," he said. "I hope you can forgive my behaviour earlier. It's your own fault really, though. You shouldn't have been so difficult."

Ruby Watson's eyes remained fixed on Marlo, but the expression on her face didn't change. She looked guarded, cautious and afraid. On the other hand, anger flashed over Lila George's face. She clearly had a temper.

She would be fun to play with.

He walked over to them, slowly, and smiled as they cringed away from him and tried to push themselves further back against the wall. It was pointless, of course. There was no way they could get away from him.

"See, there's no need to make me angry. It's much nicer when you are good girls, isn't it?" Marlo reached out a hand and stroked Ruby's hair.

She closed her eyes and turned her head away.

"What's wrong? Am I not your type?" he asked, licking his lips.

"Please, just let us go. We won't tell anybody what you did," Ruby said. Her head was still facing the wall, and she refused to look at him.

He tugged on her hair, not too hard, but hard enough to show her who was in charge here.

"Now, now. We are getting along so well. Don't ruin it."

"Get your hands off her," Lila George spat. "You're going to regret you did this. You'll never get away with it."

He had been right. Lila George was definitely the most hotheaded of the pair.

"Really?" Marlo drawled. "I seem to be getting away with it so far."

"The police will be out looking for us. They'll find out where you're holding us, and you will be going to prison for a very long time."

Marlo cupped a hand behind his ear. "That's funny. I can't hear any sirens. To be honest, I'm not sure anyone has even missed you, Lila. I mean, they might notice you're gone when they need you to babysit again. Family, eh? Can't live with them, can't live without them."

The look of shock on Lila's face gave Marlo a thrill of pleasure. She had underestimated him. She didn't realise he had done his homework and planned this abduction very carefully. Although they'd only been planning to take Ruby, Marlo wasn't about to look a gift horse in the mouth. He managed to get two girls for the price of one and used his smarts to find out about Lila George and her family.

He'd been disappointed to realise the family didn't have money. They wouldn't be able to lay their hands on much cash to pay the ransom, but Marlo was determined to get his payment all the same by having a little fun with the girls.

Marlo grinned at Lila. She wasn't looking quite so brave anymore.

Ruby still had her eyes closed, so Marlo reached up and ran his thumb gently along her cheek.

She shuddered at his touch.

"I guess I'm just not your type," Marlo said. "I thought girls were supposed to like bad boys. Maybe you've got a crush on the retard? Is he more your type?"

Marlo chuckled and lowered his hand, stroking Ruby's neck before he slid his fingers beneath the material of her blouse.

The front door slammed.

Startled, Marlo let his hands drop to his sides and spun

around. Rob appeared in the doorway, staring in at him accusingly.

"What are you doing?" he demanded. "Get out here. We need to talk."

* * *

Marlo left the bedroom and closed the door behind him.

Rob had stalked off into the kitchen, and after locking the door, Marlo followed him in.

Benny stood by the fridge holding a glass of milk. He cringed back against the wall as though he wanted to make himself smaller. But there was no chance of that.

"Did you get the recordings?" Marlo asked.

"Yes," Rob spat back. "What the hell did you put in that last container? The bloke's clothes were smoking. You really are sick, Marlo."

Marlo raised an eyebrow. Charming. He didn't really care what Rob thought of him, but he was eager to see the videos, though. He was proud of the little twist he'd used to surprise Rob. Although Rob didn't realise it yet, he was also participating in the game.

Marlo had lulled him into a false sense of security by giving the first woman paint. He would have loved to have been there to see the look on Rob's face when he realised the second container contained acid. Rob's face must have been a picture as he watched the victim melting before his eyes.

Marlo chuckled.

"What the hell are you laughing at? I've had enough of this, Marlo. That's it. It's over." Rob was really shouting now and getting incredibly worked up.

His brother didn't like it one bit. He put his glass of milk on the counter and then covered his ears with his hands and began whimpering.

Marlo rolled his eyes. "Don't make such a fuss, Rob. It's just a bit of fun. We won't be getting any money out of Lila's parents so we need to get our kicks where we can."

Rob pushed his face up to Marlo's then stabbed a finger at his chest. "That is not how I want to get my kicks," he growled.

That was the last straw for Marlo.

He glared down at Rob's finger that was rudely prodding him in the chest. Rob had crossed a line and needed to be punished, but Marlo wasn't stupid.

Rob's punishment would come, but right now he still needed a man on the ground.

"Come on, let's not fall out. We've got a big payday coming. I realise you're not as into this game as I am, so I'll tell you what. We'll compromise. We'll do one more game and then ask for the money. Just one more."

Marlo thought he was being incredibly reasonable, but from the flush on Rob's face and the way he gritted his teeth together, Marlo realised he wasn't really in a compromising mood. Well, tough. Marlo was in charge here, and the sooner Rob realised that, the better.

He shot an irritated glance at Benny whose whimpers were growing louder. "Can't you shut him up?"

Rob glared at him and then put a gentle hand on Benny's shoulder, leading him out of the kitchen and back into the sitting room.

He could hear them talking but tuned them out.

This was a complication he could do without. He hated having to pander to people like Rob, weak-willed individuals, who didn't realise when they were onto a good thing. They wanted everything Marlo could give them, but they weren't prepared to work for it.

"Rob," Marlo called out, finally getting bored and losing his patience. "We need to talk."

Rob came back into the kitchen. "I need to take Benny home. He's really upset."

That was not happening. Marlo shook his head. "No, you can't do that. He has to stay here."

Rob shook his head. "You don't understand... When Benny gets upset –"

"I don't care," Marlo snapped, cutting Rob off. "He is not going anywhere. We can't trust that daft sod not to spill our secret. Now let's go to the pub down the street. I need to get out of here, clear my head and have a drink. We can talk things over there."

CHAPTER TWENTY-FOUR

AT WOOD STREET STATION, Mackinnon walked over to the coffee machine. They had a large pot brewing and would probably have the machine working through the night. He poured himself a large mug, and when he turned around to walk back to his workstation, Evie caught his eye and waved him over.

"We've got some information back from the mobile phone companies. They are pay-as-you-go, and the phones were purchased online by a Mr Albert Banks. According to the phone company, they were delivered, but he says that his credit card was stolen and he never received the phones. We've checked, and he did report his credit card stolen shortly after the phones were delivered. But it might still be worth talking to him."

Mackinnon nodded. "You're right. I'll go myself and check him out. Can you send me the details?"

It was a common enough occurrence, and they had expected that the phones would have been purchased with a stolen credit card. If Albert Banks wasn't involved in the crime and the phones were delivered to his address, that meant the kidnappers would have had to be waiting for the parcel ready to intercept it before Albert Banks took delivery of the phones.

Potentially Albert Banks could provide some useful information, particularly if he had any idea who may have had access to his credit card. They could crosscheck any names he gave them.

Mackinnon thanked Evie and carried his coffee back to his desk.

On the way, he passed Charlotte, who was looking at some archived articles on the web. On her computer screen was a blown up image of Mr and Mrs Watson dressed for a night on the town.

They were wearing full evening dress. Mr Watson was in black tie, and Claire Watson wore a full-length, silver gown set off with dazzling jewels.

"What are you working on?" Mackinnon asked.

Charlotte looked up and smiled. "Still working on potential motives. There's been a recent takeover of a medium-sized British company by Peter Watson, which could have created some bad feeling among the old employees. That is something worth looking into, but more and more it looks like they were targeted because they were rich." Charlotte pointed at the image of Claire Watson on the screen. "Her earrings alone must be worth a couple of grand, and that necklace..." Charlotte shook her head. "I can't even imagine what that is worth."

Mackinnon took a sip of his coffee as he stared at the image. Finally, he said, "Sure, they are wealthy, but something about this case seems to be personal. And I don't understand why they've targeted Lila George as well. Her family are... well, not in the same league as the Watsons. I doubt they could gather together much money for a ransom."

Charlotte sighed and nodded, rubbing her eyes, and then reached for her half-full cup of coffee.

She took a mouthful and then grimaced. She'd obviously let it grow cold again.

"How is your Nan doing?" Mackinnon asked.

Charlotte smiled. "She's fine. I went to hers for dinner last night. She can still talk the hind legs off a donkey."

"And are your parents still living in Spain?"

Charlotte nodded. "To be honest, I think they've got the right idea. I think they're a bit worried about the outcome of the referendum, though. I might go out there for a holiday once all this is over and take a few days leave. How are things with you? Didn't your parents retire to Dorset?"

"They're in Devon now. I'd like to see them more often, but it's such a trek to go for the weekend, especially when Chloe and the girls have things planned. I was thinking of going down on my own in a couple of weeks, maybe surprise them."

Charlotte smiled and pushed her coffee cup back on the desk. "And how are things with Chloe and the girls?"

Mackinnon paused before answering. Things were going well apart from Sarah's issues. It seemed like that girl always had something going on. "They're good. I'm still a little worried about Sarah, though."

"Has she been giving you more grief?"

"To be honest, I hardly ever see her these days. Since she went to university, she rarely comes back home, but I'm worried about her." As Mackinnon spoke the words aloud, he realised they were true.

"Worried? Why?"

"She acts like she's angry all the time, but she's vulnerable. I can't help thinking she's going to get herself into trouble."

Charlotte frowned. "Does Chloe agree?"

Mackinnon shook his head. "Forget I said anything. I'm just a bit distracted today, and I clearly haven't had enough caffeine." He raised his cup and took a large mouthful to prove his point.

Charlotte nodded slowly. "I'm sure she'll be fine. She probably just gives you a hard time because you've moved in with her mum. She's used to having Chloe all to herself."

Mackinnon nodded. To a large extent, that was true. He tried to stay out of it when Chloe chastised Sarah for her behaviour. He knew it wasn't his place to intervene, but after the conversation he'd had with Sarah that morning, he couldn't help thinking she was in more trouble than she let on.

"I'm heading out now, to talk to Albert Banks. The phones were purchased on his credit card. It doesn't look like he's got anything to do with it, but we need to check it out anyway."

Charlotte stood up and stretched. "Let me know how it goes. I'm going to get another cup of coffee."

"Don't let it get cold this time," Mackinnon teased, even though he knew she would.

Mackinnon drained the last of his coffee and asked Collins to tell DI Tyler where he'd gone and then headed back to the Towers Estate to talk to Mr Albert Banks.

CHAPTER TWENTY-FIVE

MACKINNON DECIDED to walk to the Towers Estate from Wood Street Station. He needed the fresh air to clear his head and wanted to use the walking time to think over the questions he had to ask Albert Banks. He picked up a ham and cheese sandwich and an orange juice from Boots and ate them on the way.

In cases like this, the individual whose credit card was used usually had absolutely nothing to do with the criminal activity, but they couldn't rule anything out when Ruby Watson and Lila George were still missing.

Albert Banks lived at number twenty-seven, Lily Tower. A section of the Towers Estate had blocks of flats, lanes and alleyways named after different flowers. Mackinnon thought it was an odd choice. The place was a mass of concrete and brick, and there wasn't an inch of green anywhere, apart from a few squares of scraggly grass and most of that was yellow.

It wasn't the worst area in the Towers Estate, though, and

although there was a touch of graffiti here and there, the area was generally clean and tidy.

Albert Banks lived on the second floor of Lily Tower so Mackinnon took the stairs. Before he knocked on the front door, he could already hear the TV blaring out from inside and knew someone was home. He rapped on the door and waited.

A short man with dark brown skin and a bald head opened the door. He wore a frameless pair of glasses and blinked up at Mackinnon. "Yes?"

Mackinnon showed his warrant card and introduced himself. "I'd like a moment of your time. It's about your stolen credit card, Mr Banks."

Albert Banks' raised his eyebrows. "Oh, I have gone up in the world. I didn't think the police gave a damn about my stolen credit card when I reported it. Now they've sent a detective sergeant to discuss the matter. I couldn't get five minutes with a PC when it happened."

He stood with his hand on the door, as though he expected Mackinnon to barge his way in. He hadn't asked a question, and Mackinnon wasn't going to launch into a defence of the police service. Instead, he said nothing and waited.

Eventually, Mr Banks' tense body relaxed, and he took a step backwards into the hall. "I suppose you'd better come in."

Mackinnon followed him into the dark, narrow hallway as Mr Banks waddled along towards a brightly lit room at the end of the hallway. It turned out to be the kitchen.

Albert Banks rubbed his hip as he stood by the kettle.

"It's arthritis," he said. "I've been sitting still for too long. Can I get you a drink?" He nodded to the kettle, and without waiting for an answer, grabbed two mugs from the cupboard by his head.

"Thank you. I'd love a cup of tea."

As Albert Banks set about making the tea, Mackinnon took the opportunity to look around the kitchen. It was clean, tidy and well-maintained. The microwave looked new, but there was an ancient-looking radio on the windowsill.

He would reserve judgement until he had seen the man's television, but usually, if someone was involved in credit card fraud, they often gave the game away by having their home kitted out with the latest gadgets. Of course, that wasn't reliable one hundred percent of the time, but it was a good indication.

Mr Banks handed Mackinnon his tea. "I've added milk, but I hope you don't take sugar because I don't have any."

Mackinnon shook his head. "I don't, thank you."

"Do you mind if we sit in the front room. I have been suffering with my hip today."

"Not at all."

Albert Banks led the way into the sitting room. There was a three-seater, patterned sofa under the window and a single armchair in front of the TV. A large dresser was set against one wall, which dominated the small room. The door that led out onto the balcony gave a perfect view of the concrete block opposite. The television was large, but it wasn't the latest model by any means. Mackinnon guessed it was at least a couple of years old. Albert Banks reached for the remote control and muted the television.

"Did you find the person who stole my card?" Mr Banks asked, although from the scowl on his face, Mackinnon guessed he already knew the answer to that question.

"I'm afraid we haven't yet," Mackinnon said. "Credit card fraud is becoming more common, and although city police are trying to crack down on it, the people involved can be incredibly sneaky." Without giving Albert Banks a chance to reply, Mackinnon started to ask his questions. "According to our reports, the credit card was stolen on the twenty-fifth of April. Is that correct?"

Mr Banks thought for a moment and then said. "That was when I reported it missing. To be honest, I usually use my debit card, and I hadn't needed to use it for a while. It could have been missing for a little while before I noticed."

"How long is a little while?"

Albert Banks bristled and looked offended.

"I don't like the way you seem to be inferring that it was my fault. I'm incredibly careful with my cards."

"I'm not inferring it was your fault," Mackinnon said and took a sip of his tea. "There was an item purchased with your credit card on the twenty-second of April, and it was delivered to this address."

Albert Banks opened his mouth and closed it again. "I hope you're not suggesting I lied about the fact my credit card was stolen?"

"Mr Banks, I'm not suggesting you lied. I'm just trying to find out what happened. Do you know what happened to the items that were ordered on the twenty-second of April and delivered here?"

Albert's forehead creased in a frown, and he shook his head. "No. The card must've been missing by then. But I'm sure nothing was delivered here. I suppose it could have been when I was at work."

"Do you have a mobile phone?"

Albert nodded. He looked around the sitting room, searching for it. These days, most people knew exactly where their phone was at any time so they could check their messages every five minutes.

He got to his feet gingerly. "Yes, it's around here some-where. I don't really use it very much."

As he puttered around looking for the phone, Mackinnon continued to question him. But as more time passed, the more Mackinnon was convinced Albert Banks had absolutely nothing to do with this abduction. Either that or he was a very good actor.

"Ah, here it is," Albert Banks said, grinning broadly as he opened a drawer in the large dresser and pulled out a brick-sized mobile phone. It had to be at least ten years old. It didn't even have a colour screen.

Mackinnon drained the rest of his tea and got to his feet. "Thank you very much, Mr Banks. You've been very helpful. We believe the people who stole your credit card are involved in another crime, and hopefully, we will be able to track them down soon. We'll be in touch."

Albert Banks' face brightened. "Oh, that is good news. I mean, the credit card company were very good about it and refunded my money, but the worst thing is the stress of it all, the thought of somebody using my identity online. I'm glad you haven't given up on it."

He led Mackinnon out and then waved him off cheerfully.

Mackinnon wished there was more they could do about credit card fraud. Although City Police led the country in their drive to tackle cybercrime, sometimes it seemed as though the culprits were always one step ahead.

CHAPTER TWENTY-SIX

MACKINNON WAS HALFWAY BACK to the station when his phone rang. He fished it out of his pocket and saw that it was DI Tyler.

"Mackinnon."

"Jack, I'm heading to the Watsons' now. I'm going to talk to them and emphasise how important it is they don't leave the apartment. I don't want them replying to any text messages without telling us about them first. I'd like you to go and speak to the George family and make sure they understand that, too."

"Not a problem," Mackinnon said, turning around. "I'll head over there now. What do you want to do about Glenn Calvert? He's relatively new at this, and I imagine today's been pretty stressful for him. Is there an FLO taking over from him."

"We're pretty stretched at the moment. I was hoping he would be able to stay with the family tonight, but have a word with him. If he's not happy, I will sort something out. Let me know how you get on."

"Will do," Mackinnon said and hung up, slipping the phone back in his pocket.

It was a warm day, and most residents in the area had their windows open so Mackinnon could hear music and the noise from televisions as he walked back towards the Towers Estate.

He used to live in a flat in London, and he had been used to the almost constant noise. Even at night, there was still a background hum of activity. In Oxford, it was different. The first few nights he'd stayed at Chloe's he hadn't slept well, and at first, he hadn't been able to figure out why.

He'd lain awake in bed, staring at the ceiling, and finally realised it was because it was so damn quiet. He just wasn't used to it.

He'd grown accustomed to it now, though, and occasionally found the constant buzz of London annoying. Still, he supposed he got to experience the best sides of both. When he was in London, he stayed with his friend Derek, in Hackney, and got to work in the city. When he was in Oxford, he had a more relaxed pace of life. It wasn't all Inspector Morse and punting down the river, but it was definitely a gentler pace of life, more peaceful.

He reached the Georges' building and headed up the stairs. He knocked on the front door and within seconds Glenn Calvert answered. He looked stressed.

"Everything okay, Glenn?"

Glenn wasn't able to meet his eye. "I'm really sorry about earlier. I had no idea she'd left, and I know that's ridiculous. I should have kept a closer eye on her."

"Glenn, these things happen. Claire Watson left her apartment without being seen as well. We just need to keep a close eye on the parents now. If another text message comes in, we need to know about it."

Glenn nodded.

"I've just had a word with DI Tyler. He wants to know if you're all right to stay here tonight. If you don't think you can make it through until morning, we can get somebody to relieve you."

Glenn shook his head. "No, that won't be necessary. I'll stay here."

Mackinnon nodded, and then Glenn took him through to the sitting room where the Georges were sitting on the sofa and staring blankly at the TV set.

"I'll make us a cup of tea," Glenn said, collecting the cups from the coffee table.

Mackinnon sat down in the armchair opposite the Georges.

"How are you bearing up, Janice?"

It was a stupid question. He could tell exactly how she was bearing up just by looking at her. She was a nervous wreck. Not only was her daughter missing, but she had thrown acid over a stranger to try and get her daughter back.

"I suppose you're here to give me a stern ticking off. Or have you come to arrest me?" Janice said.

"Don't talk like that," her husband said. "Of course, he is *not* going to arrest you. Your daughter is missing. Tell her," he said, looking at Mackinnon.

"There will be consequences from today, Janice. That's out of my control. But right now, we need to move past that and concentrate on getting Lila home. The best chance we have relies on you telling us everything you know. There can be no more running off to do things in secret."

"That's easy for you to say," Janice said bitterly. "The text message said if I didn't go alone they would kill Lila. What was I supposed to do?"

Mackinnon nodded. He couldn't even imagine being forced to make such a choice.

"I know you want to believe what they say. But you did what they asked, and they didn't return Lila. You need to trust us."

Janice shut her eyes and clutched her hands together in her lap.

"It's all right, Detective," Toby said. "Janice knows the lie of the land now. If we get any more messages, we will tell you about them straightaway."

Mackinnon nodded.

"Have you made any progress?" Janice said.

Mackinnon nodded. "We have been tracking down the phones that were used by the abductors and hope that could lead us to them."

He saw Janice's face light up, and her body grew rigid as she hung on his every word.

"But it's early days. We will be working all through the night. There's a whole team back at the station who are trying to track down the person who last saw your daughter. We are doing everything we can to make sure Lila comes home."

Janice put her head in her hands. "I know you are trying, but you haven't found her yet. She is out there somewhere, with God knows who, and you haven't found her. What do you think they are going to do next? Do you think they're going to give me another task? What happens if I don't do it this time?"

The thought chilled Mackinnon to the core. He had no idea what the abductor's next move would be.

CHAPTER TWENTY-SEVEN

AT THE KINGS ARMS PUB, Rob sat at the table in the corner by the fruit machines, and Marlo brought over the drinks.

He put a pint and a whisky chaser down in front of Rob.

Rob knew what Marlo was trying to achieve, but alcohol wasn't going to persuade him.

As Marlo sat down, Rob demanded, "What are you playing at, Marlo?"

Marlo took a sip of his beer instead of answering, so Rob continued, "I've had enough of all this. It's over. It stops here. I am taking Benny home."

Marlo put his beer back on the table. "Okay, let's relax and talk about this like adults. You're right. There's no point risking getting caught if we don't have to. That's why I've decided we should do one more little task and then we'll get the money."

Rob stared at him and shook his head. Marlo was delusional. Why did there always have to be one more thing...

One more job... Why couldn't he just give up while they were ahead?

Marlo pulled out two phones from his jacket pocket. Each mobile was in a see-through plastic bag.

"Obviously, we can't text the parents again on the same number. The police will be tracking those now and keeping a close eye on those naughty mothers, but I think they'll still want to play the game."

He pushed the phones across the table to Rob.

"No more games!" Rob said.

Marlo's eyes grew cold as he smiled. "One more job and then we ask for the money. It's your choice, Rob. You can walk away now with nothing, or you can do one more job and get paid. It would be a shame to lose everything after all the hard work you've already put in."

Marlo smiled and knew he had Rob over a barrel.

Rob pushed his beer away and reached for the whisky. He took a large gulp, which burned his throat on the way down. He slammed the glass back on the table.

"And how exactly am I supposed to get the new phones to the parents?"

Marlo grinned. "I'm glad you asked. I've got you a nice disguise. You're going to be a delivery driver."

Rob's eyes widened. Surely this couldn't be happening.

"Don't be ridiculous," he snapped.

Marlo grinned even wider. "Trust me."

Rob shook his head. Marlo was the least trustworthy person he knew. But he needed that money... and it wasn't as if he was actually hurting anyone. "I won't do it if it is something dangerous. I don't want to have anything to do with acid."

Marlo nodded sombrely. "Cross my heart and hope to die.

It's got absolutely nothing to do with acid. It's a harmless little game."

Rob shrugged, feeling defeated. "I'll think about it."

"Don't be such a baby," scoffed Marlo.

That was the last straw.

"I said I'd think about it!" Rob shouted the words, and a number of people in the pub swivelled towards them.

"Look what you've done now," Marlo said mockingly. "You've drawn attention to us."

Rob shakily got to his feet, pushing himself away from the table. He couldn't stand to look at Marlo for another minute. "I need some air."

* * *

MARLO RETURNED from the Kings Arms in a bad mood because Rob had stormed off in a strop to goodness knows where, and now Marlo had to handle things himself. He didn't like getting his hands dirty and preferred to have a partner to deal with the nitty-gritty. Marlo was a planner. He had played his part by coming up with the big ideas in the first place and wasn't keen on doing all the work himself. That's why he had involved Rob and offered him a cut, but if Rob thought Marlo would still cut the money fifty-fifty after this, he was mistaken. Thanks to Rob behaving like a spoilt child, it looked as though Marlo didn't have any choice. He would have to handle everything.

He wouldn't forget this. Rob would pay for his little tantrum.

He walked down the steps to the basement flat and paused to listen before he opened the front door. All was quiet. He smiled and put his key in the lock. As he walked inside, the huge, hulking figure of Benny standing silently in the doorway to the sitting room made him jump.

He hid his nerves with anger.

"What are you looking at?" Marlo demanded.

"Where is Rob?"

"How should I know? He probably got bored of looking at your ugly mug."

Benny's lower lip wobbled.

As if it wasn't bad enough that Rob had done a runner, leaving Marlo to execute the plan, he now had to deal with Rob's slow-witted brother, Benny.

He'd had enough of both Morris brothers. Rob's sulking and spineless attitude had pushed Marlo to the point of no return. He couldn't punish Rob as he wasn't here, but there was one way he could get to him...

Marlo looked at Benny and smiled.

"Rob really shouldn't have left you here, Benny. Who knows what could happen to you when he isn't here to keep an eye on you."

Despite the overt threat in Marlo's words, Benny's blank expression didn't change at first. His eyes searched Marlo's face, and his forehead puckered in a frown.

"Are you going to let the girls go home now?" Benny asked.

The big lump really didn't know when to keep his mouth shut.

Marlo's temper roared to the surface, and he slammed the side of his fist against the wall.

"Will you shut up? Unlike your brother, I'm not going to put up with a halfwit asking me questions all the time."

Benny may not have been able to pick up on the subtle threat behind Marlo's words, but he did pick up on his anger.

He took a step backwards, his eyes widening in fright.

"Sorry… I didn't mean it."

But it was too late for Benny's apologies. Marlo had had it up to here with Rob and his stupid brother.

Marlo raised a hand and crooked a finger at Benny, beckoning him forward.

"Come here. Do you want to see the girls?"

The terrified look left Benny's face and he smiled tentatively. He blinked a couple of times and then nodded eagerly.

"Fine. Knock yourself out then."

Marlo dug in his pocket and selected the key to the bedroom the girls were held in. He walked down the hallway and unlocked the door, pushing it open.

"In you go," he said smiling nastily at Benny.

For a moment, Benny wasn't sure what to do. He stood still, looking at the open doorway.

Marlo clapped his hands. "You wanted to see them, didn't you? Get in there."

Benny shuffled forward slowly, and when he reached the doorway, he stopped again, craning his neck around the corner into the dark room.

"Why is it so dark in there?"

But Marlo wasn't going to answer any more of Benny's questions. He used his full weight to give Benny a huge shove from behind, pushing him into the room and then quickly shutting the door behind him and locking it.

Benny must have been shouting at the top of his lungs, because despite the soundproofing, Marlo could still hear him. He battered the door, trying to get out, but it was too late.

Marlo was going to leave him in there with the girls for the foreseeable future, at least until Rob got back.

What the hell did Rob think he was? Some kind of babysitter?

That would teach Rob not to throw temper tantrums like a two-year-old. He smiled, imagining the look on Rob's face when he came back and realised that Benny was locked up with the girls.

CHAPTER TWENTY-EIGHT

BENNY WAS STRUGGLING TO BREATHE. His heart was beating so hard and blood was rushing in his ears.

He gasped for air and slammed his hands against the wall, which was covered in a soft, spongy material.

It was pitch black in the room, and Benny hated the dark.

A single tear trickled down his cheek. Why had Rob left him here? Why did he leave him with someone nasty like Marlo?

Benny hollered again even though he knew Marlo had locked him in here on purpose.

He'd raised his fist to bring it down again when he heard a voice behind him. Benny turned around in terror and put his back flat against the wall. His eyes searched the darkness.

"Benny? Is that you?"

Benny squeezed his eyes tightly shut. That sounded like Lila. She was his friend. Lila wouldn't hurt him.

When he opened his eyes again, it was still dark.

His hands fumbled for the light, trying to feel for the

switch, but everything he touched was covered in a horrible spongy foam.

"Benny? It's Lila."

Benny gulped down two large lungfuls of air and stared into the darkness. The only light in the room was coming from the small crack around the door. There wasn't enough light to see properly, but Benny thought he saw two dark figures moving at the back of the room.

"I'm sorry," Benny said, his voice quivering. "I'm sorry for what happened."

"Who are those men? Why are they doing this?" Lila asked.

"Don't ask him that. They could be listening. If we don't know anything, they can let us go." Benny recognised Ruby's voice.

He began to relax a little as his eyes adjusted to the dark room. Although there wasn't much light coming in from around the doorway, there was enough to drive away the complete darkness that terrified Benny. He was glad he wasn't alone. Ruby and Lila were here, and they wouldn't hurt him.

"If you think they're just going to let us go, you'd better think again. If we want to get out of this, it's down to us to get ourselves out," Lila said.

"Why is it so dark?" Benny asked. "I can't find the light switch."

"Don't bother looking for the light switch, Benny. They've taken the light bulb out. It's okay, though," Lila said. "Your eyes will get used to the dark soon."

When Lila spoke again, her voice was much closer to Benny and made him jump.

"Benny, we need to get out of here. Can you help us?"

"I don't know what to do." Benny leaned back against the

door and slowly slipped down until he was sitting on the floor.

He put his head in his hands and began to cry.

* * *

A QUARTER OF A MILE AWAY, Rob sat on a wooden bench in a small park, watching people walk their dogs and joggers sweating as they ran passed him.

They were all busy living their normal lives, not sparing a second glance to the man sitting on the bench. They had no idea what he had done.

He leaned back against the wooden slats, feeling them digging into his ribs and spine, and looked up at the cloudy sky.

What was he going to do? He couldn't believe he had let things get this far. There were two girls being held against their will because of him. If he hadn't helped Marlo and persuaded Benny to lure the girls into a trap, they'd be finishing their day at work right now.

He wished he could draw a line under everything and take Benny home. He'd like to give the girls back, but he wouldn't be able to do that without recriminations and punishment.

Why had he thought this would be easy? He should have known it would be a disaster, especially with someone like Marlo involved.

He pulled out his mobile phone and checked the time. He was being selfish. Benny would be worrying and wondering where he was, but he didn't want to see Benny right now. He couldn't face looking into his big eyes and seeing confusion and hurt there. Benny had always looked up to Rob. He'd worshipped him, and Rob had always been there to look out for Benny. It was the least he could do for the unconditional adoration Benny gave him.

There had been times in the past when Rob felt he'd let Benny down.

When their mother had first fallen ill, Benny had gone into sheltered housing. It had been a major shock for him, and the adjustment hadn't been easy.

But Rob told himself it was for the best because Benny would mix with other people like him and learn to support himself. The truth was, he just didn't want Benny getting in the way of his social life. He'd visited his brother once a week, and on every occasion, Benny was so overjoyed to see him, it made Rob's heart grow heavy with guilt.

Both brothers had taken their mother's death hard. She'd been a strong woman who handled everything life threw her way without complaining. She'd always supported both her boys financially and emotionally in a way that made them feel confident and safe, and when she was gone, Rob felt lost and Benny was distraught.

More than ever, he'd look to Rob for guidance. He thought Rob had all the answers.

Rob shook his head. If only. He'd gone from one extreme to the other. After she died, he'd taken Benny out of the sheltered housing straightaway and moved him into his flat. That was a stupid move. He'd completely underestimated how much time Benny would take to adjust to his new surroundings, and that meant Rob needed to take a lot of time off work and had ultimately caused Rob to lose his job.

He didn't have much comeback after being sacked. It had been a cash in hand job. His mother had warned him about that. She had told him to get a proper job and make sure he was on the books, paying taxes and National Insurance, but

Rob had thought he'd known better. He hadn't expected to have a full-time dependent, but he couldn't let Benny down.

They were close to being evicted from their flat, and if that happened, Rob wasn't so worried about what would happen to him because he could crash on a friend's floor or maybe even sleep rough in a hostel for a couple of nights, but Benny couldn't do that. He was sure if he got back in touch with Benny's old caseworker, they would arrange accommodation for him, but Benny would be distraught and would think Rob was rejecting him.

Rob took a long breath in and then exhaled slowly. There was nothing else for it. He would have to do Marlo's bidding one more time and get the money. After that, he and Benny could have a fresh start.

CHAPTER TWENTY-NINE

JANICE GEORGE LIFTED her head from the toilet. It was the fourth time she'd thrown up in the last hour.

She closed the lid, pushed herself away from the toilet and leaned against the cold bathroom tiles. Closing her eyes, the same image that had haunted her for the last few hours returned with crystal-clear clarity.

The man's name had been Sam Markham, and Janice would never forget the sight of his burnt flesh as he stripped off his T-shirt in front of her.

He was going to be scarred for life, and she was responsible.

All for the promise of getting her daughter back. Only it hadn't worked. She'd done exactly what they'd asked, played their stupid game, but she hadn't heard anything more from the abductors since the awful moment she'd thrown acid over that poor man.

Absolutely nothing. She hadn't even received a text message to tell her she'd won or lost the game. The bastards still had Lila, and she was no closer to getting her back, despite causing devastating pain to Sam Markham.

Janice put a hand to her belly and took a deep breath, trying to fight back the nausea.

She'd been worried that the sickness was due to inhaling some of the contents from the container, but the doctor had said it was shock. Her body was quite literally rejecting the fact this was happening to her.

She reached for some toilet tissue and wiped her mouth.

No doubt, she would be charged eventually for what she had done, but right now, they were treating her with kid gloves. Of course, that didn't mean she would get away with it. She had maimed a man for life. You didn't just walk away after doing something like that.

Janice gingerly pulled herself to her feet and flushed the toilet.

She washed her hands and face and then looked at herself in the mirror, barely recognising the woman looking back at her.

Her eyes were wide, her hair mussed up, her cheeks red, and she looked like a crazy woman.

On the street where Janice had grown up, there used to be a woman who shared her house with sixteen cats and spent her days muttering to herself. The locals called her Mad Mary, and that was who the face reflected in the mirror reminded Janice of. She'd lost touch with reality. Nothing in the real world mattered anymore. She only cared about getting her daughter back. She had promised the police she would show them any new text messages, and she wouldn't do anything the kidnappers asked, but that was a lie. She knew, deep down, she would do absolutely anything they asked to get Lila back.

The police had asked her to trust them, but that was a joke. They were useless, especially that poxy family liaison officer, Glenn Calvert. He just sat around drinking tea and chatting inanely about pointless things.

She'd had enough.

Even if she did listen to the police, and kept her promise to refuse to participate in any more games, who could say the mother of the other abducted girl wouldn't take part in the game...

Janice would never forgive herself if Lila died because of something she refused to do.

The fact of the matter was, the abductors had said only one girl would live.

Ruby or Lila.

Janice was determined to make sure it was her daughter who survived.

ALMOST AN HOUR HAD PASSED since Rob had run off and left Marlo at the Kings Arms. He'd said he needed a little time to think about things, but Marlo hadn't realised he was going to be such a tart about this whole operation. He was acting like an amateur.

At the end of the day, Rob had promised to take this job on. Marlo was prepared to fulfil his side of the bargain and give Rob more money than he'd ever clapped eyes on in his life. But if he didn't start pulling his weight, Rob wouldn't see a penny.

Benny had stopped banging, and it was finally quiet. But instead of enjoying the peace and quiet, Marlo was feeling anxious and tense.

Why should he be the one waiting around for Rob? He was the brains behind the outfit and had things to do. He was fed up of pandering to Rob and his stupid brother.

Marlo stood up and pushed back his sleeves. He didn't care about Rob. Sod him. He had a job to do whether Rob was going to help him or not.

It was almost time to trigger the next stage of the game. He needed to check on a couple of things to make sure everything was going according to plan.

As usual, Marlo had been meticulous in his research, but he knew he could never be too careful.

He walked out of the sitting room and into the hallway, pausing by the bedroom door and listening. There was no sound from inside. Good. He glanced at the front door. It was time to go.

He left the basement flat without his jacket, although the sun was setting, the early evening was still muggy and warm.

He set off at a brisk pace, and it only took him ten minutes to reach the primary school.

Bryant Lane Church of England school was a red-brick, single story building attended by less than three hundred pupils, aged between five and eleven.

A man hanging around the school gates during school hours would be noticed and probably reported quickly, but in the evening, there was nobody around to notice Marlo.

His eyes took in all the little details as his mind finalised the plan. Everything relied on timing, but schools, by their nature, demanded things happened on schedule, and that played into his hands.

After a few minutes, he left the school and walked to Barnes Street, which was only a couple of minutes' walk away.

Three-storey houses lined the pavement, most of them with a basement. Their grilled windows and stairs to the lower level meant it was easy to peer down and look into people's homes.

He walked until he reached number thirty-three. The lights were on in the house, illuminating a homely scene of a family having dinner.

He watched them as they smiled, chatted and passed each other the serving dishes. The mother stood up and piled pasta on her two daughters' plates.

She said something to her husband, who frowned and finally put down his mobile phone.

The two little girls started to eat straightaway.

How nice to see a family sitting at a dining table, enjoying dinner together.

"Enjoy it while you can," Marlo muttered, grinning.

One of the little girls looked up and seemed to look directly at Marlo.

He gave her a little wave. "See you tomorrow," he whispered.

Noticing the child was gazing at something through the window, her mother looked up sharply, but Marlo stepped back into the shadows, and she couldn't see him. She frowned and shivered and then stepped forward to pull the curtains shut.

Marlo smirked. That wouldn't help her. Not with what he had planned.

CHAPTER THIRTY

BENNY HUGGED his knees to his chest and rocked backwards and forwards.

It would be okay. Rob would be back soon and would take him home. As soon as Rob got back, he would find out Marlo had locked him in the dark room and rescue him.

Benny felt something touch his shoulder and shrieked.

"Relax, Benny. It's me, Lila."

She was so close he could feel her breath on his cheek. *Lila.* Lila was nice. Lila wouldn't hurt him.

"You have to tell me who they are, Benny. What are they going to do to us?"

Benny shook his head and tried to explain. "It's okay. They're not going to hurt you. Rob's my brother, and he wouldn't hurt anybody."

"They did hurt me!"

Lila raised her voice, and Benny flinched. She grabbed his hand and pulled it up to her face.

It was too dark in the room to make out more than shadows, but under his fingers, he could feel her swollen flesh and the dried blood on her lip from when Marlo had hit her.

"I'm sorry. So sorry. I didn't know. Rob said I could have an Xbox. He said it was just a game –"

Lila let out her breath in a hiss and dropped Benny's hand. "A game? A sodding game!"

"Shhh, Lila."

That was Ruby's voice, coming from a little further away.

He could just see the outline of her body as she shuffled towards them. "Listen to me, Benny," Ruby said. "You did a bad thing."

Benny shook his head frantically. "No, no, I didn't."

"Yes, Benny, you did, but you can put it right."

Benny shook his head. He didn't understand what she meant. "I don't like the dark. I'm scared."

"So am I, but we need you to break down the door so we can get out of here. Are they still in the flat?"

Benny shook his head. He couldn't do that. "My brother will be angry."

"I don't give a toss about your brother, Benny. He's an evil bastard. He must be otherwise he wouldn't have done this to us." Lila said.

"Lila!" Ruby's voice was harsh. "You're not helping. Listen to me, Benny. The other man who hurt Lila… The man who wore the baseball cap –"

"Marlo?"

"Yes, Marlo. He is forcing your brother to do this, so you have to break down the door and save Rob and us."

"I can't."

"You can, Benny. We are not strong enough to break it down, but you are. Please try."

Benny couldn't answer. He was trembling too hard.

"Have they gone out, Benny? Have they locked us up and left us alone in here?" Ruby asked. "Do you know where we are? Are we still in London?"

Benny put his hands over his ears. There were too many questions. They made his head spin.

"Please, Benny. We need your help. Once we get out of here, I'll get you that Xbox straightaway."

Benny began to cry. "I don't want the Xbox anymore. I just want to go home."

Lila reached for his hand and squeezed it. "That's what we want, too, Benny. Let's go home together. Come on get up."

Lila tugged on his hand until Benny did as he was told and got to his feet.

She felt her way across the padded wall and pulled Benny with her until she found the door.

"Okay, Benny. I think it's better if you kick the door right by the lock... that's here."

She took his hand and pushed against the door. He could feel the handle poking out beneath the soft foam covering.

"If that doesn't work, you'll have to use your shoulder," Ruby added.

Benny was so scared he couldn't speak.

"It's going to be okay, Benny," Ruby said. "You just need to break the door down like in the films. You'll be just like a movie star."

Benny smiled. "I saw someone do it on EastEnders once."

"See, it won't be that difficult," Lila said. "Ready when you are, Benny."

Benny took a deep breath. It was so quiet in the room.

He didn't know if Marlo was still out there or if he'd gone out. What if Rob came back and got angry with Benny for breaking the door?

He moved forward, almost scared to touch the door, and gave it a little shove followed by a kick.

The door didn't budge.

"You need to do it harder than that, Benny," Lila said. "Give it some welly. Like they do on the TV."

This time, Benny kicked it hard and heard the sound of wood splintering beneath his shoe. But still, the door remained closed.

"That's more like it Benny, now try and push it with your shoulder," Ruby said. "Take a run up."

Benny did as he was told. He couldn't wait to get out of this dark room. He took two steps backwards and then ran at the door, flinging his whole body at it.

It gave way easily this time, and Benny tripped and went sprawling into the hallway, landing on top of the fallen door.

He heard the girls' anxious whispers behind him and blinked happily in the bright light of the hallway.

"Good work, Benny. Now, get up, quick," Ruby ordered. "We need to get out of here. Is the front door locked?"

Without waiting for an answer, she ran to the front door and rattled the handle.

She spun around. "It's locked, Benny. Where is the key?"

Benny pushed himself up to a sitting position. "The spare key is in the kitchen."

He opened his mouth to say something else, but he saw a shadow at the door behind Ruby, and his eyes opened wide.

"What is it, Benny?" Ruby asked. "What's wrong?"

But Benny didn't need to answer. Lila did that for him, "They've come back. They're at the door. Quick!"

But before Ruby could get away, the front door opened.

Marlo stood in the doorway.

The initial shock on his face when he saw Benny on the

floor and the girls roaming free in the hallway, soon gave way to anger.

He stepped inside, shut the front door behind him and raised an eyebrow. "Well, you have been busy while I've been gone, haven't you?"

CHAPTER THIRTY-ONE

MACKINNON RAN a hand through his hair and muttered a curse. He'd forgotten to call Chloe and let her know he would be working late tonight. They had been together long enough now that she would probably have guessed it was going to be an all-nighter, but she still deserved the courtesy of a phone call. He also felt guilty after leaving her to deal with Sarah's money problems alone, though Mackinnon wouldn't dream of interfering, he could still offer support just by acting as a sounding board.

He reached for his mobile phone, drained the last mouthful of coffee from his mug and headed outside.

He could have called Chloe from the incident room, but he wanted to get some fresh air. It felt like they were due for a thunderstorm. The air was thick, humid and heavy as Mackinnon stepped outside Wood Street Station.

Chloe answered after the second ring.

"Don't tell me, it's going to be a late one, isn't it?"

"I'm afraid so. It doesn't even look like I'll be getting back to Derek's tonight."

Mackinnon had sent Derek a text earlier, letting him know he might be crashing at his place later that night, but it was looking more and more unlikely.

Detectives working a case like this put in long hours because the time it took to get somebody else up to speed on all the information coming in was a huge time suck they couldn't afford, especially during the first twenty-four hours the girls were missing.

"Did you speak to Sarah? She turned up right before I had to leave for work."

Chloe paused for a beat and then said, "Yes, I did, but she didn't stay long."

Chloe didn't volunteer any further information, and Mackinnon wondered if Sarah had even mentioned the fact that she needed cash.

"She asked me for money," Mackinnon said. "I couldn't help thinking she was in some kind of trouble. What did she tell you?"

He heard Chloe sigh heavily on the other end of the phone. "She didn't tell me much to be honest. I gave her five hundred pounds, and when she left it was not on the best of terms."

"Did she say why she needed the money?"

"No, she didn't say much other than she'd borrowed some money from a friend and needed to pay it back."

"A friend?"

Mackinnon had been worried Sarah had borrowed money from a less than salubrious outfit. He'd heard reports of loan sharks targeting university students. It wasn't the customer demographic one might expect. Moneylenders usually operated on housing estates, focusing on the poorest populations, but just recently, a number of lenders had moved onto the student population. They preyed on youngsters who were away from home for the first time and not managing their money well.

From their point of view, it seemed to be a good option. They were broke, and then all of a sudden a nice chap offered to lend them some money. It was only later they learned of the extortionate interest rates and the penalty for not paying on time.

It was a win-win for the moneylenders because most of the students had parents behind them who would bail them out.

"That's what she said," Chloe said. "I tried to get more out of her, but you know what she can be like."

Mackinnon did know. He was well aware that Sarah didn't often tell them the whole story.

"So she didn't stay long?"

"Only long enough for me to transfer the money into her bank account. When I tried to discuss the matter with her afterwards, she suddenly had a burning need to get back to Kingston. She said she had to work tonight." Chloe gave another sigh. "But I had a lovely day with Katy. It was nice to spend some time with her. She's growing up so fast."

"Did she enjoy the show?"

"She loved it. So do you have any idea when you might be back?" Chloe asked.

"Not yet. It's quite a big case and could go on for a while. I'll probably be staying in London for the next few days. I'll give you a ring later, though."

After Mackinnon hung up the call, he stood outside Wood Street Station and looked up at the clouds gathering in the sky. He had a feeling that this situation Sarah had got herself into was going to get worse before it got better.

As he stepped back inside the reception area, he saw Charlotte saying goodbye to an ex-boyfriend of Lila George's she had just finished questioning.

After she watched him leave, she turned to Mackinnon. "I don't think he is involved. He was in Manchester until lunchtime." She sighed. "Are you staying at Derek's tonight?"

Mackinnon nodded. "Probably. How is Tyler bearing up?" Mackinnon asked. He knew Tyler had been conducting interviews with Charlotte.

They headed around the duty sergeant's desk towards the secure door at the back of the reception area. Charlotte swiped her card, and they both entered.

"He's under a lot of stress." She shook her head. "I used to think it would be nice to get to detective inspector level, but now I'm not so sure."

"There are definitely easier jobs," Mackinnon said.

"Did Tyler rip into Glenn Calvert after Janice George went missing?" Charlotte asked.

Mackinnon shook his head. "No, he was very supportive, and I think Glenn will keep a close eye on Janice from now on. To be honest, it's not easy keeping tabs on the parents. Claire Watson managed to get out on Kelly Johnson's watch, and she's a very experienced FLO. Save locking them up, I'm not sure what we can do to make sure they stay at home."

THE FIRST THING Marlo did when he returned was raise his fist and give Lila George a backhander.

It sent her slamming into the wall, and she slumped down onto the carpet, stunned.

Ruby had screamed for Benny to help them.

"Stop him, Benny. Don't let him hurt us!" she'd screamed with wide terror-filled eyes as Marlo advanced on her.

If Benny had either brains or balls, Marlo would be in trouble. Big trouble. But the pathetic lump of quivering flesh sat down on the broken door with his back against the wall, trembling and not even daring to look up at Marlo.

It was easy enough to subdue the girls and put them in the other bedroom. Luckily that also had a lock, but unfortunately, no soundproofing. It was a pain in the arse because that meant he would have to keep the girls quiet. He'd used duct tape to cover their mouths.

Ruby had sobbed while he was doing it, but Lila George had glared at him with fury, pulling away from him as he yanked the duct tape around her head.

He needed money for the girls, so he couldn't do much more than give them a couple of slaps. He didn't want damaged goods on his hands.

Benny, on the other hand, was just a nuisance, and Marlo didn't have to put up with him any longer.

He turned around to look at Benny, who hadn't moved from his spot on the floor.

He leaned down, put his head very close to Benny's and said, "Get up, you stupid lump of lard."

Benny grimaced and started to cry, and Marlo's lip curled back in disgust.

He had to get rid of him and fast. He had a plan but he was on borrowed time. He needed to have it done and dusted before Rob returned.

CHAPTER THIRTY-TWO

THE WATSONS' family liaison officer, Kelly Johnson, stifled a sigh.

Peter Watson had been berating his wife for the last ten minutes. As a family liaison officer, she trod a fine line. She needed to be supportive, providing the family with information and keeping the channels of communication open between the police and the family.

She was an experienced officer and had worked on many harrowing cases, but the very worst thing, in her opinion, was seeing a family turn on each other and rip each other to bits, especially when they needed the support of their loved ones to get through the tough times ahead.

Both Peter and Claire Watson were in the kitchen, and Kelly sat on a sofa in the living area. She was facing the large windows, pretending to look out at the London cityscape. Listening in to an argument between husband and wife felt like the worst kind of prying, and she tried to give them some space, but at the same time, she needed to listen in case any relevant information came to light.

"I can't believe you thought it was a good idea to go alone," Peter Watson said for the tenth time.

He leaned heavily on the marble kitchen counter, glaring at the kitchen sink, as though he couldn't force himself to turn around and face his wife.

Claire Watson stood in the middle of the kitchen and let his angry words wash over her before replying.

"I told you. I went alone because that's what the text message instructed. I couldn't risk –"

"She is my daughter, too. Don't you think I should get a say in it." Peter Watson slammed his fist on the counter. "What if you'd messed it up, and they'd killed Ruby *and* you because of your recklessness?"

Kelly stood up and walked over to the open-plan kitchen. The argument was turning nasty and things were going to be said that couldn't be unsaid.

"I think the best thing we can do now is move on and focus on what's going to happen next," she said. "Claire made a mistake, but an understandable one, and she needs your support, Peter."

Peter Watson turned his icy-cold eyes on Kelly. "I don't remember asking for your opinion."

But Kelly stood her ground. She wasn't easily intimidated. You needed to be calm and confident as a FLO, even when people where hurling insults left, right and centre.

She maintained eye contact with Peter until he looked away, shamefaced.

"I know feelings are running high, but recriminations won't help at this stage."

Peter Watson whirled around and jabbed a finger in his

wife's direction. "She still should have told me about the message."

Claire Watson's quiet demeanour suddenly snapped. "Oh, will you shut up? I'm sick to the back teeth of you. What would you have done in my position?"

Her voice was high-pitched and verging on hysteria.

At that moment, the Watsons' son walked out from his bedroom and wandered into the open plan kitchen, looking at his parents with interest.

"I think it's best if we all take a break for five minutes to cool off," Kelly said, trying to diffuse the situation.

Curtis shrugged and picked up an apple from the fruit bowl. "Oh, don't stop on my account. I'm used to it." He bit into the apple and then walked through the kitchen, ignoring his parents, and headed towards the front door. "I'm going out."

"Wait," Kelly said hurriedly. She didn't have the power to make the boy stay here, but surely even he could see it wasn't a good idea to leave the apartment in the current situation.

Kelly began to walk towards him, planning what she would say to convince him to stay, but before she got to him, Claire Watson was at Curtis' side.

She grabbed him by the shoulders, shaking him. "Please, Curtis, don't go. I can't... Please..."

She gripped the material of his sweatshirt so tightly her knuckles turned white.

Curtis paused for a moment and stared at his mother. After a brief hesitation, he shrugged.

"Okay. I'll stay."

Claire released him and then covered her face with her hands, gulping down large breaths of air.

Peter watched all this without saying a word and then

strode from the kitchen to take up his spot by the floor-to-ceiling windows and resume his pacing.

CHAPTER THIRTY-THREE

MACKINNON ARRIVED at Drake House to touch base with the Watsons. He'd travelled on foot and reached the front of the building, intending to use the street-level entrance, but before he got there, he saw the familiar figure of Claire Watson standing outside and talking to someone.

There was a plain-clothed detective across the street, and Mackinnon wondered whether he had a better view of the woman talking to Claire Watson.

Mackinnon's pace slowed as he studied the two women. He couldn't see her face as she had her back to him, but she had brown hair and a thick-set figure. She wore a pair of loose-fitting trousers and a startlingly white pair of trainers.

That and her straggly hair with a half-grown out perm, which didn't look as though it had seen the inside of a salon for quite some time, told Mackinnon she probably wasn't a resident of Drake House.

As he drew nearer to the two women, Claire Watson suddenly looked up. When she saw Mackinnon, her face tightened, and she whispered something to the other woman who quickly darted away without looking back.

"Who was that?" Mackinnon asked as he reached Claire Watson and nodded at the woman who was now crossing the road.

Claire Watson shook her head. "I don't know."

She was lying. But Mackinnon didn't know why.

"You were talking to her."

"So? I just said good evening. It's hardly important in the grand scheme of things," Claire Watson snapped. "And I could do without the third degree, thank you."

Mackinnon turned to see the retreating figure take a left off Moor Lane and disappear from view.

He turned back to Claire Watson, but she'd already started to walk back inside Drake House, heading towards the penthouse lift.

He didn't know why, but he knew for sure that Claire Watson was hiding something.

Mackinnon travelled up with Claire Watson in uncomfortable silence. She clearly had something else on her mind.

When they entered the Watsons' apartment, Kelly walked over to say hello.

Mackinnon gave them a brief update, trying to reassure the Watsons that they were making progress. When he'd answered their questions, Claire Watson informed them all she was going to have a lie down.

"Leave your phone out here," Peter Watson snapped, glaring at his wife.

Claire Watson hesitated. She pulled the phone out of the pocket of her beige chinos and looked at it, as though she were very reluctant to let it out of her sight.

But finally, she took a deep breath and set it down on the coffee table before walking off to the bedroom.

A phone rang from somewhere else in the apartment and Peter Watson sighed. "That's the phone in the study. I'll have to take it. I won't be long."

Now alone in the open-plan living area, Kelly turned to Mackinnon and asked, "Do you want a coffee?"

Mackinnon shook his head as they walked towards the kitchen. "No, thanks. I had one not long ago. How is everything going here?"

Kelly shrugged as she switched the kettle on.

"It's not been easy. He is very angry, and she is remorseful on the surface but… underneath, I'm pretty sure she would do the same thing again given half the chance."

Mackinnon nodded. He agreed with Kelly's analysis. "Have you got kids?"

Kelly nodded. "Yes, a girl, Stephanie. She's ten next month. I have to say I think any mother would have done the same thing in Claire Watson's shoes." Kelly sighed and reached for a mug. "It's an impossible situation. Are you sure you don't want a drink?"

Mackinnon nodded. "I'm fine. I saw Claire Watson talking to someone downstairs, an older woman. Has anyone visited the apartment?"

Kelly frowned and shook her head. "No, the only people who have been in the apartment are family or police. They've been keeping the news quiet, so we haven't had anyone outside of Peter, Claire and Curtis here."

Mackinnon nodded, and in a low voice, he said, "She was definitely talking to someone and was quite defensive when I asked about it. I'm not sure it has any bearing on the case, but keep an eye out for Claire communicating with anyone other than us, her husband and her son."

Kelly nodded as she spooned instant coffee into her mug. "Will do," she said. "How is Glenn doing?"

Kelly knew how hard it was to be a family liaison officer, and she knew Glenn was relatively new at the job. She understood how personally he would have taken the fact that Janice George had run out of the apartment on his watch. The same thing happened to Kelly, but she was experienced enough to know that there was no point blaming herself.

"He is okay," Mackinnon said, "but he's being a bit hard on himself."

As the kettle came to a boil, Kelly reached for it and poured steaming hot water into her mug. "I thought DI Tyler was going to blow a gasket when it happened."

"I think he came close, but he's a good detective. He is doing his best."

Kelly picked up her mug and nodded. "That's all we can do."

Both Mackinnon and Kelly turned when they heard a noise behind them.

Curtis had walked out of his bedroom.

"Oh, it's you," he said as he looked up at Mackinnon. "Do you have any idea who took my sister yet?"

He lifted the apple he was holding to his mouth and took a final bite before throwing the core into the bin.

Mackinnon said, "We're still working on it."

"Is it true what they say that it's usually someone you know who committed the crime?"

"It depends on the crime," Mackinnon said.

Curtis nodded thoughtfully and then he said, "You should

talk to Ruby's friend, Kirsty. She is out of the country at the moment, but you should be able to get her on a video call."

"We've tried but haven't been able to get in touch with her yet."

Curtis nodded. "Have you spoken to Mr Addlestone?"

Mackinnon frowned. "Who's that?"

"He is Ruby's English lit teacher and a bit of a letch, apparently."

"We'll talk to him. Thanks, Curtis."

Curtis shrugged. "That's all right. I'll tell you if I think of anything else."

"At first, I thought you weren't too worried about your sister's disappearance."

Curtis smirked. "I hoped she'd come back on her own. We're not the closest of families, but that doesn't mean I don't care. You know I'm adopted, don't you?"

Mackinnon nodded. "Yes, your parents told us both you and Ruby were adopted."

"Well, it's not easy being as intelligent as I am. I suppose my parents told you I was a child prodigy, didn't they?"

Mackinnon exchanged a brief look with Kelly. The Watsons hadn't mentioned that, no doubt because they were a little too preoccupied with Ruby's disappearance to sing their son's praises.

Curtis didn't pick up on Mackinnon's reaction.

He continued, "I don't feel very connected to them, my parents, I mean. I don't find them…interesting."

Kelly's eyes widened. "Interesting?"

Curtis sneered. "Yes. They are just predictable."

Curtis turned around and walked back to his bedroom, signifying that the conversation was over.

Mackinnon turned to Kelly after Curtis was out of hearing range. "What do you make of him?"

Kelly stared at Curtis's closed bedroom door. "I don't know. He's definitely odd, but it could be an act, a type of self defence, but if it is, he keeps it up all the time."

Mackinnon nodded. "Right, I'd better go and get the teacher Curtis mentioned checked out."

"Do you think it's a good lead?"

Mackinnon shrugged. "I hope so. We really need one."

CHAPTER THIRTY-FOUR

"Now, Benny, you've been a very naughty boy. What do we do with naughty boys?"

Benny was silent.

Marlo kicked him with the edge of his shoe. "Answer me!"

"I don't know," Benny whispered.

"They have to be punished," Marlo said.

Benny bit his lip and took a step backwards. "How?"

"I haven't decided yet." He held up his hand and crooked his finger. "Follow me, Benny. We're going for a little walk."

He lifted the broken door, leaning it against the wall. The lock and one of the door panels were shattered, so it wasn't as though he could fix it and hide what had happened from Rob, but he'd cross that bridge when he came to it.

Marlo left the girls locked in the other bedroom, and he and Benny stepped outside into the balmy evening. There was a rumble of thunder in the distance.

Benny followed Marlo up the steps to the pavement. "Where are we going?"

"We are going to the allotments. It's a lovely evening for it."

Benny looked up at the sky, narrowed his eyes at the dark clouds and shook his head. "You're not supposed to go to the allotments after dark. I know because my mum used to have an allotment. You can't grow bananas. It's not warm enough here, but my mum grew tomatoes. We had to give it up after she died because Rob's not got time. He's too busy."

Marlo nodded and pretended to listen to Benny warbling on as they walked towards the bus stop.

Benny was happy enough once they got on the D7 bus. Once they were outside the basement flat, Benny appeared to relax in Marlo's company. It seemed as though he put all the bad experiences of the flat behind him and felt he was safe now he was out in the real world.

Benny was about to get a rude awakening.

They reached the allotments, which were fenced off and locked. They'd had trouble with kids hanging around and breaking into sheds, so they'd taken to locking up at eight p.m.

Marlo didn't let that bother him. It was only a normal padlock, and with practised ease, he picked the lock.

Benny watched him with wide eyes. "You shouldn't do that," he said. "You'll get in trouble."

Marlo didn't bother to reply. He walked along the small pathway between the rows of runner beans, heading for a shed right at the back of the allotments.

He'd spent a few nights here a couple of months ago, trying to lay low, so he knew exactly where he was going.

"Hurry up," Marlo said, and stepped off the path, skirting around a vegetable patch.

He waited for Benny to follow him and then knelt down at the back of the shed.

It was already getting dark so Marlo used his hands to feel along the wood panels at the back of the shed. When one of them gave way, he smiled. It still hadn't been fixed. Good.

He pushed two of the panels to one side and then looked back at Benny, scowled at the size of him and removed two more panels.

He took a quick look round but nobody else was there. There was a gentle hum of traffic from the main road behind the allotments, but otherwise it was quiet.

He jerked his thumb, indicating that Benny should go inside the shed.

Benny's eyes widened, and he shook his head.

"It's dark in there. I don't like the dark."

"I don't care what you like. Get in there now before I lose my temper."

Benny slowly ducked his head in the dark hole and squeezed his huge body inside.

He took his time about it, and Marlo kicked his backside with the tip of his shoe. When Benny was finally through the gap, Marlo followed him inside. It was dark and smelled of earth and potting compost.

Benny stood and whimpered in the corner as Marlo scrabbled about under the bench to find the candles he had stashed there.

He had chosen this shed in particular because it was clear the owner didn't visit very often. The people who ran places like this were very particular on standards and expected everybody to pull their weight. All allotments had to be kept clean and tidy, and that included weeding the flower beds and vegetable patches. But the bloke who owned this shed had been in hospital for a while, and even the allotment manager wasn't cruel enough to take it away from him while he was ill.

"Right, Benny, sit in that chair and look straight ahead," Marlo said as he lit a candle and stuck it on the bench.

Benny ignored his instructions, and the light from the candle flickered across his large face, giving him an eerie appearance.

"I said sit down," Marlo growled.

Benny let out another pathetic whimper but did as he was told and sat down in the chair.

Marlo moved behind him and reached for the cable ties.

As he began to fasten him to the chair, Benny spoke up. "No, I don't like it. I want Rob."

"We are just playing a little game, Benny."

Marlo worked quickly to fasten his wrists. He had to tie him up because the big bastard was strong. He couldn't take the risk of Benny fighting back, but despite Marlo's concerns, Benny only struggled half-heartedly.

When he was finished, Marlo could breathe more easily. Only now that Benny was safely secured did Marlo allow him to see the steel blade. It was long and pointed, like one of those fancy letter openers they had back in the day.

Marlo had picked it up during a robbery a few years ago. It had coloured glass embedded in the handle, and although he knew they weren't real jewels, he liked the blade for its elegance and had kept it with him.

Benny's face was a picture.

"What's that? What are you d...doing with the knife?"

Benny bucked against the fastenings, and for a moment, Marlo was truly concerned he might get free. But despite his strength, Benny didn't have a violent nature, and his struggles soon gave way to sobs.

As soon as he'd stopped moving around so much, Marlo lunged forward and buried the knife in Benny's gut.

Benny's eyes flew open and fixed on Marlo's face.

Marlo held his breath in anticipation.

He wanted to see the life drain out of Benny's eyes, but he closed them only a few seconds later.

Marlo stood there, staring down at him, feeling cheated.

He'd died much faster and less violently than Marlo had expected. He reached down, and with some effort, managed to pull the knife out of Benny's body.

The fact that Benny didn't even flinch told him everything he needed to know.

Benny was gone.

CHAPTER THIRTY-FIVE

WHEN MACKINNON LEFT DRAKE HOUSE, he phoned DI Tyler straightaway to ask him about Ruby Watson's English teacher.

They had questioned a number of Ruby's friends and teachers, and Mackinnon wanted to know if they'd already spoken to Mr Addlestone.

As soon as Tyler answered, Mackinnon said, "I have just had a word with Ruby Watson's brother, Curtis. He mentioned that we might want to speak to Ruby's English teacher, Mr Addlestone. Curtis said, and I quote, '*he is a bit of a letch*'."

Tyler paused on the other end of the phone before saying, "Addlestone. The name rings a bell, let me check."

In the silence that followed, Mackinnon looked up at the sky. In London it was never truly dark thanks to the number of street and residential lights.

Large clouds moved quickly across the sky as the wind picked up. It wouldn't be long before a storm hit.

Tyler came back on the line. "We haven't spoken to him

yet. He is on the list, but we had no reason to put him at the top. We will probably get to him tomorrow…unless you think it's worth bumping him up the list."

Mackinnon didn't need to think about it. Immediately he replied, "Yes, move him to the top of the list. In fact, I could go and see him right now if you have his address."

The fact that Ruby's brother mentioned him, made Mackinnon unwilling to leave this for another day.

Tyler hesitated for a brief moment and then gave Mackinnon the okay. He reeled off Terrence Addlestone's address, and Mackinnon thanked him and hung up.

Mackinnon took another look at the sky and hoped the rain would hold off until he reached Addlestone's residence.

The walk would only take him ten minutes, and he set off at a brisk pace. When he reached Addlestone's road, Market Road, the first fat raindrops were just beginning to fall.

Addlestone lived in a three-storey terraced house that had been converted into three flats. Mackinnon pressed the buzzer beside the communal door and stepped underneath the covered doorway, sheltering from the rain.

A reedy voice came over the intercom, and Mackinnon identified himself.

After a brief pause, a low pitched buzz sounded and the door clicked unlocked.

Inside was a small entrance hall with old-fashioned wooden shelves converted into pigeonholes for mail along one wall. A staircase was on the right.

A door at the far end of the entrance hall opened, and a tall, thin man stepped out into the hall.

"Mr Addlestone?"

The man nodded. "Yes. What's wrong?"

"I'd like to have a quick chat with you about one of your students."

Terrence Addlestone's face paled.

He reached up to run a hand through his hair, which Mackinnon noticed had started to thin on top. Addlestone was in his early forties and according to their records he wasn't married.

"One of my students? I hope they haven't been getting themselves into trouble." Addlestone gave an uneasy chuckle. "I can't be held accountable for what they get up to out-of-school hours, and it *is* the school holidays."

"Could we go inside, please, Mr Addlestone?" Mackinnon asked.

The tentative smile left Addlestone's face and he nodded, now looking truly concerned. "Of course, it is just through here."

Mackinnon followed him into a small but tidy ground floor flat.

A great deal of work had been done on the property.

Walls had been knocked-through so the entire living space was open plan. The remaining walls were painted magnolia and most of the furniture was in warm shades of oak.

Addlestone went and stood beside a black leather sofa and indicated for Mackinnon to take a seat.

Mackinnon sat in one of the matching black leather armchairs and turned to Addlestone to ask his first question.

"How long have you worked at City College?"

Addlestone's eyes drifted over to the dining table, which was standing in-between the sofa and the open plan kitchen. On top of the table was an open MacBook.

Addlestone cleared his throat. "Four years. I worked at a private school in Berkshire before that."

Mackinnon leaned forward. "I'm here because one of your students, Ruby Watson, has been abducted."

He paused to gauge Addlestone's reaction.

"God, how awful."

He looked suitably shocked, but it was possible he was just a good actor and had been expecting a call from the police.

"So, how can I help you?" Addison said nervously as his eyes shifted once again to the open laptop.

"We are talking to everyone Ruby came into contact with on a regular basis. When was the last time you saw her?"

"I haven't seen her since school broke up for the summer holidays. I can't think of anyone who would want to hurt her. Are you sure she hasn't gone off somewhere on holiday? You know what young girls can be like."

Mackinnon didn't answer straightaway, allowing the silence to add to Addlestone's discomfort. He had started to sweat.

Finally, Mackinnon said, "Her passport hasn't been used, and we have strong evidence to suggest she has been abducted."

Addlestone nodded. "I see. Sorry, I didn't mean to sound flippant. I am not sure I can tell you much. She's been in my English literature class for the last year. She's a good student who gets consistently high grades." Addlestone shrugged. "I do know that her parents are rather wealthy perhaps that's why she's been targeted."

Addlestone glanced for a third time at the laptop, and Mackinnon made up his mind.

He reached into his pocket. "Sorry, I did set it to silent, but it's on vibrate, and it's my boss. I'd better take this. I will be back in just a moment," he lied smoothly.

Mackinnon took his phone outside the flat, stepped into the entrance hallway and quickly dialled Tyler's number.

Speaking quietly, he filled Tyler in.

"We need a search warrant. Something about him is off."

He heard Tyler sigh on the other end of the line. "We need more to go on than that, Jack."

"He's hiding something. He is extremely nervous and keeps looking at his computer. We need a warrant."

"Well, a police officer has just turned up at his home out of the blue. His nervousness might have nothing to do with our case. Have you got anything to go on besides your instincts?"

"No," Mackinnon said honestly. "But trust me, he's hiding something."

"Okay, Jack. I'll initiate the process. Keep talking to him and try to get something concrete at least. This will be my neck on the line if we screw up, and I could do without another bollocking today."

Mackinnon hung up and paused before he went back into Addlestone's flat. He didn't normally work like this. It was usually Tyler going on his gut instinct, and Jack played things by the book, but in this case, there was something about Addlestone that didn't sit right with him. He couldn't let it go.

He pushed open the door to Addlestone's flat, and saw the man standing in front of the laptop.

He hadn't heard him enter, so Mackinnon moved quickly and quietly to look over his shoulder. He was dragging files and emails to the trash can at the bottom of the screen.

"What are you doing?" Mackinnon asked.

Addlestone jumped and whirled around. "Uh… Nothing. I was just checking my email."

"Do you mind if I take a look?" Mackinnon asked, his eyes already scanning the screen.

Addlestone closed the lid of the laptop. "Yes, actually I do. They're private."

Mackinnon stared at him as he sweated and looked more and more uncomfortable, but he finally decided not to push it. He would wait until they got the warrant.

He smiled. "Fair enough. Shall we sit down and continue our conversation?"

Addlestone shuffled off back to the sofa, looking like it was the last thing he wanted to do.

"I really don't see why you're questioning me. I don't know anything about this."

"I hoped to get a different viewpoint into Ruby's life. Sometimes, teachers can offer a clearer insight than parents."

Addlestone nodded. That seemed to satisfy him and he settled back onto the sofa.

"Well, I do like to take a modern approach to my teaching. I am younger than most of the students' parents, and I do my best to bridge the generation gap. I teach mainly sixteen to eighteen-year-olds, and it's a difficult time for them. I think a teacher can play an important role in helping students develop confidence to take the next step in their lives, on to university or employment."

Mackinnon nodded. "Do you know a girl called Lila George, or have you heard Ruby mention her?"

Addlestone frowned. "No, I can't say I recognise that name."

"Ever heard of Benny Morris or Rob Morris?"

Addlestone shook his head. "No, were they involved in the abduction?"

Mackinnon didn't answer, and instead, pushed on with his own questions. He kept one eye on the clock as he did so. He planned to keep Addlestone talking as long as possible, giving Tyler time to get the warrant.

Mackinnon was convinced as soon as he left Addlestone would be immediately trying to get rid of evidence.

* * *

HE CONTINUED CIRCLING Addlestone's story, testing for holes, but finally after an hour had passed, Addlestone lost patience.

"I am sorry, detective, but I've got nothing else to tell you. To be honest, you would be better off out there looking for her." He pointed at the rain-splattered window.

Mackinnon didn't bother to push it and outstay his welcome. He got to his feet, thanked Addlestone for his time and wished him good night.

Outside, there were large puddles beside the curbs, but at least it had stopped raining. Mackinnon could see the window to Addlestone's flat from the road, it was brightly lit, but the blind was down. He could only guess what Addlestone was doing now.

Mackinnon kept a close eye on the window as he called Tyler and asked about progress on the warrant.

"I can't perform miracles, Jack," Tyler said. "These things take time."

"He is in there destroying evidence. I know it."

"He can't delete it all. If there is something to find, we will find it."

"So what am I supposed to do now? Just wait?"

"Yes, that's exactly what you're supposed to do."

After he had hung up, Mackinnon put his mobile back in his jacket pocket and walked away from the front of Addlestone's flat. Based on the unlikely possibility he hadn't already started to destroy evidence, Mackinnon didn't want his lingering presence to tip Addlestone off.

He walked around the corner and stood, partially hidden, beside a brick wall. The tall lime tree beside him helped shelter him from view and shaded him from the streetlights.

It was beyond frustrating to think that he was unable to act while Addlestone could be destroying evidence that would ruin their chances of a successful prosecution.

There had been no signs in the flat that he was involved in either girl's abduction. Perhaps Tyler was right. Perhaps he had something else to feel guilty about. Whatever it was, Mackinnon was determined to find out.

On the other hand, if he *was* involved in the girls' abduction, then he was obviously keeping them somewhere else.

Mackinnon turned up the collar on his coat as the rain started to fall again. He managed to shelter from the worst of it by standing beneath the tree.

He was staring at Addlestone's flat, wondering what was going on inside, when the front door opened.

There was a streetlight immediately in front of Addlestone's building, and Mackinnon could see him clearly as he stepped out onto the pavement with a plastic bag in his hand.

Addlestone looked around furtively and then walked over to a brown wheelie bin in front of the property.

He looked around once more before placing the plastic bag in the bin.

He wiped his hands together, turned around and disappeared back inside.

Mackinnon couldn't resist the temptation. He quickly walked forward, crossed the road and headed directly to the bin as he pulled a pair of blue nitrile gloves from his pocket.

He slipped on the gloves and lifted the lid. Looking inside, and grimacing at the smell, he prodded the bag.

There was some kind of clothing inside. A navy blue, extremely short pleated skirt – the type of skirt girls wore for PE at school. Now, this was definitely suspicious.

Mackinnon looked back at the flat and narrowed his eyes.

This would nail Addlestone.

"Got you," he whispered.

CHAPTER THIRTY-SIX

Rob Morris got back to the basement flat and stuck his head in the sitting room.

The television was off, and Benny was nowhere to be seen. The door to the room where the girls had been held had been smashed off its hinges. Splintered wood still lay on the floor, and the door was propped up against the wall.

"Benny? Marlo, what the hell has happened here?"

Marlo stepped out of the kitchen and into the hall, wiping his hands on a tea towel.

"Oh, the wanderer returns. It's about time you got back. I don't appreciate being left in the lurch."

Rob shook his head and pointed at the door. "How did that happen?"

Marlo licked his lips. "The girls did it. They are stronger than they look."

Rob frowned and shook his head. He didn't believe it.

There was nothing in that bedroom they could have used

as a battering ram, and he couldn't imagine how either girl would have been able to break down the door like that.

"No way," Rob said.

Marlo walked forward and ran a hand along the broken door.

"It had started to rot, and the frame was already weakened. I have put the girls in the other bedroom. That door seems fine."

"But there's no soundproofing in the other bedroom."

Rob cocked his head to one side and listened. He couldn't hear the girls or Benny.

"Yes, I know. It is a pain in the arse. I had to put duct tape over their mouths and tie them up. I don't think they'll be trying anything again."

Rob stared at Marlo, unsure whether he was telling him the truth, but why would he lie? What reason would he have for spinning Rob a story?

"Where's Benny?"

"Oh, he is fine. I gave him some cash and sent him out to get us Chinese."

"What? Why did you do that? He doesn't know this area. He'll get lost."

"Don't be ridiculous. I gave him instructions, and it's only two streets from here. He'll be fine."

"I'd better go and find him."

"There's no time for that. You've been missing for long enough already. Now it's time for you to pull your weight. Unless, of course, you've decided to walk away from the money?"

Rob took a deep breath and shook his head. "No, I'll do it."

"I'm glad you've come to your senses."

Marlo walked into the kitchen and returned with the

two mobile phones still in their plastic bags. "Take these. You need to give one to Janice George and the other to Claire Watson. I have sent instructions to the email address set up on your mobile. The email contains everything you need to know — where to leave the phones and how to communicate with the mothers to tell them where to find them."

Rob breathed a sigh of relief. "You mean I don't have to give them the phones directly?"

"Of course not," Marlo shook his head. "That would be madness."

Rob took the mobile phones. "There will be police crawling all over the place. How am I supposed to let them know where the phones are without being noticed?"

Marlo grinned. "I think we've been working together long enough for you to realise I always have a plan. Anyway, you're wasting time. The instructions are on your phone and you can read them on the way. Chop chop."

Rob turned to go and then hesitated. "Are the girls all right?"

Marlo gave a cold smile. "Yes, they are fine. I haven't heard a peep out of them. Go on, hurry up. If you are lucky, Benny and I might even save you some Chinese."

BY THE TIME Mackinnon returned to Wood Street Station he was soaked to the skin. Addlestone had been brought in for questioning and a search was currently underway at his property.

When he reached the incident room, Mackinnon realised he had missed all the excitement. People were talking in hushed whispers, and Tyler was currently holed up in Brook-bank's office.

Mackinnon made his way to Collins' desk. "What's going on?"

Collins looked at Mackinnon's bedraggled appearance and raised an eyebrow. "Is it raining?"

"Very funny."

Collins smiled. "I do my best." He pointed in the direction of Brookbank's office. "Tyler is furious. The DCI has just announced Cracker is turning up."

"Sorry?"

"A behavioural analyst. They're supposed to tell us who we are looking for, you know, bullied as a child, trouble forming long-term relationships blah, blah, blah."

"I see. When are they supposed to arrive?"

"Any time now, I think. Coffee?" Collins got to his feet, picked up his mug and started to walk over to the coffee machine just as the door to Brookbank's office opened, and Tyler stormed out.

His cheeks were red and he didn't look at all happy.

"Collins, you will be questioning Addlestone with me, but first we have the pleasure of talking to Ms Zelda Smith, who is going to provide us a tremendous amount of insight into our case."

There was no mistaking Tyler's sarcasm.

"Everyone, briefing room, now," Tyler added, looking grim.

As Mackinnon filed into the briefing room with every-body else, he got his first glimpse of the behavioural analyst.

She certainly didn't look anything like Robbie Coltrane. Her cool, blonde good looks were a marked contrast to

Tyler's harassed appearance as he walked to the front of the room and shook her hand.

She was tall, slim and wore a beige trouser suit, and as she shook Tyler's hand, she didn't crack a smile. Although, to be fair, neither did Tyler.

Tyler muttered a few words and then said in a louder voice to the rest of the room, "Let's make a start."

Tyler began the briefing by bringing everybody up-to-date and giving them the latest information on Terrence Addlestone.

When he had finished summarising the man's character and background, he turned to Zelda Smith.

"Do you think he fits the profile?" Tyler asked her directly.

Her features tightened, and it was clear she didn't appreciate being put on the spot.

"Possibly. With the limited information I have to work with so far, it is hard to say for sure one way or the other."

Mackinnon heard Webb mutter behind him, "Well, that's about as useful as a chocolate teapot."

"Right," Tyler said. "Well, thank you very much for your input, Ms Smith. Now, I'm sorry but I'm going to have to draw this briefing to a close. Collins you're with me. If the profiler can't tell us whether or not Addlestone abducted the girls, we'll need to find out the old-fashioned way, by questioning the suspect."

CHAPTER THIRTY-SEVEN

AT THAT MOMENT, Claire Watson was lying fully-clothed on her bed, worrying herself sick. Out there somewhere, some evil bastard had her daughter, and he was treating it like some kind of game.

Claire was being forced to compete with another set of parents for her daughter's life. What kind of sick mind could think up something like that?

She'd been horrified enough to find herself prepared to throw paint over a random stranger, but it could so easily have been her with the container of acid. She couldn't imagine how the other woman had felt in that situation.

Claire closed her eyes and swallowed hard. She had to harden her heart against the other parents. She couldn't feel sorry for them or imagine what it was like to be in their position because that would drive her mad.

But, Christ, it must have been awful to throw acid over someone.

She now knew how far the other mother was prepared to

go for her daughter, which meant Claire had to be ready to go one step further.

Peter was a wreck. He wanted to be the protector, the provider, but the abductors had snatched that from him. Not only had they taken his daughter, they had also taken his identity. Under different circumstances, Claire may have been more sympathetic, but right now, she didn't have the emotional strength to deal with Peter's crisis.

She needed all her energy to focus on her missing daughter.

In a perfect world, they would get both girls back, but nothing about this situation was perfect. If only one girl came back, Claire was determined to make sure it was Ruby.

Usually, Claire was content to assume the role of nurturer and defer many of the family decisions to Peter, but not this time. They had taken her daughter, and she would fight to the death to get her home. Traditional marital roles and Peter's identity be damned. Claire would not take a backseat in this. The police were trying to get both girls back, but when it came down to it, there was only one person she knew who would do absolutely anything to get her daughter back, and that was her. She couldn't trust anybody else.

Her mind reeled through the possible things the abductors could ask her to do next.

What would be the next stage in this twisted game? Whatever it was, Claire knew she would do it without question.

There was a knock on the bedroom door. She held her breath and sat up.

Don't get your hopes up, she ordered herself.

But it was no good; she bit her lip as she rushed to pull the bedroom door open.

"I thought I'd come and see if you were all right. I am sorry for what I said earlier," Peter said.

Claire hid her disappointment. She wasn't interested in Peter's apologies. She only wanted news about her daughter.

"That's okay. We are all under a great deal of stress," Claire said mechanically.

He smiled and reached up to tuck a lock of hair behind her ear. "We need to stick together. We're stronger that way."

Claire struggled to raise a smile.

Instead of going back into the bedroom, she followed Peter out into the hallway and walked towards the open plan kitchen.

Kelly, the family liaison officer, was there as usual. Her constant presence was already starting to grate.

She smiled at Claire and offered her tea.

Claire nodded. "Thanks. Tea would be nice. Is Curtis still in his bedroom?"

Peter nodded.

The phone rang in Peter's study. He hesitated, but Claire told him to go and answer it. As Peter walked away, through the sitting area, the doorbell rang.

"I'll get it," Claire said to nobody in particular and walked towards the front door.

ROB HAD APPROACHED the entrance to Drake House feeling absolutely terrified. He'd stared at the glass-fronted building and tried to control his nerves.

He lifted the enormous bunch of flowers in his arms up high so they obscured most of his face, but it wouldn't be enough. The amount of cameras they had in London these days meant he was bound to be spotted.

Marlo hadn't given him any instructions about what to do if he got caught, but Rob had already decided that if he was apprehended, he would tell the police someone had given him a tenner and asked him to deliver the flowers.

Rob took a deep breath and then pushed open the glass door and stepped into the foyer of Drake House.

A bored-looking doorman sat behind the reception desk. "Can I help you?"

Rob licked his lips and looked around nervously, searching for the cameras.

"You all right?" the doorman asked.

Rob needed to get a hold of himself. The doorman was already looking at him with suspicion.

"I need to deliver these," Rob said, nodding at the flowers.

"You'll have to sign in," the doorman said and pointed to a book on the reception desk. He handed Rob a pencil, and Rob scrawled his name in a scribble that wouldn't be recognised.

The security guard appeared to be satisfied. "Who are the flowers for?"

"Mrs Watson."

For one horrible moment, Rob thought the doorman had sussed him out. He looked him up and down and then finally nodded and pointed behind Rob's shoulder.

"You want the lift on the left. That goes straight up to the penthouse."

Rob thanked him and quickly walked off to the lift.

He could feel the doorman's eyes burning into his back and was convinced as soon as he was in the lift the doorman would be on the phone to the police.

His hands were trembling as he stepped inside the lift and pressed the button for the penthouse.

He felt sick to the stomach at what he was doing and was sweating so much his shirt was sticking to his back.

He hadn't thought it was possible to feel any more nervous, but when he stepped out of the lift into the lobby and saw the front door to the Watsons' apartment, his stomach churned, and for a moment, he was convinced he was going to throw up there and then.

He put a hand against the wall to steady himself and took a couple of large breaths, trying to calm down. He wasn't helping himself by acting this way. He needed to get the job done and get out of there.

If he got caught, God knows what would happen to Benny.

On his way to Drake House, he'd gone past the nearest Chinese takeaway to see if he could find Benny, but there was no sign of him. But Rob wasn't too concerned yet, he knew there were another couple of Chinese takeaways in the vicinity, and Benny could have gone to one of those.

It wasn't Benny's absence so much as Marlo's behaviour that triggered alarm bells.

Something about Marlo just seemed off.

Rob straightened up and walked towards the Watson's front door.

He held the flowers up high in front of his face, and holding his breath, he rang the doorbell.

As the door opened slowly a lump grew in his throat, and Rob was scared he wouldn't even be able to talk.

The woman he recognised as Claire Watson stood in front of him.

Thank God.

That made things a little easier.

It was the first time he'd seen her up close. Her eyes were bloodshot, and her hair was messy.

"I am sorry to trouble you so late," Rob said.

Claire nodded, but she wasn't looking at Rob, she was frowning at the huge bunch of flowers in his hands. He had to admit Marlo had been clever on that account. Nobody looked twice at a delivery driver these days.

He held the flowers out to her, feeling like a lowlife. "Delivery for you."

"Who are they from?"

"I… I am not sure," Rob stammered. "I am just the delivery driver. There is a card, though."

As soon as Claire took the flowers, Rob turned away. He had to force himself to not run for the lift.

"Wait!"

Rob turned around with his heart in his mouth.

She knew. He'd been made.

It was all over.

"Don't you need me to sign something?" Claire Watson asked.

Rob could have cried with relief. He shook his head. "Oh, no, there is nothing to sign," he said and then turned around and dived for the lift.

AT WOOD STREET STATION, the investigation was still rolling inevitably onward. Interviews were being cross-referenced and entered into the system. A couple of team members had retired to get a few hours' sleep. From now on, they would be working in shifts.

He was starving and pleased to see Collins had ordered in pizza. Mackinnon took a slice of ham and mushroom and then stood beside Zelda Smith, the behavioural analyst.

"You're here late," he commented.

"Your DCI asked me to stick around," she said pointedly, looking in disapproval at the pizza. "I know my ideas are not popular around here, but I am just doing the job I was paid for."

Mackinnon had clearly stumbled onto a touchy subject.

He held up his hands and almost dropped the pizza. "I didn't mean any offence."

Zelda Smith looked up at him with startlingly blue eyes. "Do you believe behavioural analysis can be helpful to police enquiries?"

Mackinnon took too long before answering.

"I thought so," Zelda said wryly.

Mackinnon frowned and swallowed his mouthful of pizza. "You didn't give me a chance to answer. I'm for anything that can help us catch whoever has taken those two girls."

Zelda watched him carefully, and Mackinnon had the uncomfortable feeling she was analysing him.

"It is not magic. It is science. I'm not saying I have all the answers, but along with all the other tools the police use in an investigation, behavioural analysis can help."

Mackinnon took another slice of pizza and offered the box to Zelda. She pulled a face and shook her head. "No, thank you."

"What's your take on Terrence Addlestone?" Mackinnon asked, hoping to move onto safer ground.

"You were the officer who first suspected him, right? I heard your Detective Inspector talking about it. You *thought* you were acting on instinct, but really you were performing your own version of behavioural analysis, just on a smaller scale."

Mackinnon shrugged. "He was twitchy, and he was definitely hiding something on that laptop."

Zelda nodded. "I believe you, but I don't think he has the organisational skills or the narcissistic tendencies needed to create this game. If he was involved in the girls' abduction, he isn't the mastermind behind it."

Mackinnon took a bite of pizza. That wasn't what he had hoped to hear. "The tech team have found photographs on his laptop. Surely that counts for something."

Zelda raised an eyebrow. "Yes, but they weren't photographs of Ruby Watson or Lila George. They were photographs of Ruby's friend from school, Kirsty."

Kirsty Jones, the girl Curtis had mentioned. Even if he wasn't involved in the abduction, Terrence Addlestone was still in a great deal of trouble. Kirsty was in the same year as Ruby at City College, and Addlestone taught them both. Kirsty was eighteen now, but Addlestone would lose his job over the photographs found on his laptop, deservedly so in Mackinnon's opinion.

Mackinnon polished off his second slice of pizza and then shrugged. "True, but he was deleting stuff from his computer. Maybe the tech unit will be able to find more before the night is out."

Zelda smiled confidently. "Perhaps, but I'm sure he's not the ringleader. Whoever they are, they are still out there."

That was a sobering thought.

CHAPTER THIRTY-EIGHT

CLAIRE WATSON LOOKED at the flowers with disgust. What good were sodding flowers? She had no idea who had sent them. Closing the door, she peeled back the cellophane around the flowers to get at the card and carried them into the kitchen.

"Oh, they look lovely," Kelly said.

Claire smiled weakly.

At least they weren't lilies, she thought. Funeral flowers.

"Shall I get a vase?" Kelly asked, trying to be helpful.

Claire nodded. "There is one in the cupboard by the sink."

As Kelly bent down to get it, Claire opened the card and the world seemed to tilt on its axis.

Another message.

Claire only looked at it for a second before she crushed it in her hand and stuffed it in the pocket of her trousers. Kelly was saying something, but Claire wasn't listening.

She put a hand to her forehead, trying to concentrate. It was a message from the kidnappers, so did that mean the delivery man was involved? Did he know where they were keeping Ruby?

Surely, he had to know *something*.

She dropped the flowers on the floor and ran out of the kitchen and then the front door.

She could see the lift wasn't free. The delivery driver was probably still inside it, getting away and taking his information with him.

She ran for the fire escape and took the stairs two at a time. She was vaguely aware of some voices behind her, but she ignored them.

Then she heard Peter's voice shout, "Claire? What's going on?"

But there was no time to explain. She still had another three sets of stairs to go until she reached the lobby.

Her heart was hammering so hard she could barely breathe.

Please let him still be there.

She burst out into the lobby just as the delivery man was walking out onto the street.

"Evening, Mrs Watson," the doorman said.

She ignored him and ran outside, frantically looking for the man who had brought the flowers.

There he was, on the opposite side of the road.

"Wait!" she screamed.

He turned around, and she saw it on his face – – *he knew*.

Claire ran. She had never been good at running, but the need to catch him and find out where Ruby was gave her the power to sprint.

At first, she gained on him, but not for long. He was too fast.

Peter was close behind her, and she could hear him calling

her name, but she didn't dare turn away in case she lost sight of the delivery driver. He was getting further and further away, but her lungs were burning, and her muscles were slowing already.

Panting for breath, she pointed at him. "Someone stop him!"

No one did. Passersby gave her strange looks as though she were a crazy lady.

And then, in the blink of an eye, he'd gone.

Disappeared.

The street was dark, and Claire turned in a circle, unable to believe she had lost him.

A bus went past. Did he get on that? Or had he darted into a side street?

Distraught at losing sight of the one person who could tell her where her daughter was, she sank to her knees and barely noticed when Peter reached her side and tried to pull her up.

"He knew. He knew."

That was the only thing she could say.

"Who knew?" Peter asked.

"The man who brought the flowers. He knew where Ruby was."

"Why would you think that?"

Claire tried to explain about the look of horror on the man's face when she'd confronted him.

"Didn't you see it?"

Peter pulled back and shook his head. "No. I think you're overwrought. I'll call the doctor. Maybe he can prescribe something to calm you down."

"No!"

Claire pulled away. It had been on the tip of her tongue to tell Peter about the card, but she didn't. She wanted to scream at him and demand to know why Peter hadn't tried to catch him.

"If he had nothing to do with the abduction and was just a normal delivery man, why did he run, Peter?"

"I didn't see him run." Peter sighed and shook his head sadly. "You were just running wildly up the street, causing a scene."

"Causing a scene?" Her voice was so high-pitched she barely recognised it. "Our daughter is missing, and you're concerned about me making a scene?"

"Claire, you are sitting in the middle of a busy pavement. Come on, let's get back home."

She shook his hand off her arm. "Let go of me."

"Please, Claire, calm down. You are trembling."

She was trembling, but not with fear, with rage.

CHAPTER THIRTY-NINE

KELLY JOHNSON REPORTED the incident to Tyler, and he immediately set about assigning officers to look into it.

"We can access the security cameras in Drake House. It's probably easier if one of us goes over there to look at them now," Tyler said.

DC Webb was sitting in a desk at the front of the incident room and spoke up, "Do we think the flower delivery guy really has something to do with it, or was she overreacting?"

Tyler shook his head. "We don't know that yet. There was no card with the flowers so we don't know who sent them. Claire Watson said she didn't recognise the man who delivered them. The scrawl he left in the signing book is illegible so that won't help us. One thing we know from his description was that it definitely wasn't Benny Morris."

Tyler turned to Collins. "Please tell me we are closer to tracking Benny Morris down?"

Collins pulled a face and shook his head. "I am afraid not,

sir. There has been an officer stationed outside his residence all day, but he hasn't returned yet."

Tyler muttered a curse under his breath and then addressed the room.

"The delivery driver may not have any relevance to this enquiry. Claire Watson is quite clearly emotionally on edge. Her husband doesn't appear to think there was anything suspicious about the delivery, at all, but nonetheless, we need to look into it."

There was a murmur of voices around the room and then Tyler turned to Mackinnon. "Jack, can you get over to Drake House and have a word with Claire Watson, and take a look at the CCTV while you're there?"

Mackinnon nodded. "No problem."

Tyler then turned to Charlotte.

"Charlotte, give Glenn Calvert a ring and tell him to be extra careful about delivery drivers calling at the Georges' place. If this is an attempt to make contact by the abductors, then it is quite likely that they'll target the Georges as well."

Charlotte nodded. "I'll do it straightaway."

"Do we think the abductors are no longer going to contact the parents via text message?" Collins asked.

Tyler shook his head. "We're not assuming anything. We are keeping an open mind."

"You know what happens when you assume, don't you?" DC Webb asked with a broad, inappropriate grin on his face. "You make an ass of u and me."

A collective groan sounded around the room.

Tyler moved a pile of paperwork on the desk in front of him. "We need to keep monitoring their phones, but also be on the lookout for any other method of communication. For some reason, they are using this situation to get the parents to compete against each other."

Charlotte finished talking to Glenn Calvert as Tyler ended the impromptu briefing and walked into Brookbank's office to give him another update.

She picked up her coffee, walked over to Mackinnon and perched on the edge of his desk.

"What do you make of this latest development?"

Mackinnon shook his head. "It is a puzzle. We've been working on the assumption this is about money, due to Ruby's parents' wealth, but I think it has far more to do with the abductors exerting control over both sets of parents.

Charlotte took a sip of her coffee. "It's getting too late to process any more interviews now. Have you heard how Collins and Tyler got on with questioning Addlestone?"

"He's pretending that the items in the bin weren't his. He denied putting them in there, even though I saw him do it with my own eyes."

Charlotte raised an eyebrow. "It was dark. You were on the other side of the road…"

"I know what I saw," Mackinnon said firmly.

Charlotte put her hands up. "I am not doubting you for a minute, but you know that's what they will say in court. God, wouldn't life be easier if criminals would just confess?"

"It would certainly be refreshing," Mackinnon said. "They are giving Addlestone some breathing space now, but they're going to be going back in for another round of questioning soon. Brookbank is eager to get Zelda Smith's analysis and input into the next round of questioning. You can just imagine how that went down."

"I bet Tyler is over the moon."

Mackinnon smiled wryly and picked up his jacket. "He is not a happy bunny."

* * *

CLAIRE WATSON HAD LOCKED herself in the bathroom. It was the only place she could be assured of privacy.

Peter was watching her like a hawk as though he expected her to have some sort of emotional breakdown, and the family liaison officer had been watching her almost as closely as Peter.

Claire pulled the note from her trouser pocket, and with her heart in her mouth, she read it again.

A new phone is waiting for you in a cardboard box by the communal ice machine.

Don't delay.

We will be sending more instructions to that phone at midnight.

Claire put a hand to her chest and could feel her heart racing. How was she supposed to get the new phone without anybody seeing her?

She knew she was meant to tell the police the kidnappers had been in touch. That was the right thing to do. But if she told the police, they would prevent her from communicating with the abductors and following their instructions.

She couldn't risk it.

If the other mother kept quiet and took part in the next stage of the game, she would win.

Claire couldn't chance it.

She wasn't prepared to be a team player or a good citizen. Let the other mother tell the police. Let her risk her daughter's life.

A knock on the bathroom door made Claire jump.

She shoved the note back into her pocket and gripped the side of the sink.

"Claire, darling, DS Mackinnon is here to see us. He wants to talk to you about the er… incident earlier."

Claire swore under her breath.

That was the last thing she needed. She leaned heavily on the sink and looked at her reflection in the mirror, shaking her head at her ungroomed appearance.

She barely recognised herself.

Careful to keep her voice steady, she said, "Okay. I will be out in just a moment."

She splashed some water on her face and smoothed back her hair.

A ball of fury grew inside her chest. That stupid, interfering police officer. All she wanted to do was go and get that phone, but she couldn't do that with a police officer hanging around.

The card had said there would be a new message at midnight, so she still had time. All she had to do was get rid of that damn police officer as quickly as possible so she could locate the phone.

Claire unlocked the door and put her hand on the handle. She took a deep breath.

It was time for her to put on the performance of her life.

CHAPTER FORTY

JANICE GEORGE WAS on her balcony smoking a cigarette. She might not live in the nicest part of London, but she liked her flat, and they'd been happy until those bastards had taken Lila. She frowned at the sound of revellers leaving the pub across the road and wished she lived higher up.

They'd requested a move from the council plenty of times, but they never heard anything.

They'd only managed to secure this place as council tenants because Janice had been a single mother at the time, after she and Toby had split for a couple of years.

After they'd got back together, the council could hardly kick them out on their ear, so they'd managed to keep their three-bedroom place, which was more than many families had.

It's not that they didn't deserve it. They paid their rent on time every month, but accommodation wasn't easy to come by in the capital and council places were getting rarer and rarer unless you came from another country and had a boat-load of kids.

Janice took another puff on her cigarette, breathing the smoke deep down inside her lungs.

It was fully dark now, and out there somewhere, Lila was scared and alone.

With a shaking hand she viciously stubbed out the cigarette on the metal railing.

She was just about to go in when she saw a flash of white just below her, something skimming through the air.

She peered over the edge of the balcony. It was too late for birds. What could it have been?

She saw a figure moving below, and then she scowled. It must be bloody kids messing about, chucking rubbish around probably.

Then she saw it again – that bright flash of white, soaring into the air.

This time, it nearly took Janice's eye out. She pulled back just in time.

"Oi, what do you think you're playing at? Stop throwing stuff around," Janice shouted.

Woe betide anyone who tried to cross her today in the mood she was in.

"It's a message," a voice hissed.

Janice's heart thudded in her chest.

She leaned over the balcony railings as far as she dared, trying to see who it was down there.

"Wait! I'll come down."

But before she had a chance to pull back, the white object zoomed passed her ear. Startled, she drew back and then saw it was a sheet of paper, fashioned into a crude paper aero-plane. It landed on the balcony next to her feet.

Janice reached down to grab it.

Janice held her breath as she unfolded the paper aeroplane. A message was scrawled across the paper in black ink.

This was sick. They were sending paper aeroplanes as though this was some kind of child's game.

The paper trembled in her hand. They were going to set her another task at midnight, and she wasn't sure if she could do it. She still pictured Sam Markham's scarred skin every time she closed her eyes.

She held her breath as she read the message.

A new phone is waiting for you in a cardboard box by the rubbish chute.

Don't delay.

We will be sending more instructions to that phone at midnight.

She folded the paper into a compact square and clutched it tightly in her hand as she pushed open the balcony door and stepped back into the sitting room.

Her husband was sitting on the sofa next to the annoying family liaison officer, Glenn Calvert.

The television was on, but Toby wasn't watching it.

Janice tried to keep her voice level as she said, "Toby, could you come and give me a hand settling Ella?"

Toby looked up, surprised, and she gave him a look, trying to silently communicate that she needed to talk to him alone without Glenn Calvert suspecting they were up to something.

Come on, you dopey bugger. Get your backside off that sofa.

Finally, Toby pushed himself up from the sofa and followed Janice into the baby's room.

He walked over to Ella's crib and looked inside.

"She's fine," he said. "She's fast asleep."

"I know that. I just needed to talk to you in private, and this was the only thing I could think of."

Toby opened his mouth to ask her why, but instead of answering, Janice handed him the piece of paper.

Toby put a hand to his mouth, and his eyes widened as he read. "Christ."

"What should we do?" Janice said, hearing the note of desperation in her voice.

Toby was quiet for a moment, thinking, and Janice went to sit in the comfy chair beside the baby's cot.

Toby perched on the arm of the chair and put his hand on her shoulder. "I'll go to the rubbish chute and get the new phone."

Janice nodded and watched her husband sneak out of the room and head for the front door. She chewed on a fingernail anxiously. What would they do if the phone wasn't there? Some of her neighbours didn't exactly have high moral standards. They would think nothing of pinching a mobile phone left unattended.

She could only hope Toby got there in time. They had until midnight to wait for the next message, and already Janice was panicking about what they might ask her to do.

She'd always considered herself a strong woman, but the cracks were starting to show. She could only take so much.

It would be different if they'd acknowledged her last task or given an indication Lila was okay. That would have given her hope.

She was starting to think they would never get Lila back.

She leaned over baby Ella, who was sleeping peacefully, and stroked her soft cheek. She remembered when Lila was the same age. They were so much easier to look after when you could keep them with you all the time.

She looked up sharply as Toby slipped back into the room. "Did you get it?"

His face looked gaunt and drawn in the soft light coming from baby Ella's nightlight.

He nodded and held up the phone. "There was already a text message on it."

He held it out so Janice could read the message on the screen.

Level I unlocked. Await further instructions at midnight.

"What the bloody hell does level one unlocked mean?"

"I suppose they mean the first stage of the game."

"Should we tell the police?"

Toby shook his head. "Not yet. The police haven't told us anything about the other family getting a message, have they?"

Janice shook her head. "No. I don't know if they got one."

"Think about it, Janice. Of course, they got a message, too. That's the whole idea behind this sick game. Two sets of parents competing for their daughters' lives. They would have got the message, and they haven't told the police. If we don't do what the abductors ask, and the other parents do, then we lose by default, don't we?"

Janice held her head in her hands and stifled a sob. "Oh God, what are they going to ask me to do this time? I don't think I'm strong enough, Toby."

Toby leaned down to press his lips against Janice's forehead. "You've played your part already, love. It is my turn this time."

Janice looked at her husband through watery eyes. "Can you? I mean, it was my phone they sent the message to originally. Doesn't that mean only I can do it?"

"There's only one way to find out."

Toby tapped a couple of buttons on the mobile phone and started to type a text message.

He had just pressed send when the door opened, and Glenn Calvert stuck his head in the room. Toby quickly shoved the mobile phone between the chair cushions.

"Is everything all right? I was just going to make another cup of tea," Glenn said.

Janice wanted to tell him to mind his own business and stick his bloody tea, but Toby was more polite.

"Everything is fine. We were just reading Ella a bedtime story."

Glenn Calvert glanced at Ella, who was fast asleep, and then looked back at Toby and Janice. "Do you just make it up as you go along?"

Toby frowned in confusion. "Sorry?"

"You're not reading the story from a book."

"Oh," Toby said, nodding. "Yes, I know the stories off by heart now."

Glenn Calvert seemed to accept Toby's answer and nodded before closing the door.

A second later, there was a muffled beep from underneath the chair cushions, and Janice scrambled for the phone.

They had a new message.

Either parent can take part in the game.
We don't discriminate.

CHAPTER FORTY-ONE

WHEN ROB RETURNED to the basement flat, he had been horrified to realise that Benny still wasn't back.

Marlo had watched him with amusement as he tried to explain how dangerous it was for Benny to be out on his own alone at this time of night, especially in an area of London he didn't know that well.

The smirk on Marlo's face made Rob want to knock him out.

"I need to find him," Rob insisted. "I'll have to go look for him. Sorry, Marlo, you'll have to do the rest yourself."

"You're overreacting. Benny is not as stupid as you think. He just got lost and he's probably made his way back home by now. He's been banging on about going home all day."

Rob nodded and could have almost smiled with relief. Of course, why hadn't he thought of that? Benny would have gone straight home. He would probably be safe at home in their flat, sitting on the sofa watching TV.

"You're right. He's probably gone to the flat. I'll go and check he is okay."

"No, you won't."

"What? What do you mean?"

"The police will be watching the flat. They won't be looking for Benny, but they will be looking for you after your screw up earlier."

"My screw up?"

"Your face would have been caught on the cameras at Drake House. They'll be looking for you."

"That wasn't a screw up. I did what you asked!"

Marlo shrugged.

Rob felt sick. He knew Marlo was right. His face would have been captured by cameras at Drake House. It wouldn't take the police long to piece together the footage and find he had been at Monument Underground station, too... and at the bus stop when Janice George threw acid over that poor bastard.

"You may as well stay here and enjoy the rest of the game," Marlo said.

But Rob had shaken his head. He'd had a really bad feeling about this from the start. Why hadn't he paid attention to his own instincts?

Benny was more important than any stupid game.

This whole thing had been about Rob hustling together some money to pay the rent on their flat, and now Rob couldn't even go back there.

This game had ruined his life.

"Are you telling me I can't even go back to my own flat?"

Marlo smirked. "What's the big deal? You were going to get chucked out anyway. You can just move somewhere else."

That had been the final straw. He turned around and

stalked out of the basement flat, determined not to come back.

He'd been looking for Benny for the past hour, checking at all Benny's favourite places, but he was nowhere to be found. He even slipped back and stood outside their block of flats. He didn't dare go inside, but he could see the windows to the sitting room and Benny's bedroom from where he stood on the pavement.

There were no lights on. That wasn't a good sign. Benny hated the dark and insisted his nightlight was left on all night.

So where was he?

Wherever he was, Rob knew he would be scared.

Shoulders slumped, he shuffled away from the block of flats and walked the streets mindlessly until he saw the bright yellow of the McDonald's arches in front of him.

Could Benny be in there? Rob felt hope rise in his chest as he pushed open the glass door and walked inside. It was busy for the time of night, and about half of the tables were full.

There was no sign of Benny downstairs.

He looked around desperately and then collared a member of staff. "Do you have an eating area upstairs?"

The woman, who had been sweeping up a spilled portion of french fries, took a step back and shook her head.

Holding desperately onto the last strands of hope, Rob made his way to the mens' restrooms.

Empty.

Discarded paper towels were scattered on the floor, and the bright fluorescent light hurt his eyes.

Rob covered his face with his hands.

Oh, God, Benny. Where have you gone?

CHAPTER FORTY-TWO

CLAIRE WATSON SAT opposite DS Jack Mackinnon. The way he was looking at her made her feel nervous. He didn't believe her for one second, that much was obvious.

She smiled and tried to appear relaxed. "Today has been such a nightmare. I was confused."

"Kelly told me you were convinced the man who delivered the flowers knew something about your daughter's abduction." He glanced over at the family liaison officer, who was standing in the kitchen, pretending to make tea, but Claire knew she was listening to every word they said.

Claire took a deep breath. She would have liked to tell the man in front of her to mind his own business and leave her alone. But that wasn't appropriate, and he would realise she was holding something back.

"I was mistaken," she said. "It's hard being stuck here unable to do anything to help."

Peter leaned forward and put his hand over Claire's. He

was sitting beside her on the sofa and watching her with concern.

"The events of today have been awful, and Claire has been under a great deal of strain. She is distraught. Our doctor is on the way over to prescribe something for Claire to help her relax."

Claire gave a tight smile. *Dream on, Peter.* There was no way she would be taking anything that might dull her senses.

Peter could think again if he imagined she would swallow some prescription pills like a good little wife and settle down.

She needed to keep her mind sharp for Ruby.

If anything, Peter's reaction confirmed she had made the right choice by not telling him about the new message.

Claire bowed her head and kept up the meek, obedient wife act. It was an irritation, but one she was prepared to endure to get this police officer out of her apartment. She might be stuck with the family liaison officer, but Claire was confident she would find a way to get past her.

This detective, on the other hand, was sharper and more observant. From the way he was looking at her now, Claire was convinced he didn't believe her.

She didn't care. She just wanted him to go.

The phone was waiting for her downstairs in the communal area by the icebox.

There was a cinema room open to all residents of Drake House. Just outside was a vending area along with the ice machine. It wasn't used much, but if one of the residents went in there and discovered the phone before she did, everything would be ruined.

"And there was definitely no card with the flowers?" DS Mackinnon asked.

Claire shook her head. "No, you can ask her," she said,

nodding at Kelly. "She searched the flowers thoroughly and there was no card."

DS Mackinnon watched her carefully, and Claire had to look away and break eye contact. It felt like he could read her mind.

"Can you tell me again what he said when you opened the door?"

Claire shook her head in annoyance. "He said something like, I've got a delivery for you, then he handed me the flowers, and I asked if I had to sign anything, and he said no."

"What part of that made you think he knew something about Ruby's abduction, darling?" Peter asked.

Claire clenched her fists. Her husband really wasn't helping. "I don't know. Everything happened quickly, and I suppose I just jumped to conclusions."

She stared down at her lap, refusing to look at the police officer or her husband.

Just go, she willed him. *Get out of here.*

After another round of questioning, going over the same ground, DS Mackinnon finally left.

Peter tried to engage her in conversation and stayed sitting beside her on the sofa, but Claire answered him in a monotone voice, using one word answers when she was obliged to reply.

She watched Kelly Johnson slip into the bathroom and then Peter muttered, "I really don't know what is keeping Dr Johnson. He should be here by now. I will give him a call and chase him up."

Claire nodded and watched her husband retreat to his study.

This was her chance. Her son was in his bedroom, the

family liaison officer was in the bathroom, and her husband was in the study.

It was now or never.

Claire got to her feet and walked swiftly to the door. She opened it quietly and slipped out. Once inside the lift, she pressed the button for the fifth floor. Impatiently, she drummed her fingers against her leg.

She couldn't afford to have anyone notice her absence otherwise she'd be subjected to yet more questions. A small part of her felt guilty for not confiding in Peter, but she knew he would want to tell the police about this message, and Claire wasn't prepared to do that.

She got out of the lift, strode into the communal movie theatre and breathed a sigh of relief when she realised there was nobody there. From the entranceway, she couldn't see a package beside the ice machine.

Oh, no, please let it be there.

She rushed forward and felt a wave of relief when she saw a small cardboard box nestled against the right-hand side of the ice machine.

She leaned down to pick it up and fumbled inside, finding a small black mobile phone. She pressed a button to illuminate the screen and saw that there was already a text message waiting for her.

She opened it.

Level 1 unlocked. Your next instructions will arrive at midnight.

Her hand was trembling as she shoved the phone in her pocket, and leaving the cardboard box beside the ice machine, she hurried back towards the lift.

She made her way back to the apartment, sneaking in the front door, and returned to sit down on the sofa before anyone noticed she was missing.

She tried to keep her expression neutral as Kelly came out of the bathroom.

"Is everything okay?" Kelly asked.

"Fine," Claire said.

She could feel the hard case of the mobile phone pushing into her thigh and knew she would have to hide it somewhere, probably in the bedroom where nobody else would notice it.

The shrill ring of a mobile phone made Claire jump. Were they calling her now? But it was too early... They said midnight.

She moved to take the new phone from her pocket when she realised it was her own mobile phone ringing and vibrating along the coffee table.

She looked at the caller display and scowled. For goodness sake. As if she didn't have bigger things to worry about. She picked it up and could feel Kelly watching her as she did so. She kept her voice low so she wouldn't be overheard.

"Enough. I don't have time to deal with this now. I will sort it out later. Now, stop calling me."

She hung up and put the mobile phone back on the coffee table with a shaking hand and noticed that Kelly was staring at her with a frown.

Claire turned away.

CHAPTER FORTY-THREE

AT FIVE MINUTES TO MIDNIGHT, Claire was hiding in the en suite bathroom. She had put the new phone on silent and was staring at the screen, waiting for the text message to arrive.

Peter was still awake. He had his eyes closed, but Claire could tell from the sound of his breathing that he wasn't asleep. She could only hope that he wouldn't be knocking on the door in a minute and asking if she was all right.

The doctor had called earlier and prescribed some sedatives. Claire pretended to take them, but had thrown them in the bin when Peter wasn't looking. She needed to be alert.

Her stomach felt hollowed out and full of bile. Why did time pass so slowly when you were waiting for something? She let out a long breath in frustration and leaned back against the marble tiles. How much longer were they going to drag this out?

She had heard nothing after the last task she'd been given, and she'd done everything they asked.

Would this time be any different?

At exactly midnight, the phone in her hand buzzed.

One new text message.

She held her breath as her fingers fumbled in her haste to press the right buttons to get to the message.

Wait…that couldn't be right…

Claire bit down on her lower lip as she read the message again.

Be outside Bryant Lane Infant School at 8:55 AM. Further instructions will be sent to this phone when you get there.

Tell no one.

A primary school? Surely they couldn't be intending… They wouldn't ask her to hurt a child. She couldn't do it. She *wouldn't.*

She shook her head as her mind raced. No, she was assuming too much. It was just a meeting place, that was all. Just a landmark. When she got there, they would give her further instructions and send her somewhere else.

It probably had nothing to do with children.

Claire had tears in her eyes as she put the phone in the back of the bathroom cabinet behind a packet of cotton-wool pads.

She now had eight hours and fifty-four minutes to wait until she knew what was going to happen next.

EARLY THE FOLLOWING MORNING, Roger Sturgess entered the Stepney Allotments. Two weeks had passed since he'd last visited, and he was hoping his plot wouldn't look too shabby. He'd had an operation on his prostate a few months ago, and since then, he'd been in and out of hospital for one thing or another. He'd been starting to think he'd never get out and work on his allotment again.

Although he wasn't going to be able to do much physical work today, somehow simply being around the plants made him feel better.

He had held his allotment plot in Stepney since the early eighties, and over the years, there were occasions when it had been the only thing that kept him going. He'd lived in Stepney all his life, save a brief time as a child during the Blitz when he'd been evacuated to Cornwall.

He'd never had a garden himself, so his allotment was the only way he could grow his own food. He didn't only grow fruit and vegetables, though. He made sure to plant his fair share of flowers, too, which encouraged the bees to visit the allotment.

As he wound his way along the path towards the shed and his allotment plot, Roger braced himself. He'd put a great deal of hard graft into this place over the years, but as he grew older, he was finding it harder to maintain.

Plots on the allotment were very hard to come by, and the organisers had even closed the waiting list last year. In Roger's opinion, the council should have put some effort into creating more open spaces like this for cultivation. He thought it would help keep youngsters off the streets and out of trouble. There were community projects held in the area, but they were mostly held indoors. Roger thought the local government was missing a trick. Gardening was relaxing and reduced stress. He thought there would be considerably less violent crime if people spent more time in gardens, but it didn't bring in any money for the council, and land was at a premium around here, so he knew he was fighting a losing battle on that front.

As he turned the corner, the path snaked away and his allotment came into view. Roger breathed a sigh of relief.

It didn't look too bad, after all. In fact, if he wasn't mistaken, it had even been weeded recently.

Roger smiled. That must've been his old mate, Fred. He stood there for a moment, breathing in the smell of the warm soil and fresh green leaves. A bumblebee buzzed around him and headed for the brightly-coloured nasturtiums.

It was good to be back.

Although Fred had done a very good job on the weeding front, there was still some work to do. Some of the runner beans had grown too long for their stakes, so Roger's first job would be to reattach them. That was a nice easy job to start with.

He dug around in his pocket for his keys and then wandered over to the shed, whistling as he went.

As he pushed the door open, he sensed something was wrong. The birdsong and buzz from the insects faded into the background as he blinked at the sight in front of him.

After the bright sunlight outside, it was dark in the shed, and at first, Roger thought he was seeing things.

It almost looked like there was a man lying on the floor of his shed... But that couldn't be right.

Roger took a step forward and that was when he saw the blood on the man's shirt. With some effort, he gingerly knelt down beside the body.

What on earth had gone on here?

He gently placed his fingers against the man's wide neck to feel for a pulse. Nothing. The poor bugger.

Roger removed his hand and looked sadly at the young man in front of him.

He was a big lad, but so young. What an awful waste.

How had he ended up here? Roger shook his head. There went his relaxing morning gardening. He would have to go over the road to the shops and get them to call the police.

Roger could practically feel his joints creaking as he heaved himself to his feet, leaning heavily on the bench.

He'd turned to go when he heard a spluttering cough. Roger spun back around. Dead men didn't cough.

The big man's eyes were still closed, but Roger touched his arm and said, "Hang on, mate. I'm going to go and get you an ambulance. You just hang on."

Roger hobbled out of the shed as quickly as he could, calling for help.

CHAPTER FORTY-FOUR

AT EIGHT FIFTY-FIVE A.M., Toby George stood by the gates of Bryant Lane Church of England primary school. It had been easy enough to leave the flat without arousing suspicion. He told Glenn he needed to pop out for some cigarettes. No doubt, the police were watching them carefully after what had happened with Janice and the acid, but he wasn't sneaking off. He'd even gone into Perry's Newsagents and asked the bloke behind the till if he could leave through the back yard, so if he had been followed, that would have delayed them for a bit.

He clutched the mobile phone in his left hand. All around him, parents were dropping off their children. Why had the people who had taken Lila, asked him to come here? Why had they picked out a school?

He heard a squeal of delight and children's laughter as two boys rushed past him, racing each other into the school playground.

Toby ran a hand through his hair and looked at the mobile phone. The screen was blank, but he had four bars of signal.

He was only wearing a T-shirt and a loose pair of cargo pants, but he was sweating. He hadn't yet drawn any strange looks from the parents, but he knew he would soon. It was only a matter of time.

These people came to the school gates every day from Monday to Friday and they recognised other parents. They would soon notice Toby was a stranger in their midst, and he had no idea how he would explain his presence to a group of angry mothers.

The phone beeped and buzzed in his hand, and Toby fought back a wave of nausea as he fumbled with the phone and read the message.

Take one of the children and escort them to the corner of Milton Street.

Any child.

Toby shook his head.

No.

They couldn't be asking him to do that.

He blinked a couple of times and then read the message again. He had no idea what they would do to the child. Would they hurt them? Or was this simply a test to see if he was prepared to do as he was told.

Toby looked around wildly, imagining he was being watched by Lila's abductors right now. But he couldn't see anyone suspicious. They all looked like normal parents to him.

The children were so small and defenceless. How was he supposed to see this through?

Toby looked around at the children weaving their way past him and entering the school gates. His heart was racing.

A second beep from the mobile phone made him jump.

He read the message with a feeling of dread.

Tick Tock.

A tiny Asian girl with glossy dark hair in bunches rushed past Toby.

He called out, "Hold on, sweetheart. Your laces are undone."

The girl turned and looked up at Toby with trusting eyes. He passed through the school gates and knelt down in front of her. Her big brown eyes watched him as he tied her shoelace.

CLAIRE FELT NUMB.

She looked down at the phone in her hand and couldn't believe this was happening to her. How could she take a child? Knowing how it felt, how could she put another mother through what she was going through right now? It was sick.

She closed her eyes, listening to the sound of children's laughter and mother's nagging them to hurry up. She was out of her depth. She should have confided in Kelly rather than telling her she was going to the gym and then slipping out via the car park entrance just in case the police were watching the front of Drake House.

She looked again at the text message she had just received.

She looked again at the text message she had just received.

Take the girl with the blonde hair and the pink Paw Patrol lunchbox and bring her to the corner of Milton Road.

Claire scanned the children already in the playground but couldn't see anyone matching that description.

And even if she could, would she really go through with it?

She had no idea what they would do with the poor girl, so how could she deliver an innocent child to them?

She closed her eyes and pictured Ruby's face, trying to gather her strength.

When she opened her eyes again, she noticed a small blonde-haired girl skip past. She carried a pink Paw Patrol lunchbox. The child's hair had been scooped back into a ponytail, and her long fringe pinned back with sparkly pink clips.

She pushed back a few loose strands of hair and dislodged one of the hair clips. It fell on the ground close to Claire.

"Wait a minute, darling," Claire said and hurried forward, picking up the hair clip, a pink one with tiny kittens printed on it.

She smiled brightly at the girl. "Shall I help you put it back in your hair?"

The girl nodded. The fact she was so trusting twisted Claire's stomach and made her chest feel tight.

"Thank you," the little girl said.

Claire's hands were shaking so much she found it difficult to put the hair clip back in place.

A voice behind her said, "Hello, Claudia."

The fair-haired little girl smiled and looked at someone over Claire's shoulder. "Hello, Mrs Clark."

Claire turned to see an attractive brunette, wearing bright pink lipstick, looking down at them.

"I don't think we've met," she said, looking at Claire with open curiosity. "Claudia is good friends with my daughter, Ella."

Claire turned back and smiled at the fair-haired girl. "Go on, sweetheart. You don't want to be late."

She turned to the woman and tried to act naturally. "I am Ruby Watson's mother."

The brunette's forehead puckered in a frown. "Oh, I don't think I know Ruby. Is she in the same class as Claudia and Ella?"

"She is new," Claire said. "Well, I'd better go. I've got a hundred and one things to do this morning. It was nice meeting you."

Claire turned and walked briskly away.

* * *

TOBY LEANED back after he'd finished tying the girl's laces. "All done," he said.

The girl smiled at him, and he saw she was missing her front tooth. Memories of Lila at the same age and her overwhelming excitement over the tooth fairy leaving fifty pence under her pillow flooded Toby's mind.

He put his hand over his mouth. What were these people trying to turn him into? Some kind of monster, like them?

He wouldn't do it.

He was not going to take an innocent child.

He stood up and watched the child as she ran off towards the school, feeling further away from Lila than ever.

* * *

MARLO WAS WATCHING from the other side of the road.

He held his phone in front of him, recording the scene. Today hadn't started off well. He had planned to have Rob here, recording the events, but there had been no sign of Rob since last night.

The bloody idiot was probably still out looking for his stupid brother. Rob was supposed to act as a buffer. Marlo didn't want his face captured on CCTV, and this morning he was taking a big risk, but he couldn't get out of it. He needed the recording.

He had smiled to himself as Toby George had picked out a child at random, and Claire had done his bidding and targeted the fair-haired girl as she'd been told. But then it all went horribly wrong when they'd both let the children go, and now the playground was emptying as the children filed into the school building.

It was too late for them to take any child now.

Furiously he clicked the red button, stopping the recording. The video file was too big to send via email so he uploaded it to the cloud.

Marlo cursed.

He'd performed his role to perfection, but they had let him down. They had ruined the game, and the person who was employing Marlo would not be happy when he saw this video.

He gritted his teeth and typed a text message.

YOU FAILED.

CHAPTER FORTY-FIVE

AT NINE-THIRTY, Charlotte took a phone call. She had been feeling the effects of no sleep, and the words on her computer screen had been blurring together for the last half an hour as she went over interview transcripts.

But the phone call had lit a fire underneath her and perked her up fast. She listened carefully and jotted down a few notes before heading straight over to Mackinnon.

"Jack, I think I've got something." She held up the piece of paper. "A man was admitted to the London this morning. He matches Benny Morris' description, and he's been stabbed. He's going into surgery now."

"How sure are you it is him?"

"I am not at all sure yet, but the physical description matches. He either wasn't talking when he was taken in or he was unconscious because they don't have a record of his name. He was found by a Mr Roger Sturgess at Stepney allotments.

"I've emailed them the CCTV image of Benny, but they

haven't replied yet. If it's all right with you, I'd like to go and talk to Roger Sturgess."

Mackinnon nodded. "I'll come with you. We need to fill Tyler in first. How serious is his condition? Is he expected to survive surgery?"

"It's looking touch and go."

After they had updated Tyler, Mackinnon and Charlotte headed for Stepney allotments. They'd spoken to the local force who were managing the crime scene and they confirmed the victim was Benny Morris. They had informed Charlotte that Roger Sturgess, the man who had discovered the body, was still at the allotments.

The allotments in Stepney were part of Stepney City Farm. There were enough plots for around sixty Tower Hamlets residents to grow their own fruit and vegetables. The project was set up in nineteen seventy-nine and made use of a site that had been levelled by bombs during the Second World War.

Over the past few years, it'd had a bit of a facelift and there was now a permanent cafe on site and a farmers' market held every Saturday.

As Mackinnon and Charlotte walked through the farm towards the allotments, Charlotte grinned.

"My Nan used to bring me here when I was a kid. I remember the cows frightened the life out of me!"

They passed a group of schoolchildren lining up to buy pots of animal feed so they could feed the chickens.

They'd already been to visit the crime scene, and the crime scene manager, Jacob Trent, had told them they could find Roger Sturgess sitting in the cafe, recovering from the shock of finding Benny Morris' body.

Although the cafe was busy, as soon as they stepped inside,

they were able to identify Roger Sturgess. He sat on a wooden chair, bent over a cup of tea, with a blanket wrapped around his shoulders. A woman with dark hair, pulled back off her face, stood beside him with one hand on his shoulder.

Mackinnon and Charlotte approached and introduced themselves.

When Roger began to struggle to get to his feet, Mackinnon said, "There's no need to get up, Roger. We'll join you here if that's okay?"

Roger nodded gratefully and sat back down.

The woman who was still standing beside him held out her hand to shake Mackinnon's. "I'm Leandra, I run the cafe, and Roger is one of my regulars. He's had a terrible shock."

Charlotte nodded. "It's good to see he has people looking out for him."

Leandra shot one last worried look at Roger and said, "Well, I should leave you to it, I suppose. Can I get you a tea or coffee?"

Mackinnon and Charlotte both asked for coffee.

"I hope this won't be too distressing for you, Roger. We just need to ask you a few questions," Charlotte said as Leandra walked away. "Ideally, we'd like to identify the man as soon as possible."

Roger nodded. "Of course, ask away."

"I have a photograph here. It is not the best quality as it's from a CCTV camera, but could you tell us if this was the man you found this morning?" Charlotte pushed across the image from the CCTV, showing Benny Morris standing outside Rose Hill Community Centre.

Roger leaned forward to look at the picture and then patted down his shirt, looking for his glasses.

He eventually found them in his trouser pocket and

slipped them on. He studied the image for a moment and then nodded. "I am pretty sure that is the same man."

Charlotte smiled encouragingly. "Thank you."

"What's his name?" Roger asked.

"Benny Morris," Mackinnon said. "Did he say anything when you found him?"

Roger shook his head. "To be honest, I thought he was dead. He had blood all over his stomach, and the poor lad looked so pale. I felt for a pulse but couldn't feel anything. I was about to leave him in the shed and go and call the police, when I heard him cough.

"I don't mind telling you, he gave me the fright of my life.

"When I realised he was still alive, I ran out of there shouting for help. Luckily, Derek Sythe, one of the chaps who owns a plot closer to the farm, was just on his way in, and he had a mobile phone with him so he called an ambulance."

Roger raised his mug of tea to his lips with a shaky hand. "Do you know if he'll make it?"

"He is in surgery and in a very serious condition, but if he does make it through, it will be down to you," Mackinnon said.

Everyone at the table looked up as Leandra brought Mackinnon and Charlotte's cups of coffee to the table. They thanked her and then resumed their questioning.

"Did you notice anybody else in the area when you arrived at the allotments this morning?" Mackinnon asked.

"No," Roger said and shook his head. "It was a lovely, peaceful morning. I didn't see anyone else at the allotments, and I didn't even know Derek had arrived when he did."

Roger frowned and took another sip of his tea, pulling his blanket around his shoulders. "I haven't got a clue how he even got in because the shed door was still locked when I got there."

Jacob Trent, the crime scene manager, had told Mackinnon there were a couple of loose panels at the back of the shed, and it looked as though Benny had been stabbed in situ, so somebody else had crept into the shed with him.

There were a few CCTV cameras set up around the cafe area and one set up outside the cowshed on the farm, but the allotments were a camera-free zone for the most part, so they would need to rely on the crime scene team to get some answers.

Mackinnon picked up his cup of coffee and took a sip. It was good.

Roger looked up suddenly and waved at a man over Mackinnon's shoulder.

Mackinnon and Charlotte both turned. The new arrival had wavy brown hair and a concerned look on his face.

"It's my grandson. He's come to pick me up. Did you have any more questions?" Roger asked.

Mackinnon shook his head. "Thank you for your help, Mr Sturgess. I understand you've left your address and contact details with the officer at the scene."

Roger nodded. "Yes, that's right."

After Roger left with his grandson, Mackinnon and Charlotte quickly finished their coffee and stood up ready to leave.

This wasn't an encouraging development. According to the crime scene manager, Benny Morris had been stabbed once in the stomach and left to bleed out. It looked as though the abductors were now fighting between themselves, and that was not a good sign.

CHAPTER FORTY-SIX

Marlo was absolutely fuming.

His game had been ruined, and to make matters worse, he'd just been screamed at over the phone by the prick who was organising the whole thing.

It was the unfairness of the situation that really got to him. Marlo shouldn't be blamed for other people not playing the game properly. He'd set everything up perfectly and should have been praised rather than shouted at.

He was feeling uneasy now. He wasn't used to caring what people thought of him, and he sure as hell didn't put up with people treating him like he was a piece of dirt.

He felt the smooth plastic of his mobile phone in his pocket. The anger had taken over before he could stop it. Now he'd had a chance to think, he realised cursing at the man on the phone hadn't been the most intelligent move he could have made.

He licked his lips and pulled his phone out of his pocket as he walked back towards the basement flat. Maybe he should call back and apologise? It made him feel sick to even consider it. Marlo was superior to most people he came in contact with on a day to day basis, but there was something about the chilled tone in the voice over the phone that made him anxious. Not scared exactly —Marlo liked to boast he was scared of no one— but he was wary.

He shoved the phone back in his pocket. What's done, was done. There was no point analysing it now.

Besides, he thought, smiling to himself, he had an idea. He knew precisely how to cheer himself up.

* * *

Ruby Watson was finding it hard to breathe.

The duct tape around her mouth forced her to breathe through her nose, and it felt like she wasn't getting enough oxygen. She tried to slow down her breathing, realising it was her panic causing her erratic gasps for air.

Logically, she knew by inhaling through her nose she would be able to get enough oxygen. She just had to get her breathing under control. She closed her eyes for a few moments, concentrating on each breath, and slowly her breathing rate fell back to normal, and her heart rate slowed a little.

Relieved, her eyes fluttered open. Now she and Lila were locked in the other bedroom, they had more light. A thin, long window ran along the top of the room and told Ruby it was daylight outside. But after being held in the darkness in the other room, she didn't know how much time had passed.

She wondered how her parents would be reacting. Would they have called the police by now? The thought of her mother and father made Ruby's eyes fill with tears.

She just wanted to go home.

There were so many things she wanted to do, so many experiences she hadn't had yet. Would they ever get out of here?

She didn't know what the men were planning to do with her and Lila. Ruby had been sure that the kidnappers would have demanded money by now, but surely if they had, her parents would have paid the ransom straightaway.

Because that hadn't happened, Ruby could only guess that the abductors wanted something other than money.

That sick man had duct-taped their mouths and wrists, and now she couldn't even talk to Lila and get comfort from that.

She glanced over to where Lila was sitting, leaning back against the wall. Her eyes were closed, but Ruby had no idea if she was really asleep. In the last few hours, Lila's fiery temper had faded. They were beating down her spirit.

Ruby blinked back her tears. She didn't know what had happened to Benny. Even though she wanted to hate him for leading them into a trap, she couldn't. She knew Benny didn't really mean to hurt them and had no way of understanding the consequences of what he had done.

She didn't trust that man in the baseball cap, at all. The way he'd looked at them filled Ruby with terror. She'd like to think that the kidnappers were still planning to demand a ransom, but when she looked into that man's eyes, there was an evil there that convinced her he was going to kill them and he would enjoy it.

She was so thirsty. He hadn't been back to give them water in hours, and it was hot today. The room felt so stuffy.

She needed to go to the bathroom, but the bucket he'd left was set against the opposite wall, and there was no way she would be able to go with her hands taped behind her back.

She stifled a sob, screwed her eyes shut tightly and tried to think about the future. What was she going to do when she got out of here? Maybe she would take some time off and spend the rest of the summer holiday abroad somewhere, on a beach sunbathing and drinking fruity drinks with cocktail umbrellas.

She tried hard to picture herself at the beach but suddenly she heard a key in the lock.

Her eyes flew open and she saw the man in the baseball cap standing in the doorway with a large pair of scissors.

Her heart thudded in her chest.

"I am afraid your parents aren't cooperating. They obviously need some extra motivation."

His eyes gleamed with a manic glow as he held up the scissors. "Who wants to volunteer?"

CHAPTER FORTY-SEVEN

AT NINE THIRTY, Kelly Johnson, the Watsons' family liaison officer, kept glancing at the clock in the kitchen. Claire still wasn't back. She went up to the gym just before eight thirty this morning, saying she needed to work out her frustrations on the treadmill, which Kelly had thought was a reasonable request.

The communal gym was on the fourth floor so Kelly took the penthouse lift down to check on her. She knew Peter was working, or pretending to keep busy in his home office, and Curtis wasn't out of bed yet.

Kelly walked into the gym, which was well kitted out with the latest equipment – treadmills, rowing machines and exercise bikes. A large flatscreen TV was displaying the morning's headlines, and there were three women in the gym.

None of them were Claire.

Kelly swore under her breath and raced back to the apartment. She planned to ask Peter if he knew where his wife was, and if he didn't, she was going to call DI Tyler

straightaway. She was anxious to avoid a repeat performance of the last time Claire had snuck out without her
knowledge.

Back inside the apartment, Kelly knocked on the door of
Peter Watson's study. Holding onto the hope that his wife was
in there with him.

Peter opened the door with a look of irritation on his face.
"Yes?"

"Have you seen Claire? I can't find her."

"She went to the gym."

Kelly shook her head. "She isn't there. I just checked."

The look of irritation on Peter Watson's face was replaced
by one of concern. He stepped outside the office and headed
to their bedroom. Kelly waited as he checked the en suite
bathroom.

He turned around and shook his head. "She isn't there."
His eyes flashed angrily. "If she has run off and done something on her own again, I will..." He broke off as they both
heard the sound of the front door opening.

Peter and Kelly rushed into the open plan living area just
as Claire walked into the apartment. Her shoulders were
slumped, and she looked defeated.

"Where have you been?" Peter Watson demanded.

Kelly walked up to Claire and put a hand on the woman's
shoulder. "You're shaking, Claire. Come on, come and sit
down."

"I couldn't do it," Claire said and pulled out a small, black
mobile phone, setting it down on the coffee table. "I failed."

* * *

BACK AT WOOD STREET STATION, the behavioural analyst,

Zelda Smith, was talking about Benny Morris to the officers gathered in the briefing room.

"He would be easy to manipulate. Benny has developmental delays caused by his premature birth and wouldn't be able to hold down a full-time job. It's likely he doesn't even possess the life skills required to live alone. It is possible someone has been utilising Benny for his size and his brawn, but certainly not his brain. There's no reason to think Benny would have wanted to harm the girls."

DC Webb spoke up, "But if his brother was involved, would Benny be easily led?"

Zelda Smith nodded. "I would say it was highly likely that Rob Morris is manipulating his brother."

Tyler nodded and spoke up, addressing everyone in the briefing room, "For those of you who haven't yet read the briefing notes, the man who delivered the flowers to Claire Watson, has been identified as Rob Morris."

Zelda Smith looked quite put out at being interrupted. She narrowed her eyes and then continued, "Benny craves Rob's approval, and Rob appears to be very controlling. We know that after their mother's death, he took Benny from a home where he'd been settled for the past eighteen months. That means Benny is now completely reliant on him."

Zelda opened her mouth to continue, but DI Tyler cut her off. "An officer has been posted to the hospital to keep watch in case Rob decides to come and check on his brother."

"To finish the job?" Collins suggested.

Zelda Smith said, "That is highly unlikely. Rob Morris wouldn't stab his brother. Rob has taken on the role of protector and nurturer."

"So are you saying we should be looking for a third person behind the abduction?" Tyler asked.

Zelda Smith nodded primly. "I would say there was almost certainly a third person involved."

Before she could continue, Tyler's mobile rang. His face tightened as he listened to the caller on the other end of the line. No one in the briefing room spoke. It was obvious from the expression on his face that this was major news.

He hung up and then looked around the room.

"That was Kelly Johnson. Somehow the abductors have managed to get another mobile to Claire Watson, and they have been communicating with her. They told her to go to Bryant Lane primary school and take a child."

Tyler paused as there were sounds of outrage from people around the room.

He put up his hands. "Thankfully, she couldn't go through with it. She snuck out of the car park entrance so she wasn't spotted by surveillance. I am going to go to Drake House and speak to her now. Mackinnon and Collins, I want you to go to the Georges'. I would be willing to bet the abductors have been trying to communicate with them, too. We need to make sure they haven't done anything stupid."

CHAPTER FORTY-EIGHT

"WHAT DO you mean you couldn't go through with it?" Janice practically growled the words at her husband.

Toby looked down at his shoes, shamefaced.

"I threw acid over a stranger! I should have gone myself. I knew it. I should never have trusted you."

Toby's head snapped up. "It was a child, for Christ sakes, Janice. They wanted me to take a *child*."

Janice was shocked into silence, and after a moment, there was a knock-on their bedroom door.

"What's wrong?" Glenn Calvert's voice called from the hallway.

Janice raised her eyes to the ceiling, but before she could tell Glenn Calvert to mind his own bloody business, the doorbell rang.

When Toby and Janice stepped out into the hallway, Glenn Calvert had already opened the front door. Two detectives stood in the doorway.

Janice looked at them with hatred. What good were they?

They kept hanging around here and getting absolutely nowhere. They were supposed to help people, to save poor girls like her Lila, who got into trouble through no fault of their own.

It was down to them to save their daughter, but Toby hadn't played the game the abductors wanted, and now they had failed.

It was all over.

Janice glared at the two detectives. "You're too late."

The tall officer, DS Mackinnon, stepped forward. "What have you done, Janice?"

Toby stuck up for her. "It wasn't her, it was me. You'd better come in."

DS Mackinnon and DC Collins entered the flat and followed Glenn Calvert through into the sitting room.

Once they were all sitting down, Toby began to explain how a note was thrown up onto the balcony, telling them they could find a new phone by the rubbish chute. Glenn stared at Toby in disbelief. "You told me you were popping out to get cigarettes!"

"Can we see the phone please, Toby?" DS Mackinnon asked.

He phrased it as a question, but from the look in his eye, Janice knew they weren't going to be able to refuse.

Toby got to his feet and walked off to the bedroom to retrieve the phone, and DS Mackinnon turned to DC Collins and said, "Get the crime scene guys to come and take a look around the rubbish chute. There's probably nothing there now, but it's worth having a look around."

DC Collins stood up, nodded and reached into his pocket for his mobile phone before stepping out into the hallway.

When Toby returned with the mobile phone, he held it out

to DS Mackinnon, who opened a plastic bag and asked Toby to put it inside. He sealed the bag and then looked up at Toby.

"You know you can't continue to do this. Every time you go off on your own and communicate with the kidnappers without our knowledge, you're making our job harder and harder."

Toby raked a hand through his hair. He slumped into an armchair and looked at DS Mackinnon.

"They sent a message saying I had failed. Do you think they've killed her?"

Mackinnon shook his head. "There is no evidence to suggest that."

Janice leaned forward. Her hands gripped her knees. "Do you know if the other family won the task? Did *they* take a child?"

Mackinnon shook his head. "They didn't take a child."

Janice closed her eyes and let out a shaky breath in relief. Then both sets of parents had failed. That meant Lila still had a chance.

DI TYLER WAS ABSOLUTELY FUMING.

How was he supposed to run an investigation like this when both sets of parents kept screwing everything up? If he wasn't convinced he'd be sacked, he would keep both sets of parents under lock and key until the investigation was over.

Both Claire Watson and Toby George had managed to get past the surveillance he'd set up. He was fighting a losing battle. The budget only allowed them a certain amount of manpower and it was impossible to track both parents. The officer they had stationed outside the Georges' block of flats had alerted the team to the fact that Toby had left the flat, but as the family liaison officer had confirmed he was just popping out for a packet of cigarettes, Toby hadn't been followed.

Claire and Peter Watson sat on the cream sofa opposite him. Peter looked absolutely horrified by his wife's actions, but Claire had a defiant light in her eyes.

"You don't understand. It isn't your daughter they have taken. It's all right for you, sitting there and scolding me like I'm a child, but you have no idea what this feels like. You don't *know.*"

DI Tyler could never be accused of favouring the softly, softly approach. He liked to think he was a compassionate officer, but at times like these, compassion wasn't what was needed. A good dose of common sense was required.

"I will tell you what I know," he said. "If you had come to us and told us about this new phone, we could have been there waiting for them. You do realise they would have had someone waiting and watching at the school?"

"I..." Claire's cheeks flushed red and she stammered over her words.

"If we'd known, we could have set up a sting and had a suspect in custody right now."

No one spoke. Claire Watson looked to her husband for help, but after a brief pause, he got up and walked away.

Maybe Tyler had been too harsh. Maybe he would get reported, but he was fed up of getting nowhere.

Their only progress so far was Addlestone's arrest. It didn't even look like he'd be charged for the images, as the girl in the photographs had just turned eighteen.

This labour-intensive investigation had so far produced little in the way of results. They were no closer to getting the girls home. The only progress they had made had come from Mackinnon's instincts.

Tyler stared at Ruby Watson's parents. He could lay into them again, explaining how they'd messed everything up, but he wasn't sure he was getting through to them. He needed to come at the investigation from a new angle.

As his eyes flickered between Peter Watson, who was now standing by the large windows looking out at the city, and his wife Claire, who was now staring down miserably at her lap, Tyler tried to come up with a fresh focus.

Mackinnon's instinct had got them Addlestone, and they'd only bumped Addlestone up the interview list after Curtis' suggestion.

He glanced at Curtis' closed bedroom door. If Ruby's brother had known about Addlestone, maybe there was more he could tell them.

He stood up. "I am going to have a word with your son."

Claire nodded, too upset to talk, and Peter said nothing but continued to stare out of the window.

Tyler stalked past the open plan kitchen where Kelly Johnson was busy tidying away the tea things.

He knocked once on the bedroom door and then opened it.

He stood in the doorway, eyes wide, unable to believe the sight in front of him. Curtis was sitting beside the computer, and when he saw Tyler, he quickly switched off the screen, but he wasn't fast enough.

Tyler had seen everything.

CHAPTER FORTY-NINE

CHARLOTTE HEADED for the London hospital as soon as they got word that Benny was out of surgery. He was still under the effects of anaesthetic and not fully awake, but she had seen his face clearly enough to know that it was definitely Benny Morris.

Who had stabbed him? Had they had a falling out over money or over what they were going to do with the girls?

Although they knew Benny had learning difficulties, Charlotte didn't know whether Benny was fully involved in planning the abduction or whether he'd just been carried along by the leaders.

The nurse Charlotte had been speaking to sat down at the nurses' station and pulled the keyboard towards her. "Can you give me his name and address? I'd like to be able to put in a request for his medical records and notify his next-of-kin."

Charlotte gave her Benny Morris' name and date of birth as well as his address. "I imagine his next-of-kin is his brother. We've been looking for him as well but haven't been able to track him down yet. If you do manage to get in touch with him, could you give me a heads up? It's probably best not to mention the police are looking for him, though."

The nurse gave Charlotte a guarded look. Some members of the medical profession didn't appreciate playing piggy-in-the-middle with their patients and the police. They preferred to take an impartial view and treat everyone as equals.

Life wasn't that simple, though. "When do you think he'll be up to answering questions?"

"I would say at least another hour or so. He's still very groggy."

Charlotte nodded. "Just so you know, in case you don't get his medical records in time, Benny's got learning difficulties. So he might be a little out of sorts when he wakes up, and he'll probably be scared."

The nurse nodded and glanced down the corridor in the direction of Benny's recovery room. "Do you think he'll be violent? Should I have more staff on hand?"

Charlotte shook her head. "I don't think so. He doesn't have a record of violence, but we are looking at him in connection with a crime, and obviously, he must have experienced a very violent altercation that ended in him getting stabbed. Constable Doyle is on the door, though, if you do need help subduing Benny."

The nurse raised her eyebrows as though asking for Constable Doyle's help was the last thing she would consider doing.

"I could sedate him," she suggested.

"No," Charlotte said quickly.

That was the last thing she wanted. Then she would have to wait even longer before she could question Benny.

She thanked the nurse and walked back down the corridor

towards Constable Doyle, who was sitting on a chair outside the recovery room.

Charlotte sat down on one of the chairs beside him. "I'd like you to let me know as soon as he wakes up. If he can give us any names, this could be the breakthrough we need to bring the girls home."

Constable Doyle nodded. "I will."

Charlotte nodded. "I'm going to get myself a coffee. Can I get you anything?"

Constable Doyle said, "No, thanks. I am fine."

Charlotte let her mind wander as she walked along the hospital corridors. Benny had been left to die, but he had pulled through his operation. He'd been given four units of blood to try and replace the blood he'd lost.

It would have been a scary experience for anybody let alone someone like Benny. As soon as he woke up, Charlotte wanted to be in there, questioning him straightaway. She didn't want to give him a chance to think up a story. She needed the truth.

It had been over twenty-four hours and the girls still weren't home. Every minute that passed made it less and less likely both girls would ever return home.

Rob Morris was clutching at straws.

He hadn't been able to find Benny anywhere, and he was absolutely terrified that Marlo had hurt him somehow. As a last resort, he'd started to phone around the local hospitals. He got a negative response on every occasion until he called The Royal London.

He'd started off the conversation as he had on each

previous occasion, preparing himself for the admissions clerk to tell him there had been nobody admitted by that name, but when she said they did have a Benjamin Morris registered, a gasp of surprise escaped Rob's lips.

"When was he admitted? Are you sure it was Benjamin Morris?" Rob gave the woman Benny's date of birth and address so she could cross-check.

"We believe so. He was unconscious when he was brought in, but he's been identified by the police and…"

"The police?" Rob felt an overwhelming sense of panic at those words.

"Yes, are you a relative?" I can't really give you any details out over the phone unless you are."

Rob tried to force his brain to work. It felt clogged and fuzzy from panic. He couldn't think straight.

He couldn't tell them he was Benny's brother because the police were bound to be looking for him.

"Yes, I am his…father," Rob blurted out without really thinking things through.

"Oh, then I am very sorry to tell you that Benny was brought in early this morning suffering from a stab wound. He's been in surgery where they tried to repair the damage. He's lost a lot of blood, but he made it through surgery and is now in recovery."

For a moment, Rob couldn't speak. *Stabbed.* Benny had been stabbed.

There was only one person Rob could think of who could be responsible and that was Marlo. He kicked out at the wall, clutching his phone tight to his ear.

"Is he going to be okay?" Rob's voice sounded small and distant, and he barely recognised it.

"He has a very serious injury," she replied, "but he's in the best possible hands here. When he wakes up, I will make sure he knows you called."

"Thank you. I will get there as soon as I can."

Rob pressed a button to end the call and staggered back to lean against the wall. His legs felt weak.

Benny had been stabbed, and it was all his fault.

CHAPTER FIFTY

TYLER STEPPED INSIDE CURTIS' bedroom and shut the door behind him.

"Curtis, why do you have the exact same photographs on your computer as Terence Addlestone has on his MacBook?"

Curtis turned around slowly to face Tyler. He looked younger than his sixteen years as he bit down on his lower lip and then shook his head. His shoulders slumped as he looked down at the floor.

"I didn't know what to do."

Tyler folded his arms over his chest and looked down at the boy. "I think you'd better start at the beginning, don't you?"

Curtis' face paled, and he nodded and swallowed hard.

"It all started at school. My English teacher was away, and Mr Addlestone was acting as a substitute. Anyway, the class ended, and he went outside for some reason, I think to talk to another teacher, but he left his computer on his desk at the front of the classroom.

"Everyone else had gone out, and I just thought it would be funny to get onto his computer. I was planning to post something stupid on Facebook. Just a prank, you know, something funny.

"But I found the photographs he had of Kirsty. Then he came back into the classroom, and when he saw me at his laptop, he got really angry. He pushed me up against the wall and threatened me.

"He told me if I reported him, he would make me and my family suffer."

Tyler regarded the boy steadily, watching for any signs that could indicate he was lying.

Curtis' eyes were red when he looked back up at Tyler. "I knew I should've said something at the time, but I was scared of him. It wasn't until Kirsty told me he'd been behaving really badly towards her that I knew I had to do something."

"Did you tell a teacher or a counsellor?" Tyler asked.

Curtis shook his head.

"What about your parents?"

Curtis scoffed. "They'd be the last people I would tell. They're far too busy to listen to my problems."

"So, what did you do?"

Curtis took a deep breath and then said, "I confronted him again. I did it in the corridor where there were people around so he couldn't hurt me. I told him if he didn't leave Kirsty alone, I was going to go to the police."

"And what happened then?"

"He said they would never believe me and they would think I was making everything up. He told me if I went to the police, I'd regret it."

Curtis looked miserable as he shook his head. "That's why I thought he had taken Ruby. I thought it was a warning and she'd be back as soon as he realised I wouldn't talk to the police."

"Why didn't you say anything about this before?"

"Because I was scared. You don't understand what he can be like. He comes across as a quiet, nerdy type of man, but he can be really violent."

"And how did the photographs end up on your computer, Curtis?"

Curtis shook his head and held his hands up. "I don't know. I opened an email today, and it was full of pictures of Kirsty. I was looking at them, trying to decide what to do, when you walked in.

Tyler took two steps forward and turned the computer screen on again. The images of Kirsty getting undressed were plastered all over the screen.

"Okay, Curtis. I am going to take this computer back to the station, and you need to talk to your parents."

* * *

JANICE GEORGE WAS HOLDING her head in her hands when the doorbell rang. She got to her feet slowly. It wouldn't be good news, she was certain of that much.

Toby looked up. "Do you want me to get it, love?"

Janice shook her head. "It's fine."

She walked past Glenn Calvert, who was carrying a tray with yet more tea. Janice felt like he was trying to drown her with the bloody stuff.

When Janice opened the door, she looked down into the face of a young boy, who she guessed to be about ten years old. His hair was light brown and too long, in desperate need of a haircut, and his face was covered with freckles.

He held out a cardboard box. "Parcel for you," he said.

Janice didn't even want to touch it. She stared at it and shouted for her husband.

The smile left the boy's face, and he took a step back.

"Who are you?" Janice demanded. "And who gave you that parcel?"

Toby reached the front door, closely followed by Glenn Calvert.

Glenn tried to calm the boy down as he looked like he might do a runner at any moment. "It's all right, son," Glenn said. "Just tell us who gave you the parcel."

The boy shrugged. "I don't know. A man. He gave me a fiver and asked me to bring the box to this flat."

"What did this man look like?" Glenn asked. He reached for his kitbag that he'd kept in the hallway and pulled out a pair of gloves. If this parcel had anything to do with the case, he didn't want it contaminated with any more fingerprints than was necessary.

But before Glenn was able to do anything with the parcel, Janice ripped it out of the boy's hands and peeled back the cardboard lid.

A second later, her scream reverberated around the flat.

CHAPTER FIFTY-ONE

THINGS WERE ESCALATING FAST.

Mackinnon had taken a phone call from Tyler to tell him that Lila's bloodstained shirt had been delivered to the Georges' flat.

Things were happening that didn't make any sense.

They still hadn't received a ransom request.

Everything circled back to this stupid game, and now, as if her parents weren't terrified enough, they'd received bloodstained clothing.

Mackinnon was supposed to be meeting Tyler at Drake House, but as he approached, he noticed the same woman he'd seen earlier was talking to Claire Watson outside the building again.

This time, instead of approaching them quickly and scaring them both off, he took the time to observe them unseen.

Claire looked harassed. She kept waving the other woman off as though she were trying to get rid of her, but the older woman seemed stubborn. There was definitely some heated words exchanged, but Mackinnon was too far away to hear what they were saying.

He knew the plainclothes detective was sitting in the sandwich shop two doors over, but he would have an even worse view than Mackinnon.

When Claire Watson whirled around and stormed off, going back inside Drake House, Mackinnon decided not to follow her. He was interested in the other woman, who was now heading directly up the street towards him.

He guessed she was at least twenty years older than Claire Watson. She wasn't wearing any make-up but had gold hoops in her ears. Her hair was brown, streaked with grey, and frizzy at the ends with her half-grown out perm.

She was wearing the same pair of bright white trainers, which didn't really go with her black trousers. As she walked past, Mackinnon fell into step behind her.

He wanted answers.

He followed her for two streets before she stopped to look in the window of a homeware shop.

Just before Mackinnon opened his mouth to speak, she looked at his reflection in the mirror and grinned. "Either it's my lucky day, darling, or you are a copper."

She turned around and looked up at Mackinnon.

"What's your name?" he asked.

She winked at him. "Do you want my number, too?" she teased.

"I would like some information. What is your relationship to Claire Watson?"

"Well, you can't ask ladies personal questions like that without offering them a drink first."

Mackinnon frowned, but she grinned up at him unperturbed.

"My name is Melinda Wainwright. Buy me a drink, and I'll spare you five minutes." She nodded at the coffee shop two doors along. "I'll have a full fat frappuccino, thanks."

Mackinnon played along. He bought the drinks, a frappuccino for Melinda Wainwright and a black americano for himself, and carried them over to the table where she was waiting.

"Here's your drink, where's my information?"

"That's the problem with young men these days, no patience." She closed her eyes as she took a long sip of her frappuccino. "Delicious. Now, what do you want to know?"

"How do you know Claire Watson?"

"She adopted my grandson."

Mackinnon raised an eyebrow. "Claire didn't seem too happy to see you."

"Of course, she didn't. She is trying to keep me a secret. She doesn't like me turning up at her posh pad, especially when she's got the police crawling all over the place."

"You know about Ruby's disappearance?"

The smile left Melinda's face and she nodded. "Yes, it's a horrible business."

"You don't know anything about it?"

Melinda shook her head. "Only what Curtis has told me."

Mackinnon sat back in his seat and studied Melinda. This was unexpected.

According to the Watsons, neither of their adopted children had anything to do with their blood relatives.

"Do you speak to Curtis much?"

The woman smirked. "How do I know you won't go running back and telling tales to Claire?"

"Claire doesn't like you seeing Curtis then?"

"No, she doesn't like it one bit. But she can lump it. He's my grandson."

"So, what were you talking to Claire about today?"

"I was asking her where my money was. She is late with my payment."

"Why is she paying you?"

A small smile played over Melinda's lips. "Why not? She has the pleasure of my grandson, so why shouldn't she pay for that by making my old age a little more comfortable. After all, she can afford it."

Mackinnon frowned. Something about this just didn't add up. If the adoption was all above board, then why was Claire paying Curtis' grandmother? Was she holding something over the family?

Mackinnon leaned forward. "What have you got on her?"

Her eyes widened in faux innocence, and she said, "Whatever do you mean, officer?"

Mackinnon shook his head. "Ruby Watson is missing. She hasn't been seen since yesterday morning. I don't have time for games."

Melinda huffed out a breath. "Fine. She is paying me to stay away from Curtis."

"But you just told me you heard about Ruby's disappearance from Curtis."

Melinda shrugged. "So?"

"So, you're obviously not really staying away from him."

Melinda leaned forward, her elbows resting on the table, and she looked directly at Mackinnon.

"Look, Mrs High and Mighty at Drake House doesn't want her son sullied by having a connection with his grandmother. She thinks Curtis is too sensitive to be exposed to the likes of me, but what she doesn't know is that it was Curtis who searched me out in the first place. He was the one who told me to get in touch with his mother and ask for the money."

Mackinnon took a moment to process that before he asked, "Are you telling me that it was Curtis' idea to blackmail his own mother?"

Melinda smiled proudly. "Yeah, he's a clever little bugger, isn't he?"

Clever wasn't the word Mackinnon would use.

He thought devious was more apt.

CHAPTER FIFTY-TWO

DI TYLER STOOD in the viewing room watching DC Collins and DC Webb interview Terrence Addlestone again. He was hoping to get more out of this round of questioning.

DC Collins was an experienced officer, well-trained in specialised interview techniques. DC Webb, on the other hand, was still learning, but his presence in the interview room had been a calculated choice on Tyler's part.

Whereas Collins would ask his questions in a calculated and calm fashion, his expression neutral, DC Webb had not yet learned to control his facial expressions during an inter-view. When Addlestone spoke, it was clear from DC Webb's face that he didn't believe his version of events. Tyler thought this would add pressure and lead Addlestone into defending himself, which was where Tyler hoped he would make a mistake and let loose some vital detail that would allow them to charge him.

They were getting very close to the point where they

would either have to charge Addlestone or release him. He'd only asked for the duty solicitor so far, even though Tyler was sure he could afford a better lawyer with his private teacher's salary. Perhaps Addlestone wasn't taking this seriously.

His behaviour could be interpreted in one of two ways. Either he was innocent and was sure that the police would realise that in time, or he was experienced in getting off of this kind of charge.

It would have helped their case if they'd discovered more from Addlestone's computer, but as yet, the only incriminating evidence had been photographs of Kirsty Jones getting undressed.

She wasn't under age now, though, and there was no reason to suspect she had been underage when the photographs were taken. What really creeped Tyler out about the photographs was the fact that the girl was getting undressed and appeared to be completely oblivious to the camera. Even looking at the photographs made him feel like a peeping Tom.

In the first round of interviews, Addlestone had been relaxed, too relaxed as far as Tyler was concerned, but now the cracks had started to show. Addlestone had been confronted with what Curtis had told them.

From where he stood in the viewing room, Tyler saw a light sheen of sweat break out over Addlestone's forehead.

DC Collins shuffled the stack of papers in front of him and sighed, leaning back in his seat and regarding Addlestone steadily. "Well, Terrence, somebody is lying to us. Curtis told us he found the photographs on your computer. Why would he lie about that?"

Terrence Addlestone shook his head, exasperated. Collins

had been asking him the same question, although worded in slightly different ways, for the past ten minutes.

"Because he put them there. He set me up."

Collins shook his head. "But why would he want to do that?"

Addlestone raised his fist to rub his eyes, and the duty solicitor shot him a concerned glance. "I don't know."

"So, the story he told us about you coming back into the classroom and finding him at your computer never happened?"

Addlestone shook his head furiously. "No, it's complete fiction."

"If what you are telling us is true, how did he get the photographs onto your computer?"

"I…" Addlestone stared down at the table. "I don't know. All I know is that I found them there and tried to delete them, but I kept finding more photographs in different folders." He shook his head. "I panicked. I recognised Kirsty, and I knew what trouble I could get in for having photographs like that on my laptop. I could lose my job, and the effect on my career would be horrendous. I haven't done anything wrong. I'm a victim!"

Collins nodded and then said mildly, "I think Kirsty Jones is the victim here."

Addlestone swallowed hard, his Adam's apple bobbing up and down. "Yes, of course. It must be horrendous for her, too."

"We've spoken to your previous employers, and they told us about the incident five years ago with a girl called –"

Addlestone gave an exaggerated groan and curled his lip in disgust. "The girl was a liar. I was completely exonerated. This is a witch-hunt." He glared at the duty solicitor, who so far hadn't said very much at all. "Aren't you going to do anything? They're trying to set me up."

The bald-headed duty solicitor, sitting beside Addlestone, finally spoke up. "I think we should just stick to the case in hand and not rely on hearsay."

The truth was, the incident Collins had been referring to had been largely discredited. The young girl in question had accused a large number of men of inappropriate conduct, and she was currently undergoing mental health treatment.

They certainly wouldn't be bringing this up in court, but in an interview like this, everything was fair game, in Tyler's opinion. They needed to pile on the pressure until Addlestone cracked and spilled his dirty secrets.

DC Collins gave a slight nod of the head to DC Webb.

During the interview planning stage, they had assigned a couple of questions to DC Webb. This formed part of his training, but interview techniques weren't black and white. A detective needed to play up to his or her personality strengths, and Tyler knew that better than anyone.

DC Collins was calm and cool. DC Webb was the opposite and was the perfect tool for provoking a reaction.

"Are you really trying to tell us that a sixteen-year-old boy has set you up for some unknown reason?" DC Webb asked, scepticism hung heavily on his words.

Addlestone nodded morosely.

"For the benefit of the tape, Mr Terrence Addlestone is nodding," DC Webb said.

He leaned forward so his face was closer to Addlestone's. It was the perfect challenging behaviour. Predictable, Tyler thought, but effective.

"Or are you just trying to palm off your guilt onto a defenceless, young boy."

Addlestone gave a scoffing sound and looked up, glaringly at DC Webb. "He's hardly an innocent child. He's been—"

Collins nodded, encouragingly. "Carry on. What's he been doing?"

But Addlestone bit his tongue and shook his head. Tyler could only guess at what he'd been about to say.

"Then there is the matter of the physical evidence," DC Webb said. "A girl's netball skirt was found in your dustbin. It is being analysed now but I reckon we will find out it belonged to Kirsty Jones. What do you think?"

"I have no idea. I've never seen that skirt before."

DC Webb smiled as he shook his head, folded his arms and leaned back in his chair. "Really? I find that very hard to believe. One of our officers saw you put a plastic bag containing the skirt into your dustbin. You carried it out of your house, and yet you expect us to believe you have never seen it before?"

Addlestone's eyes flitted rapidly between Collins and Webb and then he turned to look at the duty solicitor.

"You don't have to answer this, Terrence," the solicitor advised.

Terrence Addlestone groaned. "All right. I have seen it before. It was in my flat, but honestly, I don't know how it got there. Someone must've put it there."

He was really sweating now. The blue shirt he wore was changing colour, darkening as it soaked up the sweat around his armpits.

DC Webb grinned. "Let me guess, Curtis Watson put it there to set you up?"

Addlestone nodded half-heartedly. Only time would tell if the man was telling the truth. But in Tyler's opinion, if he was spinning a story, he was a very good actor.

Tyler took a quick glance at his watch as Collins and Webb continued to interview Addlestone.

He needed to arrange a briefing. In the last couple of hours, so many things had happened, and the team urgently needed an update.

CHAPTER FIFTY-THREE

TYLER LEFT DC Collins and DC Webb questioning Addle-stone and called an emergency briefing for the rest of the team. He would fill Collins and Webb in after they had finished the interview, but right now, it was important the entire team were working from the latest information.

Zelda Smith was still present, at Brookbank's insistence, and she sat at the front of the room, goading Tyler with icy blue eyes. He personally had nothing against behavioural analysts, he just wished their answers weren't so wishy-washy. They added a qualifier to everything they said so when someone was finally arrested for a crime, they could take the credit without taking the blame if they were wrong.

Tyler didn't think that was fair.

He waited for everyone to take their seats around the large oval table. There were never enough seats for everyone in an investigation this size, and some of the officers and admin staff had to stand up again.

Tyler pushed a stack of briefing notes into the centre of

the table. He wasn't a big fan of paperwork but believed in briefing notes. When there were a lot of facts to give out in a brief period of time, it was hard for the human brain to absorb them all.

Whatever was said first at the briefing, would distract people from listening to the rest of the topics. Their minds naturally tried to break the initial information down and make sense of it, which means they missed other important points that were brought up afterwards. And in this investigation, they couldn't afford to miss anything.

After everyone had the single sheet of A4 paper with Tyler's bullet points, he made a start.

"As some of you already know, I discovered photographs of Kirsty Jones on Curtis Watson's home computer. They were the same images we found on Terrence Addlestone's MacBook last night. Curtis says, Addlestone threatened his family and emailed him the photographs. He told me he believes Addlestone took Ruby as a way of warning him to keep his mouth shut.

"I've just come from the interview suite where DC Collins and DC Webb are questioning Addlestone. When he was confronted with what Curtis had told us, Addlestone insisted that he was set up by Curtis. It is not yet clear how this is related to Lila George's and Ruby Watson's abduction. It could be smoke and mirrors, and Addlestone could be responsible."

Zelda Smith raised her hand and smiled confidently at Tyler. He barely resisted rolling his eyes but nodded at her, giving her permission to talk.

She turned, putting her back to him and facing the rest of the room. "From what I have read so far, our accumulated knowledge on the Watson family tells us Curtis is highly intelligent. It is possible he could have set Addlestone up, on the other hand, Addlestone does possess some characteristics of a classic manipulator. It is important for him to be in control and in a position of authority with children or young adults. Child abusers often take jobs to come into contact with children, and Addlestone has always taught teenagers."

Tyler thought that was ridiculous. Surely, the same could be said of most teachers. That didn't mean they were all manipulative and a danger to society.

Evie Charlesworth, who stood against the wall at the back of the room and spoke up, interrupting Zelda, "Sorry to cut in, but I have something important to share."

Tyler nodded at her. "Go ahead."

"Well, we have been looking into Terrence Addlestone's background, trying to get an understanding of the man, and one thing we have been able to access is the emails on his computer. He has email receipts proving he has been making regular payments to somebody by PayPal. Not a company, a person. There is no name, though. They are only identified by an email address. If Addlestone has been set up, is it possible that Curtis is blackmailing him?"

"Even if Addlestone wasn't set up, it's still possible Curtis decided to blackmail him rather than report him after finding the pictures of Kirsty Jones. How soon can we find out who Addlestone was paying?" Tyler asked.

"It might take us a little while to access that information. We only have an email address. If we ask PayPal for information, it could take a while. But if we suspect Curtis, there is one way we could find out without waiting for warrants and approval."

Tyler nodded, interested to hear what she was going to say next.

"We now have Curtis' computer. I have spoken to the tech team and they confirmed Curtis has a mail application on his computer. We can get the address from that and see if it matches with the PayPal payments. I'm waiting for them to call me back."

Tyler nodded. He liked that idea. "Good work, Evie. We'll look into that after the briefing."

Mackinnon slipped into the room, having just arrived back at the station after visiting the Georges.

Tyler looked up. "Jack, anything to report?"

Mackinnon nodded. "Lila George's parents are extremely distressed after they received Lila's bloodstained shirt. They think it's some kind of punishment because they didn't play the game. I also spoke to the woman I mentioned seeing the other day outside Drake House.

She was talking to Claire Watson again, and when I caught up with her I found out she was actually Curtis' grandmother. I only caught the tail end of what you were saying just now about the possibility of Curtis blackmailing Addlestone, but it turns out Curtis is encouraging his grandmother to blackmail his mother."

Mackinnon paused to let the news sink in, and there were lots of puzzled frowns around the briefing room.

"So what the Watson's told us about Curtis and Ruby not having any contact with their biological families wasn't true?"

"Claire has been paying Curtis' grandmother to stay away from him, what she doesn't know is Curtis has carried on seeing her behind his mother's back, and it was his idea for his grandmother to demand money." Mackinnon shrugged. "If he's blackmailed someone once, it's pretty likely he could again."

"This is clearly a demand for attention," Zelda Smith spoke

up. "Curtis is blackmailing his own mother because he doesn't feel loved. That's why he is reaching out to another family member. I agree with DS Mackinnon, he could be targeting Addlestone. Blackmail has worked for him once, so it's not beyond the realms of possibility he would decide to do it again."

Mackinnon nodded slowly. "Only this time, maybe he has bitten off more than he can chew."

Tyler sighed. "Curtis did say Addlestone had threatened his family. It could be Addlestone's motive for taking Ruby Watson and the reason we haven't had a ransom demand."

The evidence was beginning to suggest Curtis had only been telling them half of the story.

"Can we find out if Curtis put those photographs on Addlestone's computer or whether it was the other way around?" Mackinnon asked.

Evie, who had been in communication with the tech team, nodded. "We should be able to analyse when the files were created and modified on individual computers and get a rough idea that way. The thing is, Addlestone's been deleting files on his computer, but there are techniques to find out what those files were because nothing is really ever scrubbed from the computer properly. He hadn't been using specialised software. If he'd done this kind of thing before, surely he would know to smash the hard drive rather than try and delete the files."

Tyler pondered on that for a moment before summarising the remaining developments. The rest of the team gave their feedback and then Tyler brought the briefing to a close.

Tyler felt they were getting closer, but he wanted definite answers. If they found out Addlestone had been blackmailed by Curtis, that would give him a strong motive for Ruby's abduction.

He raked a hand through his grey hair. Of course, it didn't help them understand why Lila George was taken, too, or why the abductors had decided to make it some kind of sick game. Perhaps that was Benny and Rob Morris' influence, though? Addlestone wouldn't have handled something like this himself, so it made sense he would have employed a couple of goons.

Now, they had to try and find a link between the Morris brothers and Addlestone if they were going to prove this case against him.

CHAPTER FIFTY-FOUR

MACKINNON WAS at his desk writing a report about his conversation with Melinda Wainwright when Evie hurried into the incident room.

Mackinnon looked up from his computer screen as Evie walked up to his desk, looking confident and pleased with herself. "It was Curtis' email address. We don't know what bank account the money has been going into yet, but Addlestone has been sending him money via PayPal."

Mackinnon leaned back and smiled at her. "Nice work. That is pretty strong evidence Curtis has been blackmailing him."

Evie nodded. "It is sad really. Curtis must be devastated that he's put his own sister in danger."

Curtis didn't act like a normal sixteen-year-old, and had behaved oddly every time Mackinnon had spoken to him, but surely even he realised that by blackmailing Addlestone his actions had inadvertently led to the kidnapping of his sister?

Before Mackinnon could respond to Evie, Tyler strode back into the incident room.

"Okay, listen up everyone. We've had an ID on a man who was acting suspiciously close to Bryant Lane Primary School. He was standing on the other side of the road, and it looked like he was recording the scene. We believe he could be involved in the abduction and possibly coercing the Georges and the Watsons into performing tasks. His name is Marlo Wainwright. He is a petty criminal, who served a short sentence for repeat shoplifting offences."

Mackinnon had felt a jolt when Tyler mentioned the name Wainwright. Surely, that couldn't be a coincidence.

He interrupted Tyler, "Sir, Curtis' grandmother's name is Melinda Wainwright."

Tyler's face changed in an instant. "What else do we know about the family?"

"Not much yet. Her daughter, Curtis's mother, died of a drug overdose a few years ago. I don't know whether she has any relatives called Marlo."

Tyler nodded. "Well, we had better find out. Get in touch with her ASAP."

Mackinnon reached for the phone on his desk and searched through his mobile for Melinda Wainwright's number. He prayed she'd given him a genuine telephone number.

Feeling the eyes of everyone in the incident room on him, Mackinnon felt relieved when the call connected and he heard a ringing tone.

A husky woman's voice answered the phone. The television was on in the background.

"Mrs Wainwright?"

"Yes, that's right. If you're selling something, I'm not interested."

Tyler nodded to indicate he wanted Mackinnon to put her on speakerphone, and he did by pressing the green button on the phone panel.

"It's DS Mackinnon. I spoke to you earlier today, and you were kind enough to answer some of my questions."

She chuckled. "Now, don't tell me, you're making a follow-up phone call to ask me out on a date."

Mackinnon knew he would be in for plenty of ribbing about that one later. He ignored the smirks and pressed on.

"I wanted to ask if you have someone in your family called Marlo?"

Melinda Wainwright was quiet for a moment, and her voice was guarded when she next spoke. "My grandson is called Marlo. He is my eldest daughter's boy, Curtis' cousin."

Tyler gave a broad grin.

"Marlo Wainwright. He kept his mother's name not his father's?"

Melinda gave a throaty chuckle. "No chance of that. She had no idea who the father was."

"Has Curtis met Marlo?"

"Yes, they've met a couple of times. I had a barbecue at my place a couple of months ago, and they were both there."

"Do you know where I can find Marlo?"

This time there was no hesitation before Melinda snapped, "And why should I tell you? The poor lad has had enough trouble with the police. He is trying to make a fresh start."

"I am sure he is, Mrs Wainwright."

Mackinnon glanced up and looked straight at Tyler. He didn't want to give too much away. If he mentioned the fact that Marlo could be involved in Ruby's abduction, his grand-mother could warn him and that would hamper the investigation. Before Mackinnon could decide how much to reveal, Melinda Wainwright spoke again.

"To be perfectly honest, love, I have no idea where he is. He's a bit of a black sheep. Deep down, I don't think he's a bad lad, but he is always disappearing off somewhere on the back of one of his big ideas. He'll return eventually with his tail between his legs when his current scheme has fallen through. He always does."

After Mackinnon thanked Melinda Wainwright and hung up, Tyler came and sat on the edge of Mackinnon's desk. "Well, that was unexpected. If Marlo is involved in the abduction, why would he target Curtis' sister? Is he jealous of Curtis, do you think?"

"They are cousins," Mackinnon said. "They share the same DNA, and yet, Curtis has huge advantages in life over Marlo. Jealousy is a definite possibility."

Zelda Smith walked over to Mackinnon's desk and looked directly at Tyler. "I should go and talk to Curtis. I think he's a deeply unhappy young man, and he might be able to tell us where we can find Marlo."

"I am not sure that's a good idea," Tyler said. "We could bring him in, but before we do that, we need to have a much better idea about what's going on here. Does this mean Addlestone is in the clear? Is Curtis involved, or is his cousin doing this for some kind of envy-motivated revenge?"

"I can't do my job properly if I can't speak to the people involved in this case," Zelda said sharply. "Looking through your interview notes just doesn't cut it."

Tyler narrowed his eyes and glared at Zelda. "Maybe we could bring him in after we discuss an interview strategy, but

I'm not screwing up the investigation so you can put the kid on a therapist's couch."

Zelda's eyes widened, and she looked indignant. "I think it would be much better if I talked to Curtis in his own home. He will feel far more confident there, and I should be able to get him to open up. From what I know of his personality, Curtis is feeling isolated. He doesn't feel like part of his new family but he also doesn't belong to his old family, and I think he's struggling with that."

Eventually, Tyler sighed and agreed. "Okay, you can go to Drake House and talk to Curtis. I'll ask his parents' permission, and I'll come with you."

Zelda tossed her blonde hair and gave a satisfied smile. "When shall we go?"

"We can go as soon as Collins and Webb have finished questioning Addlestone."

Zelda walked away, looking like the cat who'd got the cream, and Tyler rolled his eyes at Mackinnon before heading out to give Brookbank another update.

Mackinnon picked up the phone and dialled Charlotte's number. She needed an update because she'd been at the hospital waiting for Benny to wake up and answer some questions.

She was going to be shocked by the latest news to say the least.

CHAPTER FIFTY-FIVE

BENNY MORRIS HAD BEEN PUT in a private room to recover after his operation as the medical team were worried he could be violent when he woke up, and for the past thirty minutes, Charlotte had been walking up and down the corridor outside Benny's room, trying to burn off some nervous energy as she thought over the questions she needed to put to him.

She'd been running on empty for the past few hours. A Snickers bar from the vending machine washed down with two cups of coffee had given her a desperately needed boost. Now, she was buzzing from the sugar and caffeine.

The doctor who'd just been in to see Benny said he was still groggy, but Charlotte would be able to go in and talk to him soon. Despite their initial concerns, Benny had not been violent. That was the good news. The bad news was that Benny hadn't uttered a word since he'd come round from the anaesthetic.

"Is there any medical reason he isn't talking?" Charlotte

asked.

Dr Marina Patel shook her head as she looped her stethoscope around her neck. "No, I think it's down to the fact he's just been through a very traumatic experience. Waking up in hospital must be disorientating."

Charlotte nodded. That made sense. She could only hope that Benny would trust her enough to open up. Would he be willing to talk? The fact that he had been stabbed suggested that all was not well between the abductors and she might be able to use that as leverage to get Benny to talk.

The doctor rushed off to attend another patient, and a few minutes later, a nurse stuck her head out of Benny's room and told Charlotte she could come in and talk to the patient.

Charlotte walked forward quickly but shot a quick glance at Constable Doyle who was still sitting beside the door. He was a comforting presence.

She'd seen the CCTV evidence and knew Benny was a big guy, but seeing him in person was something else. He looked too big for the hospital bed. He wasn't fat, though. He was just big all over. His hands were easily twice the size of Charlotte's, and even his face was huge.

As soon as she stepped into the room, his big eyes locked on hers, but his face remained impassive. She didn't say a word until she'd approached the side of his bed and pulled up a chair to sit down.

"Benny, I am Detective Constable Charlotte Brown of the City of London police. I have some questions for you."

Benny said nothing but he kept his gaze fixed on Charlotte's face.

Charlotte continued, "You were brought into hospital this morning with a stab wound, Benny. Can you tell me who did that to you?"

Again, Benny didn't answer, but this time a flicker of emotion passed over his face.

"Two young women, Lila George and Ruby Watson, have been abducted, Benny. Do you know anything about that?"

Benny's lip began to wobble, and although he didn't speak, he became more agitated. His fingers twisted and clutched at the sheets, and he let out a low moan.

"Are you okay? Are you in pain?"

Benny gave a small nod, and Charlotte called the nurse, who had remained in the room. She was standing by a cupboard, sorting through some items inside. Charlotte suspected she was really staying in the room because she wanted to keep an eye on the questioning.

The nurse walked up to Benny and smiled at him. "We've given you something for the pain, Benny, but it will be uncomfortable for the next few days as you recover. We'll give you another dose of medication in an hour. Do you think you can manage until then?"

Benny nodded his head, and the nurse patted him on the back of the hand, walked back to the cupboard and continued rearranging the stock.

Charlotte frowned. Benny was responding to their questions, so he clearly understood them. He was just refusing to answer. They didn't have time for this.

"Benny, this is very important. I need you to talk to me, do you understand?"

He nodded but still said nothing. Charlotte decided to ask a question that didn't relate to the current case, one that Benny might feel more comfortable answering.

"Benny, what is the name of the community centre you go to?"

Benny licked his lips as he contemplated her question. It

seemed to take ages, but finally, he decided that it was safe to answer.

"Rose Hill community centre," he said.

Charlotte nodded. "Good."

At least she had managed to get him talking. That was progress, albeit slower progress than she wanted.

"Benny, do you know Ruby Watson and Lila George? They work at that community centre, don't they?"

Benny nodded, and Charlotte gritted her teeth. Great. Now they were back to nodding, but after a brief hesitation, Benny surprised her by asking, "Are they all right?"

"I don't know Benny. I am trying to find them and I thought you would be able to help."

Benny looked panicked. "Where's Rob?"

"Your brother?"

Benny nodded.

"I don't know. When did you last see him?"

"Last night."

"Can you tell me what happened last night?" Charlotte asked.

Benny shook his head frantically. "No."

"Did you see the girls last night?"

Benny looked away. His breathing was getting faster as he got more and more agitated.

Charlotte reached out and put a hand on his arm. "Benny, I'm a police officer and I want to help. You want to help too, don't you? You want the girls to be safe and you want to find your brother?"

Benny turned his big eyes on Charlotte as though he were weighing up whether to trust her or not, and then finally he nodded and began to talk.

CHAPTER FIFTY-SIX

MARLO COULD BARELY CONTROL his breathing. His hand was gripping the phone so tightly he thought he might crush it. The humiliation of listening to somebody, who was not even worthy to lick his boots, rant and rave and accuse him of doing a bad job made Marlo furious.

The fool thought he was so clever, but he had no idea about the real world. He wouldn't know how to pull off a job if it smacked him on the arse, and now he had the cheek to tell Marlo off for embellishing the game.

He had no style, no ambition.

But Marlo couldn't say any of that to the person on the other end of the phone, not if he wanted to get paid, so instead, he gritted his teeth and tried to explain the situation.

"I don't think you understand. I had to think on my feet. People are unpredictable, and things don't always go to plan. But I handled it."

He held the phone away from his ear to save himself from the dressing down.

He'd had enough of this.

Why was he following orders from a jumped up little prick? He shouldn't be taking orders from anybody. The person on the phone clearly had no idea who he was dealing with.

"Now, listen to me," Marlo said. "It's all very well for you to read me the riot act now, but I didn't see you here making decisions and..."

The phone went silent, and Marlo pulled the phone away from his ear and looked at the screen in disbelief. He was shaking with rage and could feel the vein at his temple pounding.

The bastard had hung up on him. Of all the disrespectful, rude things to do...

He would regret that. Marlo would make sure of it. From the start of this game, Marlo had had to abide by somebody else's rules. He'd had to promise there would be no permanent damage to the girls.

Marlo was shaking as he dropped the phone onto the kitchen counter. He'd made that promise under different circumstances. Now, all deals were off.

Marlo smiled coldly. The game was about to get deadly.

* * *

ZELDA SMITH PACED her small corner of the incident room. DI Tyler had promised to take her to speak to Curtis Watson ages ago, but he was still keeping her waiting. He thought she was stupid.

She knew he didn't think much of her profession. He didn't respect the time she'd spent studying and analysing criminal behaviour. To be honest, she had almost respected him for that when she first met him. At least he'd been honest about his opinion, and Zelda had relished the challenge to prove herself.

She'd worked on a number of cases with both the Metropolitan police and the City of London police and she often met resistance. It made the result all the more gratifying when her contribution helped solve the case and sceptical officers realised there was value in studying criminal behaviour.

After all, if you understood the criminal mind, you could predict behaviour and that was very helpful.

The trouble was, case notes, interview summaries and reports really didn't cut the mustard. It was so much easier when she got to talk to the people involved. A typed up conversation on the printed page was useless compared to looking into somebody's eyes to see whether they were lying to you.

Curtis Watson sounded like a very interesting character indeed. He was young, and struggling to find his place in the world, but it was his intellect that interested Zelda. He clearly didn't fit in with his current family, and from everything she had gleaned so far, it appeared that he didn't feel connected to them. That's why Zelda wanted to see him in person. If he really had no connection to the parents who had cared for him since he was a child that would be extremely unusual, and her professional curiosity had been piqued.

Although Zelda, believed pigeonholing people according to their personality characteristics wasn't helpful, there were some personality traits you couldn't ignore, and she knew she would be able to give more insight into the case if she could talk to Curtis and his parents. Once she'd spoken with them,

Zelda intended to persuade Tyler to let her see the Georges as well.

She had claimed a mental victory when Tyler had agreed she could talk to Curtis, but now she worried she'd celebrated too soon. She had a sneaking suspicion he just said that to shut her up and was now going to stall for time.

Zelda looked up as Evie Charlesworth made her way towards her. Evie had an open face and a warm smile. She had an administrative role and supported the team, but unlike most of the staff, who regarded Zelda with suspicion and seemed to believe she was psychoanalysing them if they so much as made eye contact, Evie was friendly and easy to talk to.

"Any sign of Detective Inspector Tyler?" Zelda asked.

"I'm afraid not, Zelda. I've been asked to pass on a message. DI Tyler is going to be at least another hour or two. You could take a break and maybe go and get something to eat?"

Zelda hid her anger well. She smiled at Evie. "Right. Thank you."

There was no point taking it out on her. After all, she was only delivering the bad news. Tyler's message convinced Zelda she had been right. Tyler was fobbing her off.

After Evie walked back to her own desk, Zelda reached for her laptop bag and umbrella. She hadn't been asking for the world, only a little cooperation, but if Tyler wasn't prepared to compromise, Zelda would do things her own way.

She gave Evie a small wave as she strode out of the incident room. Evie would assume she was going to get something to eat as she had suggested, but Zelda was going to Drake House to talk to Curtis Watson whether DI Tyler liked it or not.

CHAPTER FIFTY-SEVEN

IT WAS TAKING FOREVER.

Benny wanted to be helpful, and he did have information, but it wasn't easy to extract the details. Charlotte had been asking him question after question, trying to determine where the girls were being held.

From what Benny had told her so far, she understood that the girls were in a basement flat with long narrow windows, probably somewhere in London. She knew a man called Marlo had taken Benny to the allotments and stabbed him. It had taken fifteen minutes to get Benny to stutter Marlo's name.

According to Benny, Marlo was the violent ringleader, and Rob was a moral, honest citizen, but of course he was biased.

"What about street names, Benny? Can you think of any?"

Benny shook his head.

"Close your eyes and try to picture the outside of the basement flat. What can you see?"

Benny's eyelids fluttered closed. "It is sunny," he said.

Charlotte barely held back a groan. This was hard work.

"Are there traffic lights outside the flat?"

Benny, who still had his eyes closed, shook his head.

"What about a pedestrian crossing nearby?"

Again, he shook his head.

Charlotte sighed. The only solid information she had so far was that wherever they were holding the girls must have been within walking distance to the allotments as Benny had told her Marlo had led him there from the flat. She supposed that gave them something to go on, although she really needed something to narrow the location down further.

"When you walked to the allotments with Marlo, did you pass any bus stops? Or any tube stations?"

Benny opened his eyes and grinned at Charlotte. "Yes, we went on the D7 bus."

"Bus? I thought you said you walked to the allotments?"

Benny nodded. "We did, after we got the D7 bus."

Charlotte rubbed her forehead. Her caffeine and sugar buzz was wearing off, and she was getting a headache. Benny mentioning the D7 bus had given her an idea. She pulled out a mobile phone and did a quick Google search to check the bus route. She quickly found that it did indeed stop just outside Stepney City farm and the allotments.

Now all she had to do was follow the route back and try to get Benny to identify where he had boarded the bus. That would be easier said than done. She pulled up Google Street view, and beginning at the point where the bus started its journey, she began to show Benny the images of the streets.

She scrolled around so Benny could see. "Did you get on the bus here, Benny?"

Benny looked at the image for a long time, and Charlotte

felt hope build in her chest. But then her excitement was quenched when Benny shook his head and said, "Nope."

They repeated the same routine. She showed Benny the street view from each bus stop a further eight times before Benny finally said, "Yes, we got the D7 bus from there."

"Really, Benny, are you sure? It is very important."

Benny nodded.

She felt a spark of excitement. If they could pinpoint a smaller area, they could start questioning the local residents and shop owners to see if anyone had seen the girls and examine local CCTV footage.

Charlotte smiled. "Well done, Benny. That's a great help."

* * *

MARLO CRACKED HIS KNUCKLES. Now that he had made his decision, he was feeling much happier. He never worked well with people bossing him around.

He excelled when he was free to do what he wanted, and what he wanted was to make those girls scream.

Especially Lila George. He wanted to see that defiant light in her eyes snuffed out once and for all. He was going to enjoy this. He would take his time and squeeze every last drop of pleasure out of the moment.

He remembered Benny's pathetic face when he had first realised Marlo was taking the girls. He had been distraught when Marlo had slammed his fist into the side of Lila George's head in the alleyway.

"If only you were still around to see what I am going to do next, Benny," Marlo said with a chuckle as he walked towards the bedroom.

* * *

CHARLOTTE SPENT the next ten minutes showing Benny images on her phone of the surrounding roads and streets in the vicinity of the bus stop he'd picked out.

He jabbed his finger at the phone when she reached Marston Street and said excitedly. "Yes! That one."

"The girls are being held in this street?"

Benny nodded.

"Can you remember a door number?"

Benny was quiet for a moment then shook his head.

"It doesn't matter. You've already been a great help," Charlotte said, eagerly making a note and looking down at the street view.

"But there's no banana."

Charlotte looked up and shook her head. "Banana, Benny? What does that mean?"

Benny looked put out. "There was a banana."

Benny hesitated as he looked at her phone, and his forehead creased with a frown. "I am sure. But there's no banana."

Charlotte would have laughed if the situation hadn't been so serious. She certainly hadn't been expecting him to say that.

"I'm...not sure what you mean, Benny? What banana?"

Benny shrugged. "There was a banana."

"Right." Charlotte said, feeling her hope drifting away.

How could she rely on the information Benny had provided?

Benny grinned at her, pleased with himself, and she smiled back. She couldn't be angry with him. He was trying to help. He may not have provided the most reliable information, but it was the best they had to go on right now.

CHAPTER FIFTY-EIGHT

Lila and Ruby had been sitting back to back for the past hour, their fingers desperately working back and forth, trying to remove the duct tape from each other's wrists.

It wasn't easy, and Ruby groaned in frustration. She'd peeled the tape back a quarter of an inch only to drop it, and then when she fumbled again, trying to find the edge of the tape, it was stuck fast.

Ruby's fingers were sweaty and slippery as she struggled to grip the tape. "It's no good. It's not coming off."

"We just have to keep trying," Lila said. "No one else is coming to save us, Ruby, if we're going to get out of here, we have to do this together."

Ruby took a deep breath and tried again.

At least they'd managed to remove the duct tape from each other's mouths. That had taken ages as well. Ruby had crouched on the ground, putting her face as close to Lila's hands as she could. Lila's fingernails had scratched at the skin on her cheeks until she'd finally managed to rip off the tape, and then Ruby had returned the favour.

It was comforting to hear Lila's voice again. When they'd both been gagged, the eery silence and seeing her own fear reflected in Lila's eyes had been awful.

"Okay, stop for a minute, and I'll see if I can free myself."

Ruby paused and looked over her shoulder to watch Lila's progress.

Lila grunted in frustration and then swore when she couldn't wriggle her hands through the loosened tape.

"Let's try again," Ruby said and shuffled closer to Lila. "Even if we do get free, what are we going to do? As soon as he comes back in here and sees we have taken the tape off, he'll just put more on."

Lila shook her head as Ruby's fingers plucked at the tape. "I am going to run at him."

Ruby made a scoffing noise. "That will never work."

"Think about it, Ruby. Sure, he's stronger than us individually, but if one of us can hold him up long enough for the other to get free, we'll be able to get some help."

Ruby shook her head. "Even if we could hold him up for a short while, how would we get out of the flat? The front door will be locked."

"Benny said the spare front door key was kept in the kitchen, and every time Marlo has been in here, he has always left the key to the bedroom door in the lock."

"So?"

"So, we lock him in. That will give us time to grab the front door key from the kitchen, get out and raise the alarm."

"So one of us has to stay locked in here with Marlo?" Ruby asked as her eyes widened in horror.

Lila shrugged. "It should only be for a little while. Once we raise the alarm, the police will be on their way, and we'll be rescued."

Ruby shook her head. "And I suppose it's me who has to stay in the room with Marlo?"

Lila shook her head. "Not necessarily. I say we both rush him. Ideally, we'll both get out and can lock him in, but that's unlikely. He'll probably grab one of us, so it's up to the other person to get out, lock the bedroom door and raise the alarm. Okay?"

Ruby's heart was beating faster just thinking about it. "Okay." She managed to peel away a large section of tape from Lila's wrists. "Try again now."

"Oh, thank God," Lila said and circled her wrists and shoulders in relief as she finally slipped her wrists free of the bindings.

Then she turned to Ruby and made short work of the tape looping around her wrists.

When they were both free, Lila looked into Ruby's eyes. "Are you ready?"

Ruby nodded and tried to look confident even if she didn't feel it. She had spent the first few hours after they'd been abducted unable to believe this could have happened to her. She thought she was going to wake up from some crazy dream. Then she thought it was only a matter of time before the police burst in and rescued them, but now, finally, she was starting to think Lila might be right.

There was no point waiting around for someone to save them. They had to save themselves.

CHAPTER FIFTY-NINE

CHARLOTTE MADE her way to Marston Street. She'd left Benny happily enjoying some jelly in his private hospital room. He seemed happy enough there even though he constantly asked after his brother. One of the nurses had located Benny's medical records, and she let slip the fact that Benny had spent much of his childhood in and out of hospital with various ailments. He clearly felt at home in the medical environment.

Marston Street looked just as it had on Street View. Although Charlotte was familiar with East London, she didn't know this area very well. It was just outside city limits, and there were no sixties tower blocks, only old-fashioned Georgian houses— lots of them had basements with grilled windows, allowing some light to get to the downstairs rooms.

She guessed most of the houses had been converted to flats a long time ago. But none of the basement windows matched Benny's description. Each house had steps leading down from the pavement to a small paved or gravelled area and the basement rooms all had square windows.

She was halfway along Marston Street when a large, brightly-coloured poster on the opposite side of the road caught her eye. It was huge and hung on the side of the first building in a row of shops. Charlotte smiled. It was an advert for a type of banana yogurt, and there was a cartoon image of a banana, complete with a happy smiling face.

"Well done, Benny," she murmured. She shouldn't have doubted him after all.

The images from Google Street View had been out of date. The poster on the images she'd shown Benny had been for an insurance company.

Knowing that Benny hadn't been away with the fairies when he was describing the location gave Charlotte more confidence. She had a good feeling about this location. Benny had been telling the truth.

If the girls were still being held here, she could use some backup. She quickly called Mackinnon and filled him in. Right now, the team were focusing heavily on trying to extract information from Addlestone, but Mackinnon promised to give DI Tyler an update and said he would meet her in Marston Street as soon as possible.

Not wanting to waste any time, Charlotte began to look carefully at the buildings.

She was looking for a basement flat with horizontal, narrow windows. As all the houses in this area were terraced that meant the windows had to be at the front of the house or at the back. She couldn't see the windows at the back without knocking on every door and asking to go inside, so she decided to walk the length of the street in both directions to see if she could find any windows matching Benny's description.

She'd only walked past six houses when she saw a change

in the buildings. Instead of red brick, the next row of houses were a sandy colour and slightly taller. And more importantly, the windows were horizontal strips of glass at the basement level.

This could be it. The girls could be in one of these basement flats.

She walked quickly onwards, looking at the next row of houses and then felt disappointed to see just how many basement flats had the same horizontal windows.

She cursed under her breath. Finding the girls would take a lot of manpower. They'd need officers knocking on all these doors.

If she requested uniform's help, Tyler would ask her whether she thought Benny's information was credible. She believed him, but she knew Benny wouldn't be considered a reliable witness, which meant when it came down to prosecute this case or her bosses examined any failures in procedure, this would be something that was looked into thoroughly.

Modern police work was nothing like it was on the TV. If this was a TV show, Charlotte would barge into each flat, find the girls and rescue them dramatically. Instead, she was faced with half a street of identical basement flats on both sides of the road.

She would have to call in and speak to Tyler. He would then arrange to get local CCTV analysed, and they would narrow it down from there. A huge door-to-door operation would certainly alert the abductors to the fact the police were closing in on them and that was the last thing they wanted.

Feeling suddenly despondent, Charlotte turned and was heartened to see Mackinnon walking towards her already.

"That was quick."

"I wasn't far away," Mackinnon said, covering the distance between them in a few long strides. "What exactly did Benny tell you?"

Charlotte's gaze flickered to the huge poster and thought it was best not to mention the confusion over the banana. "Benny told me it was Marston Street. He positively identified it from images on Street View, and he also told me about that poster." Charlotte pointed to the bright yellow banana. "He told me the girls are being held in a basement flat that has thin, horizontal windows. I am guessing something like these," she pointed to one of the basement flat windows, and Mackinnon nodded.

"The Street View didn't show the windows properly, so I couldn't get Benny to ID them, but I'm reasonably confident the girls could be in one of these flats."

"Unless they've been moved since Benny was last here," Mackinnon said.

Charlotte nodded. That was a possibility, but one she didn't really want to acknowledge. If the girls had been moved, they would have to go back to the drawing board.

CHAPTER SIXTY

WHEN LILA HEARD the key turn in the lock, her stomach clenched in fear. She shot a quick glance at Ruby and saw that she was just as afraid. There was no time for reassuring words, though.

As soon as that bastard stepped inside the room she was going to run at him, and even if she didn't escape, she was determined to do some damage.

She tried to act bravely for Ruby's sake, but Marlo terrified her. She'd understood why Benny had sat quivering on the floor rather than fight back the first time they tried to escape. There was something about Marlo's eyes— dark, and dead. They reminded her of shark eyes.

Lila moved up from her crouched position as the door opened.

When he stepped inside, Marlo blinked a couple of times, surprised that the girls weren't in the middle of the room, where they had been the last time he'd checked on them. Seeing him so close and smelling his sweat paralysed Lila.

For a split second, as her mind ran through her options, she froze.

What if this was a mistake? What if this made him even more angry and he punished them and…

Lila was jerked from her thoughts by Ruby hollering at the top of her lungs and running at Marlo with her fists flying.

Lila joined in, kicking out at Marlo. She aimed for the side of his knee, lashing out hard.

She'd heard somewhere that the knee was a weak point, and it seemed to work because he went down like a ton of bricks sprawled all over poor Ruby.

The scream of terror Ruby let out made Lila's heart skip a beat.

She knew she was supposed to run. She knew the plan. It was her idea after all, but seeing her friend helpless with that monster looming over her, made every muscle in Lila's body go rigid.

It took Ruby screaming at her again to make her move. "Run, Lila. Run!"

Lila turned, intending to dart through the doorway, but Marlo was wise to her. He reached out, his long thin fingers wrapping around her ankle.

She yelped in terror as she fell forward.

His gaze clashed with hers, and she saw the smirk on his face.

He didn't think she would be able to get away. He thought he had won. He was enjoying this.

The thought made Lila furious, and she kicked out at him with all the power she could gather.

She felt, rather than heard, a satisfying crunch as the bottom of her heel smashed into his nose. The contact, made him loosen his grip on Lila's ankle, and she quickly scrambled to her feet, grabbing the handle, pulling the door closed and locking Ruby in the room with Marlo.

Thank God Marlo was a creature of habit and had left the key in the lock. She had to act fast. Who knew what Marlo would do locked alone in that room with Ruby?

He would be angry and frustrated and he was bound to take his anger out on her.

She rushed into the kitchen, remembering clearly that Benny had told them that the spare keys were in the kitchen. But was the front door key still there? And whereabouts in the kitchen did Marlo keep it?

She staggered down the hallway, bursting into the small kitchen and looked around frantically.

There wasn't much in the way of kitchen equipment, which made it easier to search. She scanned the tops of the counters first. Nothing.

She yanked open the drawers. The first one was cutlery and there was no sign of any keys, but the next drawer contained takeaway menus and a set of keys with a bright green label on the keyring.

She snatched them up quickly and ran down the hallway, trying to block out Ruby's screams coming from inside the bedroom.

Tears were streaming down her cheeks as she tried to force the key into the lock. In her desperation, she fumbled and thought for one horrifying moment that it wasn't the right key. But finally it slid in the lock and turned smoothly.

She tugged the door open and stepped outside, breathing large gulps of fresh air. There wasn't time to hesitate. She raced up the steps to the pavement level and looked around wildly for someone to ask for help.

It was a busy street. Lots of cars were passing by, and she

wondered whether she should step out in front of one of them and flag them down, or whether she should go to a neighbour's house.

Out of the corner of her eye, she saw two teenage girls approaching, holding their phones in front of them. They were chatting about Pokemon.

She turned and started to run towards them. Surely they would let her use a phone to call the police.

She willed her legs to move faster, but they felt like jelly. She didn't know whether that was because she was so scared or because she'd been sitting for so long.

"Can I use your phone?" She practically screamed the question at the girls.

They were younger than they had first appeared and looked up at Lila in horror.

She guessed she must look quite a state.

"Please, I am not gonna steal it. I just need to phone the police. I was –" Before she could finish what she was saying the two girls dodged past and started to cross the road to get away from her.

"No! Wait! I just need to borrow your phone," she considered chasing after them and then decided against it. There were other people around, other people she could ask.

She turned quickly, without looking where she was going, and slammed hard into a man's chest.

CHAPTER SIXTY-ONE

"Lila George?"

Lila looked up at the man towering over her.

How did he know her name? She tried to take a step back but his hand was on her elbow, keeping her upright, and gently but firmly preventing her from running away.

Oh, God, was he involved? Had she just escaped only to run into another one of the abductors?

"Help! Police!" she screamed out, determined to get someone to help her.

Then she noticed there was a woman standing behind the tall man. "Lila, it's okay. I am DC Charlotte Brown, and this is DS Mackinnon. We've been looking for you. You are going to be okay now."

"My friend, Ruby, is still inside with that psycho. They're both locked in the bedroom."

The tall man put his hands gently on Lila's shoulders and turned her around. "I need you to tell me which flat she's in, Lila."

Lila looked back at the female police officer, who was now talking urgently on the phone.

It suddenly struck her as odd that there weren't any police cars or sirens to be heard.

"Is it just you two? Where are all the police cars?"

"Never mind that now, Lila. Show me which flat Ruby is in."

Lila clenched her teeth as she walked quickly towards the flat. Every part of her body wanted to resist going back there, moving closer to that nasty bastard made her feel sick, but she had to for Ruby's sake.

"It's this one," she said pointing down the steps to the basement.

The front door was still ajar.

"Thank you Lila," he said. "You should go with DC Brown now. She'll make sure you're safe, and there will be an ambulance here soon, okay?"

Lila knew he wanted her to move away from the flat, but she couldn't tear her eyes away as he walked down the steps towards the basement and then disappeared through the front door.

CHAPTER SIXTY-TWO

MACKINNON HADN'T EXPECTED things to move quite so quickly. He'd assumed they would be conducting door-to-door enquiries after they'd had instructions from Tyler, but everything changed when Lila George barrelled along the pavement towards them.

She didn't look like the pretty girl in the photograph her parents had shown the team. Her hair was tangled, and she had blood smeared over one side of her face.

It was the wild look of panic in her eyes that had hit Mackinnon the hardest. She'd looked up at him with fear and distrust.

Now, he could feel her eyes burning into his back as he descended the steps, pushed open the door and slipped inside, moving as quietly as possible.

He knew Charlotte would take Lila away from the scene and wait for backup.

According to procedure, he should be waiting for back up, too, and he would have done if it had just been Marlo inside, but the thought of Ruby Watson being locked in a room with Marlo compelled Mackinnon to enter the flat. There was no way he was going to stand around, doing nothing while a seventeen-year-old girl could be being abused. He'd seen the injuries Lila George had sustained and guessed Ruby Watson would be in a similar state.

As soon as he saw Charlotte leading Lila George away, Mackinnon quickly scoped out the flat.

Directly in front of him was a narrow hallway, with bare floorboards. The kitchen door at the bottom of the hall was open and Mackinnon could see no one was inside. The open door to his right led to the sitting room and there was nobody in there either.

The door to the first bedroom had been broken off its hinges and the wooden panels were splintered. The one remaining door to his left was shut and there was a key in the lock.

He took a deep breath and reached for the key as a strangled moan sounded from inside the room.

He heard a female voice say, "No, please, don't hurt me."

Mackinnon gritted his teeth, turned the key in the lock and pushed the door open.

He didn't bother to try and keep quiet and flung the door open so hard that it crashed back against the wall.

"Police," he shouted loudly.

He wanted to make his presence known and to attract Marlo's attention, preferring Marlo to focus his anger on him rather than Ruby Watson.

Shocked, both Ruby and Marlo turned to him at the same time. Ruby moved first. She quickly used the opportunity to scramble away from Marlo and then cowered in the corner of the room.

Marlo stood rigidly still as he looked at Mackinnon.

"Who the hell are you?" he demanded, his lip curling up in a sneer.

"DS Mackinnon."

Before Mackinnon could say anything else, Ruby shouted out, "Be careful. He's got a knife."

A thin, mean smile stretched across Marlo's lips as he pulled his hand out of his pocket and held up the metal blade for Mackinnon to see.

"I think you should put that knife down, Marlo. You're already in enough trouble. There are police all around the building. I want you to put the knife on the floor and kick it towards me."

Marlo grinned as he looked Mackinnon up and down. "I don't think so. Do I look stupid?"

Mackinnon quickly assessed his chances. Marlo was tall, but still a couple of inches shorter than Mackinnon. He had a wiry build, with thin arms and legs.

Mackinnon knew he was bigger and stronger, but he had a major disadvantage.

He had no weapon.

"Why don't you let Ruby go and we can talk about this?"

Marlo shook his head. "She's not going anywhere. She is my insurance."

"What are you hoping to get out of this Marlo? Lila is outside, she's safe. It's over." Mackinnon's gaze drifted over to Ruby as he spoke and saw the relief on the girl's face.

She looked pale and terrified, and had a blue-tinged purple smudge just below her cheekbone where she'd been used as a punchbag.

He clenched his fists at his sides. What kind of animal did something like that? What had Ruby ever done to him?

"This has gone on long enough, Marlo. Put down the knife."

"I don't think it's gone on long enough. My game was just getting started. Did you like it? I bet you wondered what I was going to do with the parents at the school, didn't you?"

He was taunting him, and Marlo paused, waiting for him to reply, but Mackinnon was determined not to give him the satisfaction.

Marlo shrugged and continued his story regardless. "The parents were supposed to take a child and bring them back here. I was going to pretend I would let Lila and Ruby go in exchange for the children." Marlo lowered his head and winked. "Really, though, I was going to keep all four. Clever, huh?"

Mackinnon shook his head. "Not really. The whole thing is a bit childish, if you ask me."

The smile disappeared from Marlo's face in an instant. He moved forward and slashed the air just in front of Mackinnon with the knife.

Mackinnon stood his ground and willed him to come just a little bit closer. If he got close enough, Mackinnon could grab his wrist and... Even as he thought about doing that, he realised he was being stupid. He had seen plenty of injuries from knife wounds during his career, and the thought of somebody having to tell Chloe and the girls that he'd been stabbed on duty, stopped him from trying anything foolish.

He wouldn't tackle him physically, but he could still get at Marlo another way.

"I heard, it wasn't your idea, at all. I heard Curtis was the brains behind the abduction."

Mackinnon kept his eyes fixed on Marlo. He realised this

would be upsetting for Ruby to hear, but he wanted to get Marlo so annoyed he let down his guard.

"That's bollocks. It was all me. All right, so Curtis came up with the idea for the abduction. But the game, that was all my idea. Has he been trying to take credit for the game?"

"Curtis?" Ruby said, her voice small. "My brother?"

She drew Marlo's attention and he wandered over to her, holding out his knife.

"Marlo," Mackinnon said, the warning obvious in his voice.

Marlo chuckled and stopped a foot away from her. "Yes, Ruby. Your own brother was behind the abduction. He is actually my cousin, so technically, I suppose we're related."

Marlo grinned as Ruby's eyes widened in horror.

"Don't look so scared. We're not blood relatives," he said.

Before Ruby could reply there was a commotion in the hallway. Mackinnon heard footsteps behind him and immediately stood to one side, assuming it would be police backup.

A dark-haired man rushed into the bedroom and immediately launched himself at Marlo.

"What the hell did you do to my brother? Did you think I wouldn't find out?"

Marlo's face lost its cocky grin.

Mackinnon stayed pushed back against the wall and shot a look at Ruby, trying to reassure her. He hoped this newcomer would keep Marlo busy so Mackinnon could get Ruby out of here.

But as the newcomer turned, Mackinnon caught a glimpse of his face, and he saw it was Rob Morris, the man who'd delivered the flowers to Ruby's mother, and Benny Morris' brother.

"You stabbed him. He's in the hospital. You tried to kill him! How could you?"

Rob seemed to be oblivious to the knife Marlo was brandishing. He shoved Marlo hard. This situation was getting out of control.

Mackinnon stepped forward. "Rob. I am DS Mackinnon. Your brother is safe, and he recovered well after surgery. I just need you to calm down. We're going to let Ruby go and then we can talk things over, okay?"

Ruby began to shuffle towards Mackinnon, but Marlo took two quick steps, blocking her path. "No! You are not in charge here." He held up a finger pointing it at Mackinnon and Rob in turn. "I am in charge. This is my game. You play by my rules."

Rob laughed. "It is not a game, you idiot. Nobody is playing by your rules. You are just following somebody else's instructions."

Marlo made a jabbing motion with his knife, and Mackinnon wasn't sure if he was trying to scare Rob or whether he was really trying to stab him.

But Rob didn't step back. Instead, he continued to approach Marlo aggressively, shoving his chest and getting up into his face.

Mackinnon moved sideways, keeping his eyes fixed on Marlo and Rob, trying to get closer to Ruby. If Marlo turned on her again, Mackinnon was determined that he wouldn't be able to use Ruby as a hostage. He would be in the way.

Rob gasped and jerked forward. The atmosphere in the room seemed to change. Mackinnon could only see Rob's back, but from the way he bent double and clutched his stomach, he knew he'd been stabbed.

Marlo stared down at Rob and licked his lips as he collapsed onto his knees.

Mackinnon moved forward quickly while Marlo was distracted.

The knife was buried in Rob's torso, so Marlo was now weaponless.

Mackinnon grabbed hold of Marlo's arm, put a hand on his back and used his leg to trip him. He hit the floor hard and Mackinnon leaned over him, pinning him to the ground with one knee, leaning on his back and trapping his arm behind his back, pulling it upwards just enough to immobilise him.

For a second, Mackinnon considered pushing his arm a little harder, causing a little more pain, but then he shook his head. That wasn't him.

He wasn't a monster.

Beside him Rob groaned and turned over. Mackinnon could see he was losing blood fast. He turned and shouted at Ruby to get outside just as he heard the wail of sirens approaching.

Ruby scrambled to her feet and darted out of the bedroom door.

Mackinnon didn't let go of Marlo, but he leaned over to Rob and said, "Hold on. An ambulance is on the way."

Moments later, two paramedics rushed into the room.

They set about trying to stabilise Rob, and Mackinnon watched their desperate efforts until he realised he was surrounded by uniformed officers.

He finally released his hold on Marlo and got to his feet but swayed a little, feeling woozy.

An officer grabbed onto him as Mackinnon staggered.

"You're bleeding, sir."

Mackinnon looked down and saw the bloom of blood on

his shirt. At first, he assumed somehow Rob's blood must've transferred onto him, but then he felt the first twinge of pain. Somehow in the confusion he'd been stabbed. He hadn't even felt it. Before he knew what was happening, two uniformed officers propped him upright as they propelled him towards the stairs and out into the early evening sunlight.

There were plenty of police cars and sirens now, enough to make Lila George very happy.

As they bundled him towards the ambulance, Mackinnon caught sight of Charlotte. Her face paled as she saw the blood on his shirt. He tried to smile and raise a hand to let her know he was going to be okay. But before he knew it, he was in the back of the ambulance. Charlotte's anxious face appeared at the doors.

"What happened?"

"Stabbed, I think."

"You think? Surely you would know if you'd been stabbed."

A paramedic removed Mackinnon's shirt and said. "It's not life-threatening, a clean slice. You'll need stitches, though."

Mackinnon muttered his thanks as the female paramedic selected a dressing pad and held it to the wound. "This should stop the bleeding."

"You know Tyler will want to talk to us about this, don't you? He'll want to know why we didn't wait for back up."

"Yes, I'll tell him. It was my fault. I'll make sure he knows that."

"That wasn't what I meant," Charlotte said exasperated. "I was worried."

The paramedic stood up, and told Charlotte they were going to take Mackinnon in for stitches. "Nothing to worry about, but he's still losing blood, so we'll take him in to be on the safe side."

As the paramedic closed the doors, Mackinnon got one last glimpse of Charlotte's concerned expression and felt bad for making her worry. She'd been right. Tyler and Brookbank would demand answers, and Mackinnon needed to have some ready.

CHAPTER SIXTY-THREE

"How does that feel?" the male nurse asked. He had just finished stitching up Mackinnon's wound.

"Not too bad." Mackinnon flexed his shoulder. "It's a bit tender now, but I didn't even feel it when it happened."

The male nurse put the suture equipment in a disposable kidney dish and sealed the bright yellow sharps bin.

"It was only a surface wound, and cuts from very sharp implements often draw blood before people feel pain. Plus in a stressful situation, adrenaline takes over, and the pain an injury like this would cause under normal circumstances would be lessened.

"It isn't a deep wound, and the sutures should hold, but if you get any heavy bleeding or an increase in pain then you may need to come back in."

The nurse gathered up the cotton-wool he'd been using and wheeled the trolley away from Mackinnon before opening the curtain around his cubicle.

Tyler was standing just outside. "So, are you going to be scarred for life, Jack?"

The nurse said, "I did a good job. His scar will be practically invisible."

"Oh, don't tell him that. He was going to use the scar to get sympathy," Tyler said smirking and walked up to Mackinnon.

"How are you feeling, Jack?"

"I'm fine. I just have to get used to not moving this arm much for the next few days so I don't dislodge the stitches. Is Marlo talking?"

"Marlo won't *stop* talking. He's saying it was all Curtis' idea."

"Do you believe him?"

Tyler shrugged. "I think Curtis is definitely involved. Having said that, Marlo planned the acid attack and he stabbed Benny Morris. There's no evidence to suggest Curtis was involved in that. Curtis may be the brains behind the abduction, but there is no reason to believe he was encouraging Marlo in this weird game he was playing."

Mackinnon nodded slowly. "I thought he might try and cover up for Curtis out of some kind of misguided family loyalty."

Tyler shook his head as the nurse walked back in and handed Mackinnon his bloodstained shirt. "I didn't think you'd want to wear this, so I brought you something else." He handed Mackinnon a blue scrub top.

"Thanks very much."

After the nurse left them, Tyler said, "Actually, if anything, the family connection is what has caused Marlo to turn against him. In his mind, Curtis had all the advantages, and he got nothing."

"So what's the next move?"

Tyler let out a deep sigh. "I need to talk to the DCI. You do know he is on his way here, don't you? He wants to make sure you're all right. He'll probably be interested to know why you went inside that flat without a stab vest, too."

Mackinnon grimaced. "He doesn't need to do that. I am fine."

Tyler rolled his eyes. "I don't think he's really doing it for you, Jack. It's politics. One of his officers has been injured in the line of duty, and it would look bad if he didn't come and pay a visit."

Mackinnon let out a low whistle. "That's cynical even coming from you."

"I'm just a realist."

"So, where do we think Addlestone fits into all of this?"

Tyler shook his head. "I'm really not sure, but it's starting to look like Curtis fitted him up."

Tyler glanced at his mobile phone again.

"What's wrong?"

Tyler shook his head. "It's probably nothing. But I can't get in touch with Zelda Smith. I promised to take her to Drake House so she could talk to Curtis, but the interview with Addlestone ran over. Evie told me Zelda left the station to get something to eat, but I left a message on her answering service, and she hasn't called me back."

Tyler frowned and looked at his phone again.

"I am starting to think she ignored my instructions and went to talk to Curtis alone."

Mackinnon looked up sharply. "She wouldn't do that, would she?"

"Hopefully, she's not that stupid, but I am going to go over to Drake House anyway and check. Curtis will have heard the girls have been released. I want to see how he reacts."

"Are you going to bring him in?"

Tyler shook his head. "There's no hurry to bring him in as long as we keep a close eye on him. Now that the girls are no longer in danger, we can take our time. It is not going to be easy to pin anything on him."

Mackinnon grunted as he tried to pull on the blue top the nurse had given him. Eventually, tired of watching him struggle, Tyler stood up and helped him yank it on.

"Ow, I hope you're not considering taking up a role in the medical profession. I don't think much of your bedside manner."

"Stop complaining."

"Am I interrupting?" Collins asked cheekily, appearing behind Tyler. "I can come back later if you two would like some time alone."

"Very funny," Tyler said dryly. He patted Collins on the shoulder as he walked out of the cubicle. "I'm going to check on the girls' parents and then head over to Drake House. I will catch up with you later."

He left Mackinnon to tell Collins about the events of the last hour and relate how things had unfolded with Marlo in the basement flat.

ON HIS WAY TO check up on Ruby Watson and see her parents, Tyler spotted Charlotte walking along the corridor towards him.

She looked tired and had dark circles under her eyes.

"How's Mackinnon?" she asked.

"He'll be fine. He's all stitched up now and ready to go home. Have you seen Ruby Watson?"

Charlotte shook her head and bit down on her lower lip. "No, not yet. She looked okay when she came out of the flat, physically at least. Mentally, I am sure both girls are pretty messed up at the moment. I've just been talking to the doctor who treated Rob Morris when he was brought in. He was declared dead five minutes ago." She took a deep breath. "I'm going to go and tell Benny the news now."

Tyler sighed and put a hand on Charlotte's shoulder. "You don't have to do that. I can do it for you."

But Charlotte shook her head. "I think it would be better coming from me. I spent some time with Benny earlier today, and I think I owe him that much."

Tyler nodded, "Well, if you're sure?"

"Yes. I'm not looking forward to it, though. I know what Rob Morris did was awful, but when you listen to Benny talk about him, it was like Rob was the perfect brother who could do no wrong."

Tyler and Charlotte stood to one side as a porter came past, wheeling a bed, containing a small, frail elderly man almost swallowed up by the bed sheets.

"I have already seen the Georges," Tyler said. "They're over the moon to have their daughter back, but it's going to take a lot of time in counselling to get over what happened to them. We still have to build the case against Janice George for throwing acid with intent to harm. I'm not looking forward to that."

Both the girls would be scarred psychologically from the abduction, but their parents would also suffer from the after effect of this deadly game Marlo and Curtis had been playing with their lives.

"I'm just going to check on Ruby Watson and her parents and then I'm going to go back to Drake House."

Charlotte nodded. "Are you going to take Curtis into custody?"

"Not yet. I want to speak to Brookbank and see what he thinks is the best strategy, but I am hoping Curtis is going to do something to give himself away."

Tyler's mobile phone rang, and he quickly said goodbye to Charlotte, who headed off to talk to Benny.

At first, he thought it might be Zelda Smith returning his calls at last, but it was DCI Brookbank.

Tyler pressed the green button to answer the call, but he had a sinking feeling in his gut telling him he needed to get to Drake House as soon as possible.

Zelda Smith had been very keen to play a role in this investigation, and it wasn't like her to miss all the action.

CHAPTER SIXTY-FOUR

CURTIS WATSON HAD OPENED the door to Zelda Smith twenty minutes ago. Things were unravelling fast, and he could have done without Zelda's meddling presence.

She was trying to get at his secrets. But she didn't stand a chance. Curtis had had plenty of practice avoiding difficult questions. He'd seen dozens of counsellors and even two psychiatrists. After he'd been adopted, his parents had made him attend intensive sessions twice a week. He'd hated it at the time but now realised how much it had helped. He may never be perfectly normal, but he could pretend.

"It must be very hard for you, Curtis." Zelda Smith made another pathetically patronising attempt to get him to open up.

Before he could reply, Kelly Johnson walked into the living area from the kitchen, carrying a tea tray.

"You must be ever so excited, Curtis. Do you want to go to the hospital to see Ruby? I'm not sure when they are going to discharge her, but I could take you there."

Curtis was amused to see Zelda Smith shoot Kelly Johnson an irritated look. For someone who analysed criminal behaviour, her own behaviour was remarkably transparent.

Curtis shook his head. "No, thank you. I'll stay here and wait for Ruby to come home."

Kelly Johnson smiled, but he knew she found his reaction odd. From the tightening around Zelda Smith's eyes, Curtis knew his behaviour was setting off alarm bells. The normal thing to do would be to go and visit his sister. But he was sick of acting normal and he didn't want to go. The stress of the situation was making Curtis rebel.

Normally he gauged what was normal behaviour by watching other people's reactions to what he said or did. It was exhausting, and at times like this, it was almost too much to cope with.

Kelly chatted on for a few moments, oblivious to the fact that Zelda wanted her to shut up so she could ask Curtis more questions.

Curtis watched Kelly Johnson with interest. It was odd. She actually seemed happy that Ruby was free. Her eyes were shining as she smiled. He didn't understand. Why did she care one away or the other? It didn't affect her? She had never met Ruby. Sometimes, Curtis thought he was the normal one, and it was everyone else who was odd.

He could really do with getting rid of both of these women so he had time to plan what to do next.

He was sure that idiot Marlo would turn on him as soon as the police had him in custody. When they had met for the first time at his grandmother's barbecue, Curtis felt a bond with Marlo.

His grandmother didn't care if he smoked or drank, and so they'd sat sharing beers next to the grill. As everybody else messed about and talked about stupid things, Marlo and Curtis had had a very interesting conversation.

He knew Marlo was jealous of him, of course. He'd seen the glint in his eyes when he looked at Curtis' expensive watch.

He had money and Marlo had been brought up by a drug addict. Curtis understood that, and if Marlo had played by the rules, Curtis was prepared to share the wealth.

He'd given Marlo money – half of the money he'd received from blackmailing Addlestone but that hadn't been enough.

Marlo was greedy, and as Curtis got to know him better, he realised he had made a mistake.

He'd been too quick to judge. On the surface, they had a lot of similarities. They were both confident, and didn't feel a connection with other people. And more importantly, they both enjoyed manipulating and playing with people's lives.

He had known they were the same when he'd watched Marlo taunt their grandmother, saying something just to get a rise out of her, not because he was angry or frustrated, just because he could. But Curtis should have realised they weren't really the same.

He had never in his whole life met anyone like him. It was isolating, and so he had been too eager and too quick to invite Marlo in on his plan.

Curtis, had never loved anyone in his life, but he had nothing against his sister. He had no reason to hurt her. The abduction was just a way to get some money from his parents, who had grown miserly recently, but Marlo had turned it into some big circus event. It was Marlo's own fault he'd been caught.

If he'd followed Curtis' instructions, he would be a rich man by now, and Curtis would have added to his own wealth.

Curtis blinked in irritation as he realised Zelda was saying something to him.

"Sorry, I was just thinking about Ruby," Curtis said. "I hope she's okay."

Kelly Johnson smiled warmly at him, and Curtis knew he'd said the right thing.

"I wonder if we could have a word in private, Curtis," Zelda asked.

Kelly Johnson looked a little put out, but Curtis nodded. He couldn't really refuse as it might look suspicious. As long as he kept calm, Zelda Smith was no danger to him. The police had no real evidence, at least, nothing a good lawyer couldn't overturn with a click of his fingers.

"Why don't we go out onto the balcony?" Curtis suggested. "I could do with some fresh air."

The penthouse flat had its own rooftop garden, which was accessed via a set of stairs, but on this level there was a smaller outside area, a balcony, which looked out on the City of London and St Pauls. Curtis stood up and opened the sliding door, allowing Zelda to step outside first. He followed her and then shut the door behind them.

It was a pleasantly warm evening and the lack of haze meant the view was good. Like most people who visited the apartment, Zelda couldn't resist walking over to the edge to take a better look at the city view.

"Impressive, isn't it?" Curtis said.

"Beautiful," Zelda said.

While she was looking away, Curtis found his eyes drawn to the seating area.

The cushions had been taken inside due to the rain last night. The chairs were set around a low table, which was hollow inside and supposed to be used to store the cushions.

His mother insisted on taking the cushions inside, though, leaving the hollow centre of the table empty.

It was a great place to hide things.

He had long suspected his mother and father of snooping around his bedroom, so he had taken to stashing things out here. Right now, he was thinking about the stun gun he'd hidden there. A friend's father had brought it back from the Middle East.

His eyes travelled back to Zelda Smith, and he looked at her thin shoulders and narrow back.

She was tall but slim, and it wouldn't take much to make her fall over the edge, especially not if she was incapacitated by the stun gun first.

The idea was tempting. Curtis hadn't yet had a chance to try out his new toy...

He looked over his shoulder, remembering that Kelly Johnson was just inside.

Could he do it?

Would they believe him if he told them she'd lost her footing and fell? Maybe he could say she dropped something and reached for it. No, they would never believe him, but they wouldn't be able to prove anything.

Curtis smiled.

After the disappointing ending to the abduction, he'd been feeling a little despondent, but this could make up for it.

He leaned towards the table, ready to quickly lift the lid, when the balcony door slid open.

Curtis turned in irritation to see Kelly Johnson standing in the doorway with her mobile phone at her ear.

"Yes, sir, she is here." Kelly Johnson covered the end of the phone and said to Zelda, "It is DI Tyler."

Zelda turned around and winked at Curtis. "I am in trouble now," she joked.

Curtis smiled through gritted teeth as Zelda stepped inside the apartment and he realised he had lost out for the second time that day.

CHAPTER SIXTY-FIVE

CHARLOTTE PAUSED before she entered Benny's private room. She hated this part of the job.

It was never pleasant to tell somebody a relative had died, but in Benny's case, it seemed even worse.

Someone in Benny's position wasn't going to find it easy to make new friendships, and now his brother was dead, he had no family left. She took a deep breath and pushed the door open. The wide, beaming smile Benny gave her when she entered made her feel even worse.

"Hiya," Benny said cheerfully. "Did you find Lila and Ruby?"

Charlotte nodded and pulled up a chair next to Benny's bed.

"We did, thanks to your help."

"Are they all right?"

"They are fine. They've been brought to this hospital as well just to be on the safe side."

That was the wrong thing to say.

Benny flung back the bed sheets and went to get out of bed.

Charlotte raised her hands, resting them lightly on Benny's shoulders. "No, Benny."

He looked at her in confusion. "I want to see them."

"That's not a good idea yet. They're with their families at the moment and getting checked out by the doctors."

Benny nodded reluctantly and leaned back on his pillows.

God, this was so hard.

She should have delivered the bad news immediately, as soon as she walked in the room.

Now the right words wouldn't form in her mind, and Benny had started talking about playing on his Xbox with Lila later as though everything was fine.

Charlotte reached out and patted Benny's arm.

"Benny, listen to me. I've got some very bad news. When we rescued the girls, Rob was there, too, and he got hurt. He was rushed to hospital but he didn't make it. I am so sorry, Benny. Rob is dead."

For a few seconds, Benny didn't say a word. His eyes remained fixed on Charlotte's face.

"My Rob?" he asked eventually.

Charlotte nodded. "Yes, your brother."

Benny's mouth tightened, and his cheeks grew red.

"Did Marlo kill him?"

The fact that the incident hadn't yet been written up, and there wasn't an official line from the department, meant that Charlotte shouldn't be going into details, but she thought Benny deserved to know.

"Yes," she said, and she held Benny's hand as big tears rolled down his cheeks.

* * *

DI TYLER TRAVELLED up in the private lift to the penthouse. It had been a crazy few days. Mackinnon had been wounded, but it could have been much worse.

Both girls had been returned safely to their families. No doubt there would be an enquiry into certain events that occurred during the investigation, but Tyler didn't think he would come off too badly.

The Watsons were still at the hospital with their daughter, and Tyler purposely hadn't told them he was going to their apartment to see Curtis. His official line was that he was going to brief the family liaison officer, but he really wanted to have a word with Curtis without his parents around.

He rang the doorbell to the Watsons' luxurious flat, and Kelly Johnson opened the door.

"Fantastic news about the girls, sir. The team must be over the moon."

Tyler smiled. "Absolutely. It's a great result. Thanks for your hard work, Kelly. The family liaison officer often has the hardest job of all."

Kelly smiled happily and walked towards the living area. "We don't do the job because it's easy."

Zelda Smith was sitting on the sofa, bold as brass, and she eyed Tyler as though she were daring him to reprimand her.

Although Tyler would very much liked to have told her exactly what he thought of her actions, he turned to focus on Curtis instead.

The boy was leaning back against the kitchen counter, and he smirked at Tyler.

"Well done, detective."

"You must be very glad your sister is coming home, Curtis."

"Of course, I can't wait to see her."

Tyler smiled. "It's funny. At one stage, we thought you were responsible for the abduction."

Curtis' eyes narrowed as he stared at Tyler.

"We believed you'd planned for Addlestone to take the fall so you could get money from your parents, not that you really needed it. Maybe the abduction was just a way to hurt them."

Curtis glanced away and turned his head, but not before Tyler had seen the smile playing on his lips.

The little sod was enjoying this.

Curtis turned back to Tyler and said, "That's a very interesting theory, detective."

"It certainly is," Zelda piped up. "But Kelly said you caught the man responsible."

Tyler ignored her. He took a step closer to Curtis and lowered his voice so that only the boy could hear him.

"You won't get away with this."

Curtis' eyes shone. "Oh, I think I will, detective."

Before either of them could say any more, the front door opened, and Peter Watson entered the room.

He strode across the room to his son and put his arm around his shoulders.

Tyler could tell from the look on the man's face that he knew what his son had done. He'd heard the name Marlo Wainwright from one of the team, or from his daughter, and put two and two together. Deep down, he had to know what his son was like.

"Don't say another word, Curtis," Peter Watson said. "Unless you have a warrant, detective. I'd like you all to leave my home. I am very grateful you brought Ruby back home safely, but I think we have all had enough of the police in our lives for now."

Tyler nodded, turned to leave and gestured for Kelly and Zelda to do the same. Both women seemed very surprised at this sudden eviction.

Just before he walked out of the front door, Tyler looked directly at Curtis.

He wanted the kid to know that this wasn't over.

The cocky little sod winked at him, and Tyler knew Curtis' mocking expression would stay with him for a very long time.

CHAPTER SIXTY-SIX

A FEW DAYS LATER, most of the team were gathered at the Red Herring pub.

DCI Brookbank had bought the first round and gave a little speech, thanking them all for their hard work. He didn't stay long, just long enough to down his pint, and then he headed back to Wood Street station.

The rest of the team stuck around, though, determined to have a bit of fun and unwind. After the past few days, they needed it.

Mackinnon and Collins had ordered their usual portions of chicken wings and were laughing and joking. Tyler looked tired, as usual, but even he had a smile on his face. DC Webb had left the group and was at the bar, trying to chat up one of the barmaids, and Charlotte sat quietly nursing a gin and tonic with a frown on her face.

"Are you all right?" Mackinnon asked, pushing his plate of chicken wings closer to Charlotte. "Help yourself."

Charlotte managed to raise a smile and took a chicken wing from the plate and picked up a napkin.

"I still can't believe we're not going to be able to prosecute Curtis Watson."

Tyler took a long sip of his pint and then set it down on the table. "They've got money. A lot of it. And he's lawyered up. We could get him for blackmailing Addlestone, but Addlestone doesn't want to press charges. He just wants the whole thing to go away."

"I heard his parents were sending him abroad to finish his A-levels," Mackinnon said. "To a British school in Switzerland."

Charlotte shook her head. "So he just gets away with it?"

Mackinnon understood how she felt. Although they had a strong case against Marlo, the idea that Curtis had planned his own sister's abduction and would be getting off scot-free rankled.

Mackinnon strongly believed in justice and he hated the thought of someone like Curtis continuing his life as though nothing had happened.

He'd only been to see the Watsons once since Ruby had returned home, and the atmosphere had been strained to say the least.

Ruby was terrified of her brother, and Peter and Claire Watson seemed to be at a loss. Deep down, Mackinnon believed they knew there was something wrong with their son. But they didn't want to admit it.

They were in a difficult situation. They couldn't turn their back on Curtis, but they wanted to protect Ruby as well, so they'd made the decision to send Curtis away.

"Curtis will commit another crime and eventually he will

be caught," Mackinnon said. "He won't be able to stop himself."

Collins raised his glass to that as Tyler said, "He'll get his just deserts eventually."

"Do you really believe that?" Charlotte asked.

"I have to," Tyler said. "The alternative is just too depressing to contemplate."

Mackinnon reached for his pint with his right hand and then winced.

He kept forgetting about his stitches. He picked his drink up with his other hand. The wound was healing nicely now, and that would be helped along by a few days leave. He was looking forward to seeing Chloe and the girls and had made a decision to make more of an effort with Sarah.

Firstly, he planned to warn her not to borrow money from anybody other than her parents. She might not want to listen to him, but at least he would have tried.

She wasn't a bad kid really, and he was determined to try to improve their relationship.

He'd like to think eventually they could spend holidays together as a family, and maybe he could take both girls down to visit his own parents occasionally. He'd visited with Katy and Chloe a couple of times, but Sarah had never come along.

He glanced down and saw that Charlotte's gin and tonic was finished. "Another one? It's my round."

Charlotte shook her head. "No, thanks. There's somewhere I have to be."

* * *

CHARLOTTE TOOK the underground to Whitechapel. The market was already closed for the day. She crossed over the road, heading for the London hospital. She had already popped into Sainsbury's and bought Benny a magazine for gamers as well as a bunch of grapes and a couple of chocolate bars.

She looped the bag over her arm and climbed the steps at the hospital's main entrance.

Charlotte absolutely hated the thought of Curtis getting away with plotting his own sister's abduction and for trying to set Addlestone up.

After Marlo's confession, it was pretty obvious that Curtis had been deeply involved, and when they'd finally managed to speak to Kirsty Jones using video call on Monday, she'd told them Curtis was creepy, but she had no idea about the photos. After looking at them, she was horrified and told them they had been taken from her bedroom.

It looked as though someone had accessed the webcam from the computer in her bedroom.

She confirmed that Addlestone had never behaved inappropriately towards her. Of course, Addlestone wanted to put the whole matter behind him. He was embarrassed and worried about his reputation, so it looked like Curtis would get away with that as well.

She'd been to see the Georges and Lila with Mackinnon yesterday, and unlike the Watsons, their home had been a happy one.

The Georges were delighted to get Lila back and proudly told Charlotte and Mackinnon how Lila was starting college in September. It was outcomes like that that made the job worthwhile, and Charlotte knew she had to focus on the positive results rather than dwell on the fact Curtis Watson was getting off without any punishment at all.

Benny had been moved from his private room and was

now sharing a ward with twelve men. She thought Benny was probably finding that quite difficult.

When she walked into the ward and Benny caught sight of her, his face lit up and he waved excitedly.

"Hi, Benny, the nurse told me you're getting out of here tomorrow. That's fantastic news, isn't it?"

Benny nodded. "Yes. But I can't go back to the flat without Rob."

"No, but I hear your caseworker has found a nice place for you to live. It is very close to where you were before, isn't it?"

Benny nodded, but he still looked despondent.

Charlotte handed him the grapes and the magazine she'd brought.

"Thank you," Benny said politely as he glanced at the magazine.

Benny had no one now. He would get swallowed up in the system, and there wasn't anything she could do about it.

Charlotte turned when she heard footsteps behind her and saw an elegant woman with a short grey bob approaching.

"Hello, Benny."

"Hiya, Diane!"

The woman had an open and friendly face and she smiled at Charlotte. "I am Diane Swanson. I run the Rose Hill community centre, and I'm looking forward to getting Benny back into the IT class."

"Nice to meet you. I'm Charlotte Brown, one of the police officers who worked on the abduction case."

As they shook hands, Diane said, "I was just checking in with Benny to see if he is ready for the move tomorrow. You are looking forward to it, aren't you, Benny?"

Benny smiled. "Yes."

"I've been popping in every day, and I'm helping him arrange Rob's funeral."

Charlotte smiled. "I'm glad he has someone like you to look out for him. I have been really worried."

"We've got a good support network, and Benny is very popular at the community centre. He gets on very well with all the members of staff, and both Eddie and I have been popping in to make sure he's okay. Benny doesn't have his mum and brother any more, but we'll be looking out for him."

Charlotte smiled. "I'm glad."

After Diane left, Charlotte sat on a chair beside Benny's bed and opened the magazine, "Okay then, Benny, show me what all the fuss is about."

Benny began to tell her all about a new game for the latest Xbox.

Charlotte smiled as Benny chattered away.

In an ideal world, they would have been able to put Curtis away for a very long time, but sometimes cases didn't work out like that. The team had done their best, and on this occasion, that had to be good enough.

She chuckled as Benny turned the page, pointed out another game in the magazine and began to enthusiastically tell her all about it.

Charlotte smiled at the thought of Mackinnon, Tyler and Collins still in the Red Herring, celebrating the end to a harrowing case. They deserved a good night out. Both girls were home and they were safe. That was a good result for everyone.

A NOTE FROM D. S. BUTLER

Thanks for reading Deadly Game. I hope you enjoyed it!

I am currently working on the next book in the Deadly Series. If you would like to be one of the first to find out when my next book is available, you can sign up for my new release email at www.dsbutlerbooks.com/newsletter

If you have the time to leave a review, I would be very grateful.

For readers who like to read series books in order here is the order of the Deadly Series so far: 1) Deadly Obsession 2)Deadly Motive 3)Deadly Revenge 4)Deadly Justice 5)Deadly Ritual 6)Deadly Payback 7) Deadly Game

I also write a series of books set in the East End under the name Dani Oakley. Please turn the page to find out more or take a look at the book page on my website.

www.dsbutlerbooks.com

ACKNOWLEDGMENTS

To Nanci, my editor, thanks for always managing to squeeze me in when I finally finish my books!

I would also like to thank my readers on Facebook & Twitter for their entertaining tweets and encouragement.

My thanks, too, to all the people who read the story and gave helpful suggestions and to Chris, who, as always, supported me despite the odds.

And last but not least, my thanks to you for reading this book. I hope you enjoyed it.

Printed in Great Britain
by Amazon

22058088R00198